THE
SPANISH
DAUGHTER

THE SPANISH DAUGHTER

LORENA HUGHES

KENSINGTON
PUBLISHING CORP.

www.kensingtonbooks.com

KENSINGTON BOOKS are published by

Kensington Publishing Corp.
119 West 40th Street
New York, NY 10018

Map courtesy of Lorena Hughes and Map Effects Fantasy Map Builder

ISBN: 978-1-4967-3626-0 (ebook)

ISBN: 978-1-4967-3624-6

First Kensington Trade Paperback Printing: January 2022

10 9 8 7 6

Printed in the United States of America

To Danny, Andy, and Natalie,
mis Pepas de Oro

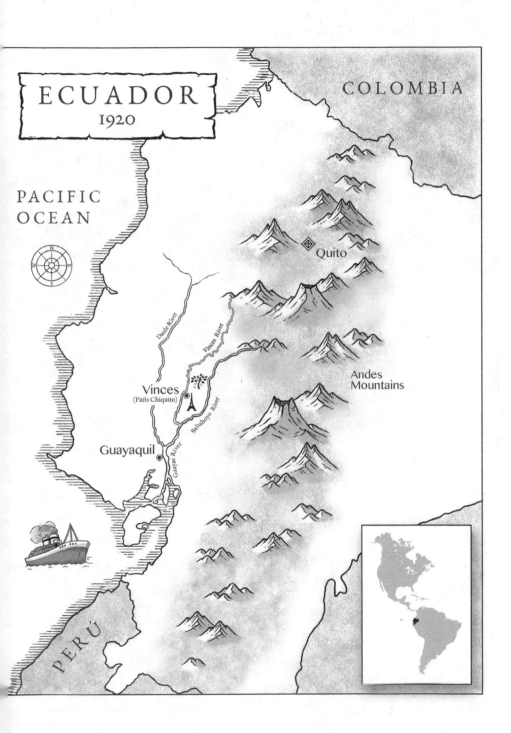

CHAPTER I

Puri

Guayaquil, Ecuador
April 1920

Surely they could all see through my disguise.

A drop of sweat slid down my forehead. I was definitely not dressed for the weather, which was akin to one of those Turkish baths gentlemen visited. The corset squeezing my small breasts was not helping matters. Neither was my husband's vest, his jacket, or his bow tie. The fake beard made my face itch. If only I could scratch it, but any wrong move might tear it off. Even worse, my spectacles were fogging up and making everything blurry.

How did I ever think I could pull this off?

A tremor rippled over my entire body as I reached the end of the pier. *Calm down, you can do this.* I took a deep breath, but my lungs didn't seem to get enough air. I did, however, get a mouthful of the stench of fish and smoke coming from the ship.

This was madness.

Herds of people waited for us to descend the plank. Some carried signs, others waved at my fellow passengers from the distance. I pictured one of them pointing at me in ridicule.

I can still go back inside.

I turned around and smacked into a shoulder behind me. With all the shouting, shuffling of feet, and dropping of bags, I hadn't seen the young man jostling in my direction. I shifted to the side and he rushed past me, ramming into an old lady strolling in front of us. She squealed as she fell on the ground.

"*¡Bruto!*" she called after him.

I darted toward her and helped her up—her bony arms as fragile as toothpicks.

"Are you all right?" I said in a low voice.

"Yes, I think so." She snatched her hat from the ground. "That man is an animal! But thank you, *caballero*. At least there are still a few gentlemen around."

I smiled at the irony but more importantly, it gave me a small measure of confidence that my disguise was working. I was about to ask her if she needed to see a doctor when a woman—older than Methuselah—approached us, leaning over a bamboo cane for support. I'd never seen so many wrinkles and spots on a single face.

"*¡Hija!*" she told the lady I'd just helped.

"*¡Mamá!*" the old lady said, hugging her mother. The women had a lot to say to each other and left without giving me a second glance.

If only my mother could be here to help me with my ordeal, but she'd passed away three years ago.

And now Cristóbal.

My throat tightened.

But I couldn't fall apart at this moment. I was already here. I had to follow through with my plan, no matter what.

A Moorish tower in yellow and white stripes rose behind a cluster of hats and palm trees. Although narrower, it reminded me of Torre del Oro, back in Sevilla, a slice of my old life appearing before my eyes to reassure me everything would be fine.

That was what my mind said. My legs told a different story. They had become as heavy as lead. At any given moment, someone—anyone—could attack me. But I had no way of knowing who or if I would be able to even move.

Get a hold of yourself, Puri. Relax.

I scanned the strange faces around me. Certainly, my father's lawyer would be among these people, though I had no idea what he looked like. I hoisted my husband's typewriter and dragged the trunk with my other hand.

Fortunately, I had given away all my gowns, which meant I only had to worry about one trunk as opposed to three. As I wandered about the harbor, I ran into several of my dresses on the bodies of other passengers. The last one of them—a pink taffeta sheath my mother had sewn for me—dissolved like foam among a sea of linen and sheer drapes.

A flock of seagulls cawed over my head. I walked past a row of canoes moored along the dock and a group of women carrying umbrellas to shield their faces from the unforgiving sun. Behind them was a man in a dark suit that stood out among the white jackets and hats like a black bean in a bowl of rice. He was holding a sign with my name; the words written in curly, black letters.

María Purificación de Lafont y Toledo.

Lafont from my French father, Toledo from my Spanish mother.

I stopped in front of him.

"May I help you, señor?" he said.

Señor. Another small mercy. He was shorter than me, but I'd always been tall for a woman. His wide skull was reminiscent of those early humans in Cristóbal's archeology books. His eyebrows were coarse and primitive, nearly joining each other.

I coughed in order to make my voice hoarser. "I'm Cristóbal de Balboa, María Purificación's husband." If I spoke slowly, I could reach the lower register of my voice.

"Tomás Aquilino, at your service."

I was right. This was the lawyer who'd sent the letter informing me of my father's death. He glanced behind me.

"Where's your wife? I thought she intended to come herself."

A sharp pain hit my chest and it had nothing to do with my corset. This ache came every time I thought of what had happened to Cristóbal. I studied every line on Aquilino's forehead, the glint in his eyes, the corners of his dry lips. Could I trust him?

I took a deep breath.

"Unfortunately, my wife perished aboard the *Andes.*"

Aquilino looked appropriately shocked. "*¡Dios mío santísimo!* How?"

I hesitated. "A case of Spanish influenza."

"And they didn't quarantine the ship?"

"No." I let go of the trunk. "Only a few passengers contracted it, so it wasn't necessary."

He stared at me in silence. Did he know I was lying? I'd never been a deceitful person and I despised having to do this.

"What a disgrace," he finally said. "We didn't hear anything about it here. My sincere condolences, señor."

I nodded.

"Help me with my trunk, will you?" I said, not as a favor, but as a command. Men didn't ask, men ordered.

Aquilino grabbed the other end of the trunk and together we carried it across the street. It was heavier than a dying bull, but I couldn't let the lawyer see how weak I was. By the time we reached the vehicle, I was panting and a layer of sweat covered my face and armpits. No wonder men sweat all the time!

He plunked down his end of the trunk next to a glossy, black Ford Model T. I hadn't known many people in my hometown who owned a car, much less an imported one. I wouldn't have imagined there would be such modern vehicles in a place that Cristóbal had called a "land of barbarians." This Aquilino must make good money as a lawyer, or maybe he was one of those men who found other means to build a personal fortune? Favors here and there, perhaps even a hand—a sort of tax, if you will—on another person's inheritance. Or maybe, he himself came from money.

I'd only traveled in an automobile a couple of times. In my native Sevilla, I walked everywhere. But when I visited Madrid to see about the expired patent to my grandmother's invention—her fabulous cacao bean roaster—I rode an automobile similar to this one, except that these seats seemed softer. Or perhaps it was my exhaustion.

Pushing on a lever by the steering wheel, Aquilino informed me that, unless I'd made other arrangements, I would spend the night at his house. We would depart to Vinces first thing in the morning to "see about Don Armand's will." He was unable to look me in the eye as he said this.

I recalled the words from the letter—I'd read it so many times

I'd already memorized it: *As one of the beneficiaries, you are required to come to Ecuador and take possession of your portion of your father's estate or to appoint a representative who may sell or donate the property on your behalf.*

One of the beneficiaries.

I'd been giving this some thought. I'd never heard of my father having other children, but one could never be too sure with men. It wouldn't surprise me if he'd started a new family here. After all, he'd left my mother twenty-five years ago to pursue his dream of owning a cacao plantation in Ecuador. It was inevitable that he should have found someone else to share his bed. The incident aboard the ship left no doubt that someone wasn't pleased with my coming. The question was who.

During the drive, Aquilino inquired about María Purificación's passing, shaking his head and clucking his tongue in apparent disappointment. It was surreal to talk about my own death, to hear my name repeated as though I weren't present. I wanted to scream at the injustice of it all. I wanted to demand an explanation on Cristóbal's behalf, but instead, I played along. I needed to make him believe I was my husband.

I looked out the window. Guayaquil was far from the village I'd envisioned and more modern than many towns in Andalucía. We drove past the river—the Guayas, he said—toward a quaint neighborhood along a hill stacked with colonial houses bursting with flowerpots in balconies and entryways. Aquilino said it was called Las Peñas and the hill, Santa Ana. The serpentine, cobbled streets reminded me of the small towns near Sevilla. The realization that I might never return to my country hit me for the first time since I'd left. Even more heartbreaking was to think that Cristóbal would never explore this new place with me. I stared at my hand, empty without the warmth of his.

Incomplete.

We stopped at a light blue house with a mahogany door and entered. In all likelihood, Aquilino was a bachelor; there was not a single feminine touch in his parlor. No flowers, no porcelain objects, no embroidered linen. Instead, stale landscapes hung on the walls and the life-size sculpture of a Great Dane stared back at me.

A door on the far side of the parlor opened and a girl with cinnamon curls entered, drying her hands on a lime apron. Her dress so loose it swallowed her.

"Lunch is served, *patrón*," she said with a soft voice.

"*Gracias*, Mayra."

The table in the dining room was much too large for just one person. My eyes set on the colorful dishes awaiting us. The girl called Mayra had prepared us fried sea bass, rice with calamari, and plantains—which they both called *patacones*.

In the last week, I'd skipped several meals—I couldn't eat after the nightmare I went through on the *Andes*—but today, I was ravenous.

Aquilino gestured for me to sit down and he took the spot at the head of the table while Mayra served us. Although I was curious about Aquilino, I didn't ask him anything. I feared that if I spoke too much, he would discover my secret. So, I said as little as possible, answering the maid with single syllables, nodding often, and shaking my head when appropriate. This seemed to suit Aquilino just fine. Like my husband, he said very little. I'd also gotten into the habit of coughing frequently to make my voice hoarse.

"Are you all right, Mr. Balboa?"

Great. The lawyer was going to think I'd contracted influenza as well.

"Yes."

I returned my attention to my plate. It was odd but impersonating a man was giving me a freedom I'd never had before. As a woman and the owner of the only chocolate shop in my hometown, I'd always been a tireless hostess. It had always been my job to make my guests feel at ease, to be the peacemaker if there was a disagreement. I often anticipated everyone's wishes (More wine? Another piece of chocolate?) and avoided uncomfortable silences. But today, I was free to enjoy my food without looking over my shoulder to make sure everyone's plates were full.

"Just wait until you try Mayra's *dulce de higos*," he said. "She picks them from the backyard tree."

Mayra set a bowl in front of me. My mouth watered at the

sight of fig preserves swimming in syrup. A slice of white cheese rested on the saucer.

"What is this syrup?" I asked, savoring the spicy, cinnamon-tasting juice.

"*Panela*," Mayra said.

If I could find a way to mix this with chocolate, I'd have a winner.

After devouring the dessert, Aquilino guided me toward the parlor, pointed at a stiff velvet couch, and sat across from me. He picked up the cigar box and offered me one. I hesitated. I'd always been curious about this mysterious male habit, but I wasn't sure I could deliver a proper exhalation. Cristóbal sometimes produced immaculate, blue circles, a source of ultimate pride for him.

At my hesitation, Aquilino's bushy eyebrows arched. Smoking was a sign of a true man, and I must pass the test. I glanced at the Great Dane by the entrance—even he seemed to be waiting for my reaction. I took a thick cigar between my fingers, mimicking Aquilino's resolve as he tightened his lips around it, and lit it.

The first inhalation hit my chest like a flame. Aquilino gave me the sort of look one might reserve for a curious insect as I coughed incessantly and hit my chest with my hand a few times, attempting to free the inferno from my body.

"You don't smoke, Mr. Balboa?"

"Only pipe," I gasped. "In my country, the tobacco is more pure." Whatever that meant. I'd heard men speak about the quality of tobacco and its purity, but to me, all of them stank in the same way.

Aquilino lit his own cigar. He had no problems inhaling or exhaling.

"I must ask you, sir," he said, his voice carrying the same solemn tone of a priest. "What are your plans now that your wife, *que en paz descanse*, is no longer with us?"

I had to tread carefully. I couldn't come across as a threat to anyone.

"I will probably return to Spain. I have no interest in either the country or the cacao business. To be quite honest, this was my wife's dream—not mine." The burn in my throat had given my voice a natural coarseness that I decided to use to my advantage. "I must ask you, Señor Aquilino, are there any other heirs?"

"Just two. Don Armand had two daughters in Vinces: Angélica and Catalina de Lafont."

Two sisters.

The news hit like a slap in the face. It was one thing to suspect something, to consider a possibility. It was something else to receive confirmation that there were, indeed, real blood relatives. My father had betrayed me and my mother. He'd raised two daughters, whom he probably loved more than me, while I'd waited for him to return to Spain for over two decades. But he was never planning to come back, I now realized. He'd made a new life without us, discarding us like an old newspaper. What an idiot I'd been—religiously writing all those letters to him, sitting for hours by the window, drawing his portrait. In my childhood innocence, I'd always expected him to walk through the front door, his arms filled with presents, and then take me on one of his adventures.

"Angélica is the eldest," he said. "Well, in reality, there is a brother, too. But he renounced his inheritance."

A brother as well. And he *renounced* the fortune?

"He's a priest." Aquilino stared at his cigar with appreciation. "He took the vow of poverty."

A priest, of all things. My father hadn't been a religious man, not according to my mother's recollections. Then how did he produce a priest? I, myself, was filled with doubts. Although I would never voice them out loud. But if it was true that this brother had renounced my father's money, had it been a voluntary vow or a forced one?

"What about their mother? Is she also an heir?"

"No, Doña Gloria Alvarez passed away a few years ago. But we'll get into all the details tomorrow."

My father had hidden so many things from us. It stung worse than his death. Good thing my mother hadn't lived to see so much deceit. Another woman, another family. Did he think he could make amends by leaving me a portion of his estate? What good would that do when I never had *him*? I would never know what his voice sounded like, what cologne he used, or feel the warmth of his hugs.

A thump against the window startled us both. We moved toward the pane in time to see a speckled bird wrecked on the pebbles outside the house.

"A sparrow-hawk," Aquilino said.

I remained silent, unable to keep my eyes from the dying bird.

"The poor creature must not have seen the glass," he went on. "It didn't know what it was getting itself into when it came here."

CHAPTER 2

Two weeks earlier

It took us a week aboard the *Valbanera* to arrive in La Habana, my first taste of the American continent with its colonial buildings, narrow streets, and tantalizing beaches. But we didn't have time for sightseeing as almost immediately we had to board our next ship, the *Andes*, a British vessel that was three times the size of the *Valbanera*. Not that Cristóbal would've agreed to any sightseeing with me anyway. He'd spent the entire week aboard locked in our cabin, typing.

The clerk at the reception desk had a perfectly bald head filled with moles, like a spotty mango.

"Your name, sir?" he asked.

"Cristóbal de Balboa, and this is my wife, María Purificación de Lafont y Toledo."

Cristóbal tapped his fingers on the desk—repeatedly—while the clerk wrote our names as if there weren't dozens of passengers standing behind us. Cristóbal had little patience for incompetence, a trait I never quite understood since he had a temperate disposition and always avoided conflict. His way of expressing his frustration was to burst into a variety of tics: tapping his foot, scratching the back of his head, loosening his tie, chewing his nails to the quick. It was as if his body expressed what his voice couldn't.

"Purificación," the clerk said slowly. "With a *c* or an *s*?"

"*C*," Cristóbal said, curtly.

My husband had little to no awareness of his many habits or the effect he had on others, especially women. He never noticed when our female customers stared at him or groomed their hair while he took their order or handed them a warm cup of chocolate. I could see why they were enthralled by him. Cristóbal was already thirty-four years old, but he took care of his appearance and of his hygiene. His beard was always trimmed and his necktie always straight. Most of all, he was attentive and kind and had an aloof quality that made women feel at ease in his presence. I couldn't deny that I'd been fortunate that my mother hadn't found me an old, fat man to marry. Ours was certainly not a problem of attraction.

Cristóbal turned to me, sighing.

Ours was a problem of affinity.

While my husband spelled out my last name for the clerk, I had a feeling that someone was watching me. I turned my head as discreetly as possible.

A man leaning against a thick column was staring at me. He averted his gaze as soon as I looked at him. There was something wrong with his face, but I couldn't see clearly for fear of appearing rude.

"Here's the itinerary." The clerk presented Cristóbal with a handwritten paper. "Your cabin is number 130 D."

Cristóbal grabbed the key from the clerk's hand before he finished the sentence. The man leaning against the column lit a cigarette. His distraction gave me the opportunity to study him.

Half of his face was burned.

The skin was thick and wrinkled from his eyebrow and cheek to his jawline. The other side of his face, however, was intact. One might even call it attractive.

For an instant, our eyes met. A chill ran down my spine, but I attributed it to the thin georgette fabric of my rose blouse. And yet, I couldn't deny there was something unsettling about him. I held on to Cristóbal's arm, pretending to stare at a marine landscape hanging on the wall above the man's head.

"Ready, Puri?" Cristóbal picked up his typewriter case.

"*Sí, mi alma.*"

The bellhop followed us with our trunks.

I didn't see the strange man again for two days. On the third day, I ran into him as I was stepping out of my cabin. He acknowledged me by tipping his hat and walked past me without further contemplation. His scent was familiar, but I couldn't quite pinpoint its source.

I considered mentioning him to Cristóbal, but by the time my husband stepped out and shut our cabin door, the man had turned the corner.

On our way to dinner, the melodic sounds of an accordion and a tambourine floated from one of the salons. Through one of the windows, I spotted a vaudeville circus.

"Oh, can't we go in?" I begged my husband. "They may have a magician!"

"Puri, I've had a breakthrough. Let's just eat our dinner and go back to the stateroom."

I clung to his arm. "Please, just this once!"

I dragged Cristóbal and his stiff legs into the salon.

The troupe consisted of three men in shiny red outfits. One rode a unicycle and sported a long, curly mustache and a top hat. His black cape billowed with the cold air drifting from the open door. Another one, a harlequin, walked among the audience on stilts, leaving the children in awe as he pretended to lose his balance above them several times. The third man had a trim goatee and was the highlight of the show. For the next fifteen minutes, he swallowed knives and balls of fire and presented us with Marina the Great, a muscular woman with a taut bun who was about to walk on a tightrope.

Cristóbal leaned over me and whispered, "Look, I'm not hungry anymore. You can go to dinner and meet me at the stateroom when you're done."

"But there's a dance tonight."

Surveying the room, Cristóbal gripped my elbow and led me outside the salon.

"I've already wasted twenty minutes on this."

"You *wasted* twenty minutes? That's what you call spending time with me?"

"You're the one who suggested that I write my novel during the trip."

"Yes, but is that all you're going to do, Cristóbal? Write your novel all day and all night? You barely eat, and when you do, it's in haste. I've spent this entire trip by myself."

He shrugged. "I can't help it if I'm feeling inspired."

"And *I* don't inspire you? You haven't touched me since before . . ."

A woman with a mink coat glanced at us.

Cristóbal coughed, his cheeks a deep red. "I don't think this is the right place to talk about this."

There were two couples nearby. I didn't care what they heard. In fact, it might be better. Perhaps their presence would motivate Cristóbal to stay, at least to avoid a scandal. Besides, I was tired of always avoiding the subjects that made him uncomfortable. I resented that he never mentioned my last miscarriage—my third one so far—as if it had never happened, as if that baby had never existed.

"I'm already doing what you wanted. Am I not?" he said.

He had a point there. I'd been the one who insisted that we sell everything in Spain, including my beloved chocolate shop, and that he travel with me to Ecuador to claim my inheritance—whatever that patrimony entailed. I'd used every tactic in my arsenal: how much this war had devastated Europe, how our shop was losing money, and my last resource: how this trip would be the perfect opportunity for him to write that novel he'd been dreaming about his entire life. But instead of letting it go, I pushed him further.

"Yes, but you make it seem like I did it for my own benefit." I couldn't control the volume of my voice anymore. "I did it for *us*!"

"Why couldn't you be happy with what we had? Why did you need more?"

"Are you serious? What did you want me to do with my inheritance? Give it away? Forgive me for looking out for our well-being. Forgive me for wanting to get us out of that tiny apartment and move to a splendid plantation in one of the top exporting countries in the world!"

"Oh, don't even start with that. I know all about that plantation. You've talked about nothing else since we received that damned letter! You're just like your father, crazed with ambition."

"You never even knew my father. *I* barely remember him!"

"It's what your mother said."

I didn't want to hear about my mother either. This trip had made me miss her even more—I thought about her every day.

"Look, Puri," Cristóbal said, softening his voice. "I don't want to argue with you. Not here. I promise I will be more available later, but now, be a good girl and let me get back to my novel."

He kissed my forehead, as though I were a four-year-old with a temper tantrum.

I took a step back. "Don't touch me!"

I'd spent an hour fixing my chestnut hair just right, reapplying my face powder—my *poudre de riz*—and choosing a lavender sequin dress that exposed my entire back. And this was what I got from my husband? A fraternal kiss? If he didn't look at me now that I was twenty-eight years old, what would happen when I turned thirty?

"Let's talk about this later," Cristóbal muttered as more people turned to look. "When you're calmer."

"No. Let's talk about it now."

Cristóbal let out an exasperated sigh. "You're being unreasonable, Puri."

Unreasonable? I couldn't even formulate a response. I would've probably insulted him if I did. I turned around and dashed out of the foyer, away from this man who had the power to infuriate me like no one else.

I climbed the ladder that led to the deck and darted forward without looking back. I didn't want Cristóbal to see my tears. I took in quick breaths, cool air clashing against my cheeks and a crescent moon over my head. I gripped the taffrail at the end of the ship.

Unreasonable, he'd said.

The black waters smashed against the hull—the sea could be so intimidating. My breathing slowed as my eyes focused on the hypnotic waves.

I supposed I was being a little obstinate. Normally, I wasn't this demanding with Cristóbal. In Sevilla, I had many friends to keep me entertained. I didn't need his constant attention. But I had no one else here. I'd been lonely for a week already and I was nervous about what awaited us in Ecuador. I needed his reassurance that everything would be all right. Had I made a mistake by giving away everything we had to chase after a dream—my father's dream?

If only Cristóbal and I weren't so different. Whereas he could live the rest of his days in a blissful immersion of his books, I couldn't sit still for more than five minutes. In the beginning of our marriage, I couldn't stand the long afternoons cross-stitching or mending socks while listening to the ticking of the clock marking the slow hours until dinnertime. The walls in our apartment suffocated me. Chocolate had been my salvation. From a young age, my grandmother—whom I'd been named after—had taught me all there was to know about chocolate. From how to transform the hard cacao beans into a silky, smooth liquid to learning what ingredients to mix in order to create a variety of textures and flavors that could be both pleasurable and addictive.

It had been my idea to transform the old bookstore, which had belonged to Cristóbal's father and grandfather, into a chocolate house. It was the most fashionable thing, it would bring some cachet to the neighborhood, I told him. And people would pay for my chocolate drinks and truffles. After all, *chocolaterías* were the fad in France—and my people wanted so much the prestige and status of the French.

Eventually, Cristóbal had acquiesced. But with time, he'd become less indulgent.

A warm breeze caressed the back of my neck.

Suddenly, I couldn't breathe.

I brought my hands to my throat, where there was an unbearable pressure, and felt a coil of rope. I didn't even have enough air to cry out.

"Shhh, María," a man whispered into my ear, "it's going to be over soon."

Who was this? How did he know my first name? My flailing hands touched two fists holding on to the rope. The man's hands were big and callused. Much larger than Cristóbal's.

Cristóbal, help me!

No sound came out. I turned my head to one side. The man with the burn scars. The pain in my neck was excruciating. I couldn't get enough air.

"Hey! What's going on over there?"

I could've sworn it was Cristóbal's voice. But maybe I was imagining things, wishing them.

My assailant's weight shifted. I stuck my thumbs between the rope and my windpipe. The pressure released a bit, but not enough.

Someone was coming.

I raked the man's shin with the heel of my shoe. The rope slowly released and I could finally take in some air. The rope fell to the ground. I gasped and coughed, catching a glimpse of the two men fighting behind me.

I spotted my husband's brown suit. His spectacles were on the tip of his nose, about to come off. Cristóbal had his arm wrapped around the man's neck, but my attacker squirmed until the two of them fell into a heap on the ground.

As much as I wanted to help Cristóbal, I couldn't stop coughing.

The man with the burn came to his feet first and drew a knife from his boot. Cristóbal stood, arching his body forward. I'd never seen Cristóbal like this, I never thought he had it in him to fight anybody. He was the kind of person who didn't think it was his place to decide over the life or death of an insect, much less another human being.

The man plunged the knife forward and sliced through Cristóbal's jacket. Cristóbal brought a hand to the wound in his arm, blood squeezing through his fingers. With a furious yell, Cristóbal lunged toward my assailant and tackled him to the ground. The knife flew out of the man's hand, but I couldn't see where it landed.

With my neck stinging, I went on a mad search for the knife, but the only thing I found was my husband's spectacles. A raspy sound finally managed to emerge from my throat.

"Someone . . . help!"

The music and laughter inside the vessel were so loud nobody seemed to hear my pleas. The two of them were rolling on the ground again. Cristóbal's body hit the railing.

I looked around for something I could use to hit the man. There was a lifeboat suspended by ropes not too far from us. I staggered toward it and climbed on the banister to reach the inside of the lifeboat. After another coughing spell, I grabbed an oar with both hands and hopped back to the deck.

Cristóbal now stood close to the edge of the ship. Something flipped inside my stomach when I saw him there, so close to falling into the immensity of the ocean. My assailant had somehow gotten a hold of the knife and stood in front of my husband, prodding at him with it. Only the handrail stood between the two of them. Cristóbal dodged the tip of the knife, holding on to the metal bar.

I lifted the oar to hit the man, but he was too close to Cristóbal and I didn't want to hurt my husband. I pointed at an opening in the railing.

"Cristóbal! There!"

Cristóbal glanced at the opening but before he could inch toward it, the man dug the knife in my husband's stomach.

"No!" I screamed, smashing the son of a bitch in the head with the oar.

The man folded over the banister, unconscious, and fell into the water, face first. Cristóbal brought his hands to the knife's handle, now buried in the depths of his abdomen. His eyes opened so wide I could barely recognize his familiar face, en-gulfed in agony and fear.

"Cristóbal!" I darted toward him, reaching out my hand to him, but a wave hit the side of the hull, making Cristóbal lose his balance and tumble into the sea, right after the other man.

I screamed so loud my throat felt as though I'd torn a vocal cord. It would take a long time for me to be able to speak again without pain.

CHAPTER 3

Guayas River
April 1920

En route to Vinces, I noticed two things: The first was the ca-
cophony of birds flying above our heads, as though we'd intruded
upon a land ruled by animals and they disapproved of our presence. The second thing was how wobbly the canoe taking us up
the Río Guayas was.

Neither my father's lawyer nor the young man rowing made
any attempt to help me onto the boat. For years, I'd taken men's
gallantry for granted. I'd never realized how much I'd relied on
them, how Cristóbal always rushed to open any door I happened
to be standing by, how he unscrewed a bottle of wine, opened a
jar of preserves, or carried logs for our chimney.

Just thinking about Cristóbal brought an enormous lump to
my throat. How could I ever move forward when *everything* reminded me of him?

I lowered my head to hide my tears.

I missed his company, his eagerness to please me, his sympa-
thetic ear (when he was listening). Strange how self-sufficient
men were. It was both an advantage and a disadvantage. In my
case, a clear disadvantage as both of these men had looked at me
as though I was less of a person when I struggled to keep my bal-

ance aboard and carry my luggage into the canoe at the same time.

Aquilino rested the side of his hand on his forehead and looked at the flock of seagulls passing by. He was sitting across from me, his legs crossed awkwardly and his long, skinny arm busily swatting mosquitoes every few minutes.

The young man taking us to Vinces couldn't have been older than seventeen. He said his name was Paco as he pushed my trunk to the back of the canoe. I supposed I should have been grateful for his help even though I sensed it had more to do with his own comfort than mine. He wore a white shirt soaked with sweat. I wondered why he even bothered wearing it as the fabric had become nearly transparent. As he rowed vigorously, two wet circles—as round and as dark as two pans—grew under his armpits. The skin on his face was hepatitis pale and his short, curly hair covered his head like moss.

"We'll go up the river," Aquilino said, pointing north. "That's where all the cacao plantations are. We call our cacao *Arriba* because of its location in relation to this river."

My father had mentioned this fact to my mother in the letters he'd sent when he first arrived. But that was when she still read his letters. After a few years, she stopped opening them and simply buried them inside a wicker basket until they turned yellow. I only read them after she passed away, though I'd been dying to open them all along.

"Our cacao is one of the best in the world," the lawyer said matter-of-factly.

"Yes, I've heard." It was becoming easier to speak in a lower tone. My voice had never been as high as other women's. My assistant at the chocolate shop, La Cordobesa, would never have been able to pull this off since she was so fond of screeching.

Paco didn't look at me once, which told me my disguise had fooled him. This fact was confirmed when he scratched his crotch enthusiastically.

From what the two of them explained, we were to navigate from river to river until we reached the Río Vinces. The Guayas

River was the longest, they said. Brown and vast, it was surrounded by abundant vegetation. I thought of the yellow plains
and olive trees in my native Andalucía. How different these two
landscapes were. Here, the trees along the river stretched out
from the earth as if yawning. They carried luscious leaves that
spread indiscriminately.

"Once we reach Vinces," Aquilino said, "we'll meet Don Armand's administrator. He'll take us to the plantation."

Paco pointed at a tree filled with yellow oval-sized fruits hanging around its thick trunk.

"That's it!" he said. "Our *Pepa de Oro.*"

I'd never seen what a cacao pod looked like before. It was hard
to believe that the dark, rich chocolate I prepared every day
came from this strange-looking fruit, this so-called golden seed,
as Paco had called it. He smiled with pride. I was just now realizing how important cacao was for Ecuadorians. I couldn't believe I
was here—I'd dreamt about it for so long. If only my father had
brought me instead of having to arrive under these bizarre circumstances.

Little else was said as we navigated from one river to the
other. The heat had rendered us mute. It was so stifling that I
wondered how wise it had been to dress like a man. I couldn't exactly remove my jacket like Aquilino did. Or undo my shirt, as
Paco had done a long time ago. The only thing I could do was dry
the sweat building over my forehead and neck with a handkerchief displaying Cristóbal's initials.

Nobody was waiting for us at the port. Aquilino suggested we
walk to the plaza to see if we could find the administrator. I offered Paco a handful of coins to watch my luggage on the deck—
I couldn't possibly haul the trunk around town as if it were a
purse.

I'd heard that the city of Vinces was called Little Paris, but I
had no idea how accurate the term was. The architecture was
reminiscent of any European city with Baroque buildings in pas-
tel colors. It even had a small version of the Eiffel Tower and a

palace in turquoise with intricate white molding surrounding windows and balconies. There were shops with French names all around us: Le Chic Parisien, Bazaar Verdú, and people who walked around in the latest fashions I'd only seen in Madrid. My father must have felt right at home here.

"There he is." Aquilino pointed ahead.

I could barely see through the fog in Cristóbal's spectacles, but I recognized a car approaching us. I removed my spectacles and wiped them with the corner of my vest.

A man in his late twenties descended.

"Don Martin!" Aquilino raised his right arm to him.

I hastily put my glasses back on before the man could see my face up close. I'd expected my father's plantation administrator to be much older, but this man seemed to be my age or maybe a little bit older. He was not handsome, at least not in the traditional sense. One of his eyelids drooped a little and his skin looked rough and uneven, as though the constant exposure to the sun had created layers upon layers of tanning that were now competing for supremacy on his face. But there was such a bright shine in his falcon eyes, I could only interpret it as aplomb.

"Good afternoon," the man named Martin said in a husky voice. "I apologize for the delay. I meant to meet you at the port."

Aquilino wiped the back of his neck with a handkerchief.

"Mr. Balboa, this is Don Armand's administrator, Martin Sabater."

Martin searched for something—or most likely, someone—behind my head. I extended my hand.

"Don Martin, meet Don Cristóbal de Balboa, Doña Purificación's husband," Aquilino said.

Martin squared his brick shoulders and shook my hand, looking me straight in the eye. No one had ever shaken my hand so hard or looked at me so intently. As a woman, I was used to a soft kiss or a gentle squeeze of the hand. Men certainly didn't hold a woman's gaze for long, unless they were close or openly flirting. I made a conscious effort to tighten my grasp with equal force.

The palm of his hand was a rock against my skin—maybe that was what the hands of all countrymen felt like. In comparison, Cristóbal had had the hands of a pianist: long and slender fingers, and as soft as a pair of velvet gloves.

I could feel my cheeks burning, uncertain of my disguise, but I held his gaze. I wouldn't be the first one to look away. Something told me that the approval of this man was paramount. But after a quick assessment of my face, Martin finally let go of my hand, seemingly uninterested.

"Did Doña Purificación stay at the port?" he asked.

"No." Aquilino gestured toward the automobile. "I will explain in the car."

The three of us entered a vehicle similar to Aquilino's, but this was a touring car with two rows of shiny leather seats rather than one. The seat offered some relief to my sore backside after the stiff canoe ride.

We stopped by the deck, where Martin and Paco loaded our luggage. On our way to the hacienda, Aquilino told Martin that Doña Purificación had perished on the ship. I tried to read something in Martin's solemn expression, but it was impossible. He turned toward me and offered his condolences without asking any details of my "wife's" passing. I couldn't decide if this was a sign of discretion or indifference.

I remained as inconspicuous as possible. I didn't want either one of them to examine my features too closely or ask me any questions. Like a mute, I listened to their sporadic chatting, which competed with the loud engine. They mentioned people I didn't know, but I supposed would meet soon. Most of the conversation, however, pertained to the weather pattern in the last couple of days and how well the crops were doing. Martin turned to me and explained that they'd already started collecting the pods. I barely nodded, as though I had no interest in the subject, but in reality, I was eager to learn everything there was to know about the business.

At the end of the road hung a handwritten sign over a sturdy fence. Martin stopped the vehicle to open the gate. I couldn't help but notice his assertive gait—the man radiated confidence. I lowered my head to read the sign through the windshield. Stunned, I read the name twice.

LA PURI.

My father had named his hacienda after me.

My father's mansion, because that was the only way to describe such a luxurious construction, was the most beautiful place I'd ever seen. It was a two-story manor with shutters and balconies all around, a solid structure painted with pristine detail in crimson, pink, and cream. Doric columns spread throughout the porch to support the second story. From the balconies hung ceramic pots with ferns and blue orchids. The porch floor was made out of the loveliest coral mosaic perfectly matching the walls. Under the shade sat a lady with a porcelain cup and a book in her hands.

Martin parked in front of the house and the two of them got out. After a moment, they turned around and stared at me. Like a fool, I'd been waiting for them to open the door for me—out of habit more than anything. I scrambled to open the door myself and got out.

The woman on the porch wore an ivory hat covering half of her face. Her silk gown in pearl tones was long, loose-fitted, and similar to the stylish dresses I'd seen so many times on the most affluent customers that came by my store. Perched on the woman's shoulder was a white cockatoo with a lengthy tail, as if to leave no doubt that her monochromatic presentation was deliberate.

As I approached the steps, I recognized my father's eyes in the woman's face. Growing up, I'd memorized every detail of my father's face through a portrait that sat on our chimney's mantelpiece.

She had to be one of my sisters.

When the woman saw us, she stood to greet us. The cockatoo remained still except for a thick yellow feather that popped on top of its head.

"Doña Angélica." Aquilino approached the young woman and kissed her hand.

She must have been a couple of years younger than me. Her body was slender, with a long, swanlike neck. There was elegance to every one of her moves, from the way she turned her head to examine us (me in particular) to the way her long fingers extended toward mine so I would kiss her hand once Aquilino had made the proper introductions. I couldn't reconcile how someone who looked so fragile would live in a rural place like this. She belonged in Madrid or in Paris, not in the country.

My cheeks flushed as I kissed my sister's hand. It felt so unnatural. The only hand I'd ever kissed had been the parish priest's (and only because my mother had prompted me to do so). One of Angélica's eyebrows lifted slightly as she examined my face more closely. I lowered my boater hat to cover as much of it as possible.

When Aquilino mentioned María Purificación's tragic demise at sea, a frown creased Angélica's brow.

"What a shame," she said, shaking her head. "I was looking forward to meeting her."

I couldn't tell if she was being sincere or just polite. Her expression revealed nothing more than discomfort, and given the strenuous heat, it might have been more of a reaction to the weather than to the sad news.

"Please come inside." She picked up a white fan from the table and opened it in one swift move, like a flamenco dancer. I couldn't help but picture my mother in her polka-dot skirt when she danced: her serious demeanor, her proud pose, the precision of her steps and the elegance of her hands. Flamenco had been her biggest passion, but she'd only danced in the privacy of our parlor; she'd always been so careful to hide her drops of *sangre gitana*.

The cockatoo adjusted its gray feet on my sister's shoulder as we entered the house.

She was very feminine and graceful, this sister of mine. The sway of her hips as she entered the hacienda held the complete attention of both Aquilino and Martin. Even I was staring, and I was a woman!

Inside, she removed her hat and set the bird on top of a cage. Angélica had her hair in a bob, very chic. As I faced my late father's oversized portrait in the foyer, I noticed how similar Angélica's complexion and coloring was to his.

The mosaic tile carried on to the foyer, but the walls inside were powder blue. Behind another column was a spiral staircase and a crystal chandelier hung above our heads.

A tall man was descending the staircase.

"Perfect timing, *cher*," Angélica told him. "Come meet María Purificación's husband, Don Cristóbal de Balboa."

When she said my name, it sounded as if she knew me well, as if she and I had grown up together, and the family talked about me often. There had been no awkwardness in her tone. It was somewhat touching, but I couldn't let my guard down. As far as I was concerned, someone in this house wanted me dead.

"Don Cristóbal, this is my husband, Laurent Dupret."

A Frenchman. I'd known beforehand that many Europeans had made their way to this remote corner of the world, but it still jarred me to find them here, looking so polished and radiant.

He wore a striped gray suit, a checkered tie, and a carefully folded handkerchief that strategically escaped his front pocket. He looked like he'd just shaved even though it was the middle of the afternoon.

"Enchanted," Laurent said, extending his hand to mine.

He had long arms and fingers that appeared to be made out of elastic rather than flesh and bone. His handshake was significantly softer than Martin's, but Laurent was manly, attractive, and had it not been for my disguise, I would've sworn his eyes scanned me with flirtation. There was something unsettling about him and I feared, more so than earlier, that he could see my true self beneath Cristóbal's spectacles. But if he noticed something, he didn't say.

I broke eye contact and followed my sister's lead to an elegant living room that smelled of polishing wax and pine. A harp sat in the corner of the room.

"Would you care for a whiskey, Don Cristóbal?" Angélica said.

I was used to light alcoholic beverages like wine, *sangría*, even champagne on occasion, but never hard liquor.

All eyes were set on me except for Martin's. After our initial introduction, he'd barely paid me any attention.

"Yes, thank you," I said slowly.

"Julia!" Angélica called. "Bring the whiskey bottle, please."

As we gathered around a marble-top table, a maid in a black-and-white uniform entered the parlor, her feet barely audible, her hair coiled in a braid around her head. She carried a tray filled with glasses and a golden bottle.

"Call Catalina," Angélica told her, picking up the bottle.

Catalina, my other sister.

You would think that as lonely as I was, I would be excited to meet my family. Under normal circumstances, I would've been. But after what had happened on that ship, I was wary, resentful. And yet, a part of me was curious to know more about them. I tried, unsuccessfully, to control the tremor in my hand as I reached for the glass Angélica offered me. As soon as my gaze met hers, she produced another smile.

"Have a seat, please," Angélica told me.

I picked a chair with a scarlet cushion.

A woman dressed entirely in black entered the room. She was much too young to be dressed with such severity. Her lace skirt covered her legs all the way to her ankles, and the long sleeves of her blouse concealed her arms entirely, but hard as she tried to hide underneath the dress, the fabric hugged her waist and hips so snugly it enhanced every curve of her body. Her eyes and eyebrows, carefully shaped and outlined, were so stunning it was impossible to look anywhere else.

She slid her hand over her tight bun and looked at me, the one stranger in the room.

"This is María Purificación's husband," Angélica said. "He came to us with the sad news that our sister perished aboard the *Andes*."

It was nearly imperceptible, but Catalina's eyes widened as she shot a quick glance at her sister. I couldn't tell if the gesture was a reaction to their sister's demise and what that meant for them, or if she had somehow discovered the truth about me.

"Don Cristóbal, this is my sister Catalina."

Catalina faced me and muttered what sounded like condolences.

"May the Lord have her in His eternal glory."

I stared at the gigantic cross hanging from Catalina's neck and nodded at her, tightening my fingers around the cold glass—I couldn't bring myself to kiss her hand, too.

"It's a pleasure to meet you," I said, mechanically.

For once, I was glad to have alcohol within my reach. I needed it. I took a shot that burned my throat on its way down, and turned to all the faces around the room, resisting the urge to blurt out accusations. One of them was responsible for the death of my Cristóbal, and yet, they behaved as noble, concerned family members, as though they cared about my fate. The only thing they might regret was not killing us both.

"Would you like something to eat, Don Cristóbal?" Angélica asked me.

"No, I'm fine."

My face was flushed, I could feel it. I leaned forward, resting my forearms on my knees, and the silence became intolerable. I could tear off my spectacles and beard, shout my name, and demand to know who killed my husband.

But things weren't so simple.

While Laurent and my sisters sat complacently across from me, Martin stretched to reach for another bottle in the cupboard. His jacket sagged open, revealing the menacing handle of a revolver.

If I became a nuisance, who's to say that he wouldn't shoot me? It would be convenient to all of my father's descendants. Nobody in this land knew who I was or had any affection for me. They could always pay off the lawyer. He owed me nothing. In fact, he'd known of our travel arrangements in detail—Cristóbal had sent him telegrams from Spain and Cuba. Anyone here could've bribed him to send a mercenary to dispose of this Spanish daughter, this pest coming to claim part of the Lafont estate.

I used to think that people were innately good. The Puri that grew up in Sevilla and befriended everyone in the neighborhood wouldn't have believed for a minute that this seemingly honorable group was capable of hurting her. But that Puri was long gone, she'd stayed behind in those Caribbean waters.

The taste of alcohol filled my mouth.

Aquilino removed a manila envelope from his briefcase, wiped his forehead and neck for good measure, and pulled out a stack of papers.

"Well," he said. "Let's talk about the issue at hand, Don Armand's inheritance."

CHAPTER 4

One week earlier

My mother always said that men were only useful when they were gone. After Cristóbal got lost in the Caribbean waters, the nostalgia of our lives together enveloped me like a cloak. There was not an hour, not a minute of the day, that I didn't think of him.

I kept reliving those last moments on the deck as though thinking about them would change anything. I should have hit the man before he stabbed Cristóbal. I should have jumped behind my husband and saved him from drowning. *I should have. I should have.* And then, after I was done tormenting myself for what I didn't do, I would try to convince myself that I did the right thing. I'd called for help immediately after Cristóbal's head got swallowed by a wave. I'd pressured the captain to stop the ship. I'd volunteered to go with the search team in one of the lifeboats. (The captain, however, denied my request. It was too dangerous for a woman, he said.) I'd stayed on the deck until dawn, my gaze fixed on the unrelenting waters, hoping to catch a glimpse of my husband.

They'd searched for hours, shining bright lights on the water's surface, calling out his name. But they couldn't find him or the vile man who had killed him. The captain offered me the consolation that my husband must have died a quick death. *He probably didn't suffer*, he said, *with that wound you mention. He probably lost consciousness from the loss of blood.*

Yes, that was my consolation. He must not have suffered.

Except that he never would've died had I not brought him to this wretched ship. Had I not fought with him that evening, he would've spent the night sleeping on top of the metal keys of his typewriter instead of in the bottom of the ocean.

Had I not, had I not.

I'd yelled at the captain when they stopped the search. I'd demanded they keep looking. I told him we were important people in Spain. Filthy rich. Plantation owners. We would pay him with gold, with land, if he found my Cristóbal. But when none of the yelling, the promises, or the threats worked, I begged. The man, his face tan, his mustache covering his upper lip, managed a sad smile and placed his hand on my shoulder.

"I'm sorry, ma'am. There's nothing else we can do. Your husband is with Our Lord now."

"How do you know?" I said, bitterly. His eyes widened a bit. I bet he'd never heard a blasphemy of this caliber coming from a Spanish woman before.

But instead of a look of reproach or a curt dismissal, he gently squeezed my shoulder and nodded.

The truth was I didn't want to think about where Cristóbal might be right now. None of the possibilities sounded good. They were downright horrific. Decomposing at the bottom of the ocean. Eaten by sharks. Bloated. Purple. I shut my eyes. I'd rather think of him coming back to me, somehow reemerging from the water and climbing the ten, fifteen meters from the waterline to the deck.

How I longed to hear the tapping of his keys now, but his precious typewriter had fallen silent since Cristóbal's disappearance, six torturous days ago. Had he thought about his novel in those last moments, about the fact that he would never finish it?

What I wouldn't give to trip over his boots in the dark.

Yes, my mother had been right about men. You only appreciated their virtues after they were gone.

Straightening my back, I knocked on the captain's door.

I'd never met a British person with a tan as deep as Captain Blake's.

"Mrs. Lafont, please come in."

By now, we'd become well acquainted with each other, but he still seemed reluctant to look me in the eye. He was the kind of man who was perfectly comfortable among other men, but terribly shy around women.

"How is the investigation going, Captain?"

"I'm glad you came, Mrs. Lafont, I wanted to talk to you about that. But please, have a seat." He pointed at an ochre leather sofa in front of the desk. A distinctive scent of tobacco permeated the room.

I obeyed. "Did you find out who that man was?"

"I'm afraid not, ma'am." He sat behind the cluttered desk; one side of his face partially covered by a globe. "We haven't found a record of anybody that matches your description of that man. In fact"—his ears turned slightly red—"I've decided to close down the investigation and rule your husband's death as an accident."

"An accident? What do you mean?" I gripped the armrest. "I told you a man attacked me! Cristóbal was only trying to defend me!"

"And I believe you, ma'am, no need to raise your voice. But I'm afraid that with the lack of evidence I can't do much. This investigation has already taken so much of my time and I have a ship to run and hundreds of passengers to tend to."

"This is ridiculous. You're going to lie, in writing, because it's easier and more convenient for you?"

"I'm not lying. Unfortunately, there's no evidence to prove me wrong."

"Is there anyone else who can take over this investigation? The authorities in Ecuador?"

"No, ma'am, this is a British ship, with British jurisdiction, so the investigation should be handled by British authorities. If the . . . incident had happened after we arrived in Ecuador, then they could handle it."

"Are you saying that I have to go all the way back to Europe to find my husband's killer? That's nonsense."

"You're welcome to file a claim with the British Consulate in Guayaquil and hire a barrister that may represent your interests in Britain."

In Britain? How were they going to find Cristóbal's murderer all the way there?

"I didn't invent that man, Captain, he was real. He knew my first name."

"Mrs. Lafont, I know this isn't what you wanted to hear. I know you wanted justice for your husband, but my hands are tied. I regret I cannot be more helpful."

I stood up, way too fast. Light-headed, I pressed my forehead with my hand.

"Are you all right? I can call Dr. Costa if you'd like."

"No," I said. "That won't be necessary."

I'd met Dr. Jaume Costa the night of the "accident." He was a compatriot of mine, a Catalonian traveling to Colombia to help with the Spanish influenza, which had taken so many lives in the last two years. After they'd stopped the search, the doctor had given me a sedative, which helped me not to go insane knowing that Cristóbal was somewhere in that terrifying ocean.

The captain stood. "If you choose to return to Spain, ma'am, I can arrange for you to get on another ship as soon as we land in the port of Guayaquil."

"No, thank you. I plan to continue my trip."

"But—forgive me for insisting—as I understand it, you'll be traveling to a small village on the coast of Ecuador. If I dare voice my opinion, I think a journey of that magnitude could be quite dangerous for a woman traveling alone."

With all the commotion, I hadn't given the rest of my trip much thought, though I'd dreaded the idea of working on a plantation without my husband's help.

"The Americas are quite different from what you're accustomed to, ma'am, especially the country. It's not my intention to scare you, but I've heard stories of missionaries—men and women—who've been attacked in the jungle and on the coast. I won't go into any details, but let's just say that the women, especially, went through some harrowing experiences."

My mouth went dry. After a moment, I found my voice.

"My father's attorney will be at the harbor to greet me and take me to Vinces." *Harrowing experiences? Like what?* "I thank you for your concern, Captain, but there's nothing to worry about."

I sounded more confident than I felt. The truth was I'd never met this lawyer, or had any references of him—of anybody there for that matter. I wondered about those women, those missionaries, the captain mentioned. Had they been raped? Were those the horrifying experiences Captain Blake hinted at? The captain had managed to make me nervous, but my pride didn't allow me to show it. I'd come too far to go back to Sevilla now, empty-handed. I nodded and walked out of the office.

I was becoming a little maniacal about Cristóbal's typewriter. For the last twenty minutes, I'd been cleaning every single key with a damp towel as if I could make them all shine. As if my husband would be coming back to finish his beloved novel. As if this would earn me his forgiveness. Once I finished with the bottom row, I started all over again from the top left corner. The letters and numbers got blurry. A tear fell on one of the keys.

A knock on the door startled me.

Have they found Cristóbal?

I rushed to open, drying my tears with the back of my hand and tightening my husband's smoking jacket across my chest.

The lady on the other side of the door must have read the disappointment on my face. Cristóbal was dead. When was I going to accept it?

"Good morning," she said. "I believe we met the other night when my husband was tending to you?"

I had a vague memory of those loose curls framing her pale face. When she smiled, her pointy canines disrupted the harmony and alignment of her front teeth, but otherwise, she was lovely, with a statuesque nose and full mouth.

"Your husband?" I said.

"Dr. Costa."

"Oh, yes, the Catalán."

"Yes. Forgive me for bothering you, but—" She looked down the hall. "Do you mind if I come in?"

"No, of course not." I opened the door wider.

"It's understandable that you don't remember me, with all that's happened." She took a seat on Cristóbal's cot, which remained as tidy as he'd left it. "I'm sorry, where are my manners? I haven't even told you my name." She extended her hand out to me. "I'm Montserrat."

"Purificación, but everyone calls me Puri."

"And you can call me Montse."

I liked her immediately. She had one of those friendly faces that promised late nights, wine, and entertaining conversation. Under different circumstances, Montse and I could've become close friends.

She removed a box of cigarettes and matches from a silver purse and offered me one. I shook my head. I'd never been one to smoke.

My vice was chocolate.

"Listen, I don't want you to think that I'm a busybody," she said, "but us compatriots must stick together, ¿sabes?" She lit her cigarette. "I just overheard something that might interest you. My husband and I were talking to Captain Blake—isn't he handsome?—about your husband's investigation. The captain said there had been no progress made and that he was closing the case and blah, blah, blah when one of his men came in with a valise." Smoke escaped her lips. "This valise was apparently found in one of the storage rooms by the galley, where they keep cleaning supplies, mops, brooms. Well, the thing is, they believe it belonged to that man who attacked you and your husband, and they think he'd been hiding in that room all along because there was a blanket on the floor."

So, I wasn't crazy. There *was* proof that the man had been here.

I stood up.

"Wait! Where are you going?"

"To talk to the captain, what else?"

"That's not going to do you any good." She uncrossed her legs. "Captain Blake asked me and my husband not to tell you anything. I think he just wants to turn the page and forget this ever happened."

"Well, I'm not going to allow that."

She smiled.

"Do you know where the valise is?" I had to see it before they disposed of it.

"I saw the captain leaving it by his desk. We should go now while they're having breakfast."

Montse stayed outside the captain's office while I snuck inside. A worn-out suitcase sat by the desk, in the same spot Montse had said it would be. I set it on top of the sofa, unclasped the draw bolts, and lifted the lid.

Beneath two shirts was a pair of trousers, underpants, a shaving kit, a box of soap. I was desperately looking for a wallet or something that would give me a name, but all I found was a book: a Bible. I nearly laughed at the irony.

I flipped through the book, scanning for his name. There was an envelope tucked inside. Glancing at the door, I opened the flap and removed two pieces of paper: one was a check, postdated, from a bank in Vinces. The beneficiary's name was left blank, and the signature was illegible.

The other paper had only one name: mine.

My suspicions were real. This man had been sent to kill me. This was enough proof to continue with the investigation, but I didn't trust the captain to do the right thing; it was too much of an inconvenience for him. He'd already proven that he wasn't interested in pursuing the case by not mentioning the suitcase and ruling the murder an accident. He wasn't a detective or a private investigator. He would simply send these papers to someone else, papers that would end up collecting dust in someone's cabinet. No, I didn't want the British authorities to handle this. Who knew how many months (or years) that would take?

I slipped the envelope inside my sleeve.

I would have to find Cristóbal's killer myself.

* * *

I didn't tell Montse about the papers. She was affable, but she'd just proven to me that she couldn't keep a secret. The first thing she'd done after the captain had asked for discretion was to come and tell me about the valise. Not that I wasn't grateful for the information. Thanks to her, I'd found the first clue I needed to discover who was behind all of this, but I barely knew the woman. I couldn't trust anybody.

I could hardly sleep that night. The little sleeping I did resulted in ghastly nightmares where I was either attacked by a group of men in the jungle or wandering by a cacao field in my camisole, lost. As I shifted positions in bed, the captain's words kept echoing in my mind: *"A journey of that magnitude could be quite dangerous for a woman traveling alone."*

I shivered just thinking about what might have happened to those missionaries the captain mentioned. If at least my final destination was Guayaquil, I could probably make it fine, but I knew nothing of Vinces or Ecuador's geography. For all I knew, this assassin—because I was certain now that my assault had not been random—could've been hired by my father's attorney. Only he knew I was coming and my arrival date. Cristóbal had mentioned the *Valbanera* in the telegram, and also the *Andes*, once we reached Cuba. For a moment, I contemplated the captain's offer to return to Sevilla.

But what did I have left there? No family, no house, not even my chocolate shop. Everything had been sold. All my possessions lay in three trunks. I sat up and turned on my bedside lamp.

The trunks rested in a pile against the wall. I hadn't given any thought to what I would do with Cristóbal's earthly possessions. It would be a strain to carry his things across an unknown land for no real purpose, just sentimentality. I ought to give away his clothes to the third-class passengers.

Cristóbal would've liked that. He'd been a charitable man. I'd once caught him feeding three beggars in the back of the chocolate shop. His jackets would go missing inexplicably, especially during the rainy season, only to be spotted a few days later on the body of a vagrant sitting outside the church steps. He always said he didn't need much to be content. Things didn't make him happy—experiences did.

I opened his trunk. His trousers, vests, and undergarments were neatly piled, just as he'd left them, and there were bow ties of different sizes and colors that I'd bought him. That was the way he liked things: orderly, predictable. I tried to imagine what he would've done had I been the one who'd perished on this ship. Would he have returned to Spain? Or would he have ventured across a foreign land to honor his wife's dying wishes? Whatever decision he would've made, things would've been much easier for him. He was a man, and as such, he was safer. Men would think twice before attacking him. Men were better fighters. Why, even someone as peaceful and intellectual as Cristóbal had put up a good fight with a criminal. He'd been much stronger than I'd ever imagined he would be. I pictured his shoulders, much wider than mine, his confident stride—so different from the delicate steps women were expected to take.

An idea flashed through my mind. I removed my husband's trousers from the trunk. They were wide, but with some minor adjustments, they might fit me. I'd always been naturally thin and so tall that as a teenager, I would often hunch my shoulders and bend my knees a little when a short man asked me to dance. It had always been a constant source of friction with my mother.

"Stand up straight," she would say, pulling my shoulders back. "Be proud. Men like confident women."

"But I'm so gawky. Nobody is ever going to want me," I would say. "Look at my arms. They go on forever!"

"Nonsense. With that body, you could be a dancer."

But I'd never been interested in flamenco. Cooking had always been my calling.

As a youngster, my biggest concern had been to be forced to marry a short man. I'd been so relieved when my mother introduced me to Cristóbal and he'd been a few centimeters taller than me.

I glanced at my face in the mirror. My eyebrows were thick and if I didn't pluck them for a few days, they might look more masculine. My nose was perky and small, but I could use Cristóbal's spectacles to cover it. After all, my father had had the same nose. I rubbed my smooth chin. I needed something to cover up the fact that I had no facial hair. Beards always made men look older. I thought of the vaudeville circus's members with those goatees and mustaches. The hair was fake—I'd seen them without beards the other day when they stepped out of their changing room to go to lunch. Perhaps I could sneak in there and take them? Maybe I would leave some money there for the trouble.

My long mane, Cristóbal's adoration, well, that would have to go. And what about my voice?

The advantage was that I didn't have a high voice. In fact, one of La Cordobesa's grievances, when I attempted to sing, was that I was trying to perform like a soprano when my voice was naturally low. Cristóbal told me once that he found my throaty voice sensual. It was ironic how the physical traits that had once been a source of shame for me—my thick wrists, my nearly flat chest, my angular hips—might help me now.

CHAPTER 5

April 1920

As Aquilino put his spectacles on, he informed me that there had been a previous reading of the will in front of this group three months ago, but he was required to read it again "to avoid any misunderstandings."

All hushed conversations ended and a tense silence followed.

Aquilino read a long and tedious document which stated that all of my father's worldly possessions were to be divided in four parts: one for each of his children. But there was one caveat, one small detail I wasn't expecting.

My father, the man I'd never really known and who, according to the will was "in full possession of his mental faculties," had left me in charge of his most prized possession: his cacao plantation. As things stood, I held 43 percent of his assets, and the other 57 percent was to be divided among my three siblings, giving each one of them 19 percent. Since Alberto had renounced his part, his portion was to be divided among the three remaining sisters, giving me close to 50 percent of my father's estate.

I was the majority holder and the one who would run the plantation.

My shoulders were so tense I had to make a conscious effort to relax them. Why had my father left me in charge when he hadn't seen me since I was two? Why not leave it to Angélica, the eldest of the Ecuadorian children, or Alberto, the only male in the family?

As Aquilino continued reading, in that monotone he used every time he opened his mouth, Angélica fanned herself faster. I resisted the urge to turn in her direction. I could only imagine the resentment that a woman like Angélica might feel about not being her father's primary beneficiary.

"Don Cristóbal," Aquilino said, lifting his head from the paper. "Ecuadorian law is specific when it comes to inheritances. With Doña Purificación's passing, her portion of the will is to be divided among her siblings." He watched each one of us over the rim of his glasses. "Heirs are only allowed to leave twenty-five percent of their assets to whoever they choose, but the rest, I'm afraid, must stay in the family."

I could feel everyone's eyes on me. The news, undoubtedly, sat well with all of them. With Puri gone, they all benefitted.

My mind was racing. Nobody in this room seemed overjoyed with the idea that Puri had inherited half of the Lafont estate. My eyes darted to the bulk in Martin's belt. If I exposed my true self right now, I would be in imminent danger. Whoever had plotted my death aboard the *Andes* would likely try again. However, if I continued to play my husband's role, I would be safe. I could freely investigate these people and find out who had set out to kill me. This descendant's clause might be advantageous. It could buy me time to find the proof I needed and then, I would expose my true identity and reclaim my inheritance.

One thought stopped me: If my husband didn't inherit anything, what excuse did he have to stay?

I set my glass on the coffee table. "Don Aquilino, you said that Puri could leave twenty-five percent of her inheritance to whoever she wanted, correct?"

"Yes." Aquilino was already putting his papers away, returning the envelope to his briefcase. "But her wishes must be expressed in writing to be valid."

I pulled my shoulders back. "Puri left her last wishes on a piece of paper. She wrote there that she wanted me to have whatever she inherited."

My sisters exchanged a quiet glance. Martin kept his gaze focused outside the window—he'd never managed to sit or open the bottle of *jerez*—and Laurent loosened his tie a notch. The cockatoo flew toward Angélica and rested on her shoulder. The bird's presence didn't seem to faze her.

"But that only entitles Don Cristóbal to twenty-five percent, right, Don Aquilino?" Angélica said.

"Correct. Doña Purificación's seventy-five percent has to be divided between you and Doña Catalina since Don Alberto renounced the will." The lawyer set his briefcase on the floor and turned to me. "Don Cristóbal, I would need to see this paper your wife signed, and of course, compare the signature to her passport. In addition, I'll need your marriage certificate and Doña Purificación's death certificate."

I wiped the sweat off my forehead. "I don't have my wife's death certificate at the moment. The ship's captain promised to send it to me from Panama after all the paperwork is completed. It should only take a week or so." I was amazed at my own ability to lie. I supposed it had to do with my self-preservation instinct. "Of course, I have no interest in staying. I know nothing about the business. In fact, I'd be glad to sell my twenty-five percent to anyone who wants it and then I can be on my way back to Spain."

Angélica sat back, petting her bird.

"I'm not a man of great ambitions," I continued. "My one and only dream has always been to write a novel. It's truly the only reason I agreed to accompany my wife on this odyssey."

Angélica smiled for the first time. "How wonderful. Laurent is also artistic. At one point, he had literary ambitions himself. Didn't you, *querido*?"

"*Oui, chérie*," Laurent said.

Martin folded his arms across his chest, as though this was the most boring subject in the world.

Even though I was lying when I told them I would sell my portion of the estate, I considered the possibility for a moment. Did I really want to spend the rest of my life surrounded by these vultures? Wouldn't it be better to go back to my country, where I still had friends who loved me, where I could see the magnificent Giralda bell tower from my window every morning, and where I could start a new business with my father's money? But if I returned to Spain, I would be going back *without my husband*, thanks to someone in this room.

This was a matter of justice, not ambition. My sisters had my father to themselves their entire lives and it was apparent that they didn't want to embrace me as one of their own, but instead, intended to wipe me off the face of the earth.

Tomás Aquilino stood. "In that case, Don Cristóbal, we can go back to town now and I can find you accommodations there."

"Nonsense," Catalina spoke in a firm voice. "Don Cristóbal is our late sister's husband and the proper thing would be for him to stay here, with family. Don't you think, Angélica?"

Angélica seemed taken aback, but remained silent.

I was torn. The only way I could find out more about these people and who was capable of murder was to stay nearby, but at the same time, I hated to admit—even to myself—I was nervous about the prospect of being so close to my potential killer, or to be discovered as an imposter.

"I wouldn't want to impose," I said. "But I do find this place most inspirational for my writing."

I was going against all my instincts, but as much as I disliked the idea of staying, I *had* to do it. If I boarded in town, how would I discover the truth?

"Of course you're not imposing, Don Cristóbal," Angélica stuttered a bit. "We'd be delighted to have you."

She held my gaze, her eyes glimmering.

"If everyone is in agreement then, I would like to get going before night falls," Aquilino said. "Don Cristóbal, once Doña Purificación's death certificate arrives, I will collect all the paperwork and we can continue with the will's proceedings. That will also give time to the other family members to decide if they want to purchase your share."

"Excellent," I said.

Everyone stood up to thank the lawyer, except for me. The whiskey gave me—albeit briefly—the courage to stay behind as

Aquilino said his goodbyes. I'd been hoping I didn't have to pose as a man any longer. I hated to be deceitful, but I saw no other way. In a week's time, I would probably know who wanted me dead and I could reclaim my portion under my own name. Assuming, of course, that they didn't manage to kill me first.

CHAPTER 6

Angélica

Three months earlier

Laurent squeezed my hand as Aquilino read a name that hadn't been spoken aloud in this house for years: María Purificación de Lafont y Toledo.

My father's Spanish daughter.

The legitimate one.

If it weren't for her, I would've been my father's favorite. Call me petty if you want, I don't care, but if you had to live under the shadow of a ghost—a perfect ghost, at that—you would know what it was like to never be good enough, to get crumbs of attention, a smile here and there, a soft squeeze on the check as payment for practicing the harp three hours a day and playing like the angels. My good disposition went unnoticed; so did my efforts to manage the household with mathematical precision after my mother's passing.

I straightened my back, listening to the long list of assets my father was leaving her. This only confirmed what I'd believed my entire life.

It wasn't that my father was cruel. On the contrary, he spoiled me with gifts all my life. But that was all I received: things. The problem was that I wasn't *her*, his firstborn; born in Europe to a Spanish mother. I wasn't passionate about the land, about those damned cacao beans and chocolate like she was—even from afar.

No, I was born in the New Continent; I was the daughter of a *mestiza*, his second not-so-legal wife and certainly not a full-blooded *hidalga*. It didn't matter that I wore the latest fashion or how light my hair was (I washed it with *manzanilla* tea every other day to keep my blond streaks). It didn't matter that I married a Frenchman, just to please my father, or that I'd memorized the name of every important wife in París Chiquito. It made no difference how meticulously I ran the kitchen, including my father's favorite recipes every week: chateaubriand, quiche Florentine, cordon bleu, soufflé, and of course, fish on Fridays, like a good Catholic family. We never skipped the rice, either—a day without rice in this country was like not fixing a complete meal at all.

But none of this mattered.

My father had no time for me. Some days, when he was speaking to Martin, I would wonder if I'd turned invisible. I would start coughing, just to get his attention, but it was often Martin who patted my back without missing a beat in the conversation.

I couldn't help but glance at Martin as Aquilino continued to read my father's last wishes with that monotonous drone of his. We were all gathered in the dining room, surrounding my father's lawyer, elbows resting on the surface of the table, mouths tightly shut. Martin pressed his hands together, his knuckles turning white. The will seemed to be having a similar effect on him as it did on me.

My father never tried to hide the fact that Martin was like the son he always wished Alberto had been. Martin was decisive, stern with the workers, and above all, he shared my father's passion for the business. Alberto, on the other hand, had been barely audible before joining the seminary. He'd spoken in monosyllables and his days and nights were spent locked in his room with his architecture, theology, and philosophy books. On the rare occasions that we did see him (during meals) he seemed to be transported to another world, and if he spoke, it would be to question things we'd never thought about or had nothing to do with our current conversation. ("Do you think goodness is innate or learned?")

Not my father. Not Martin. Their days and nights were scheduled around tree cycles. Those finicky trees were our fortune and our doom. If production was good in a given year, my father's boisterous laughter would echo in every corner of the house, and he would lavish my mother, Catalina, and me with gifts.

God help us if production was bad.

In a bad year, my father would lock himself in his study for hours on end, in a perpetual state of fasting, and the only person allowed inside was Martin (with a bottle of red wine or *jerez* as an entry ticket). My father would write infinite letters that never got mailed and ended up collecting dust in his drawers, "La Marseillaise" blasting on his gramophone again and again until we were close to tearing our ears out. Every time the door opened (mostly to let Martin in and out), I would hear cursing (*"Ce pays de merde!"*).

But apparently, he hadn't left Martin anything—an odd thing, considering how close they were and how patient Martin had been when my father was in one of his moods. Not even my mother—the saintliest of women—could stand his rotten temperament. She would invite the ladies from the *Cofradía* for an afternoon of prayer. ("Only the Virgin can help your father now," she would explain.) But my father loathed them and the sights and sounds of these devout ladies never seemed to improve his temper. Quite the opposite.

Alberto covered his mouth and coughed, but his serene expression returned almost immediately. Either he didn't fully grasp what Aquilino was saying or he didn't care.

When Aquilino finished reading the document, he raised his head and stared at each one of us.

Under the table, my legs trembled. I could barely digest that the respectable Armand Lafont had left the majority of his assets to his estranged daughter, someone who to me was nothing more than a name carved on a wooden sign that dangled at the plantation's entrance, a name that had tormented me all my life but somehow didn't seem real. Now that name was about to turn into flesh and blood and come to my hacienda to claim everything I'd managed to accrue and keep in pristine order. But where was this beloved daughter when I'd played nurse to my father during the last six months of his life? This had been the matador's final thrust.

"Oh, well," Catalina said, standing up. "What good are material possessions anyway? You can't really take them to the grave, can you?"

Of course she would say something like that. From an early age, Catalina had little use for our father's presents. It was not uncommon to see the peasants' daughters wearing my sister's gowns or playing with her toys.

"Oh, save it, Catalina," I said. "I don't want to hear a word about it!"

I managed to stand. Laurent rushed to assist me. He'd turned pale. Surely, this was not what he'd envisioned when he agreed to marry the daughter of a French landowner. Though he'd managed to fool everyone in town to think that he had his own personal fortune, he hadn't fooled me. I knew early on that Laurent's family had nothing but a prestigious last name and a lot of arrogance.

Martin avoided my eyes, like he always did, and removed a hand-rolled cigarette from his front pocket. His large hands shook slightly as he lit it, but once he took the first drag, the tremor subsided. The frown between his eyebrows remained.

"It goes without saying, Don Tomás, that my sisters are entitled to my portion of the estate," my brother Alberto said, rubbing his chin.

I still hadn't gotten used to seeing my baby brother dressed so solemnly. That white cassock made him look older, but his eyes still glistened with the same mischief and curiosity they had when he was a child.

"In that case, Padre Alberto, the law requires that your portion be divided among your three sisters."

"But Alberto doesn't even know Purificación," I said. "It wouldn't be fair! Didn't she get enough already?" My voice cracked.

"I'm just stating the facts according to the law, señora. You are certainly within your right to contest the will." Aquilino shut his briefcase. "In the meantime, I shall write a letter to your sister in Spain notifying her of your father's passing and his final will."

Laurent grasped my arm, shaking his head slightly. He leaned toward me, his warm, wine breath tickling my ear.

"Don't worry, *ma chère*," he whispered, "we'll take care of this."

CHAPTER 7

Puri

April 1920

"English or Western saddle?" Martin asked me.

At Angélica's request, my father's right-hand man was going to take me on a tour of the plantation while the maid, Julia, prepared my room. I wouldn't have accepted if I knew I would have to get on a horse.

Were all men supposed to know how to ride? I knew for a fact that Cristóbal had never climbed on one of these four-legged giants. He was as urban as they came. But I didn't want to look like a chicken in front of Martin. Something told me he didn't respect weakness.

"English," I said, which apparently was the wrong decision as the saddle was much too small and didn't have a horn to hold on to.

Martin smiled for the first time since I'd met him, but it didn't seem like a friendly gesture to me, more like a personal victory of sorts. He set a minuscule black saddle on the horse's back and pulled the leather girth under to tighten it around the belly. He'd chosen a white mare for me called Pacha, like the Incan queen, he said.

I stared at her long legs. How on earth was I going to climb this creature without tearing my pants in two?

Martin adjusted his own saddle, which was significantly larger than mine and made of a rougher leather with intricate leaf designs carved throughout. It also had a big horn sticking up on top. Was it too late to change my mind?

My pride didn't let me. I would climb on this horse and ride it even if it killed me.

In one swift move, Martin got on his horse. The saddle seemed to mold to his body. He made curious sounds with his tongue that communicated something to the animal. I had no idea what the message was, but the gelding must have understood because he shook his ears lightly and turned toward the trail.

Mimicking Martin, I rested both of my hands on Pacha's back and squeezed my left foot in the stirrup. I hoisted myself up, but the mare pulled away every time. I could sense Martin's eyes on me. My face burned. I gripped a mass of Pacha's hair with my left hand to hold her still and rested my right hand on the saddle. Then, I pulled myself up and crossed my leg over her back.

Finally!

Without letting go of Pacha's hair with one hand, I reached out for the reins, but before I could touch them, she reared. Like a marble, I slid all the way to the ground, where I landed right next to a pile of manure.

My pride hurt more than my back and buttocks, which is saying a lot because I had little cushion to muffle the fall and the pain throbbed from my tailbone to the top of my spine.

"Are you all right?" Martin asked me. His voice came out as though he were laughing. It only angered me more.

Yes, laugh all you want, Sabater, but the first thing I'm going to do when I'm the rightful owner of this hacienda is kick you out!

I supposed it would be of no use to expect him to help me up.

Being a man was dreadful.

I stood up, trying to shake the dirt off my bottom, but it was filled with mud. Pacha glanced at me with defiance. I would show her who was boss! Seizing the saddle, I hoisted myself up again, this time with more energy.

"We can switch horses if you'd like," Martin said. "Some people find it easier to ride in this kind of saddle."

"No. I'm fine."

"Don Armand liked English saddles. He said it was the only

saddle a gentleman should use. He used to say Western was for the lower class."

From his tone, I perceived some resentment toward my father. But to me, knowing that my father made the same choice was reassuring. By God, I would learn to ride as well as this man!

I attempted to balance my body on the mare's back, but my initial courage diminished as the creature started to move. *¡Madre mía!* The ground looked too far down and I didn't want to fall again. I couldn't bear the humiliation a second time. I clung to her mane with both hands and pressed my thighs against her sides.

When I looked up, Martin was staring at me.

Gone was his mocking demeanor. He'd turned dead serious. There was something odd about the way he was looking at me.

"What?" I said.

It took him a moment to answer. With his eyes still set on me, he said, "Use the reins to guide her. Right one when you want to turn right, left when you want to go left."

I told myself to calm down. He was probably just surprised that a man didn't know how to ride a horse.

"I know," I said. "I've ridden before. I'm just out of practice and this horse doesn't know me." I straightened my back and pulled on the right rein. Surprisingly, Pacha turned right, following Martin's horse.

As the mare continued down a dirt trail flanked by trees with enormous leaves, I could feel every muscle on the horse's back under my thighs. I tightened my grip on the reins, trying to concentrate on the view instead of my transportation.

After a long silence, Martin finally spoke.

"You're lucky to have come at this time of the year." He geared his horse away from the trail into a maze of overgrown vegetation. "We've just started collecting the pods so you'll see the entire process."

The horses' hooves crumpled the gray, dry leaves padding the ground. Hummingbirds chirped from the towering branches and a rooster crowed nearby. As we advanced into the heart of the plantation, the gurgle of a stream became louder. A mild scent of bananas filled the air.

"We plant banana trees to help with the growth of the cacao trees," Martin said, pointing at a shrub with leaves of a deeper green. "They provide shade from direct sunlight and also protect them from excessive winds. So do these cedars."

I raised my gaze toward the abundant branches and leaves of a few overgrown trees shielding the area like giant umbrellas.

Around me, yellow, orange, and green pods hung from V-shaped branches, like ornaments on a Christmas tree. They resembled papayas in shape and color, but smaller and with a rougher texture, as though the fruit had encountered a bad case of acne.

I had the feeling that I'd entered an enchanted forest. Cristóbal would've loved it. I couldn't help but wonder what it would've been like to live here with him, to raise our children surrounded by cedars and guava trees and, of course, cacao pods.

The children we would never have.

Even though I'd never been here before, this place felt like home, like I'd finally found the place where I belonged. If I ever contemplated the idea of selling my portion of the estate and leaving, I was deluding myself.

Hidden between leaves and branches, I discerned arms, hands, and knives cutting down pods. As we reached the peasants, they removed their hats and murmured greetings to Martin. There were about a dozen men in the area, all wearing stained white shirts and large straw hats.

A few steps away, a man with salt-and-pepper hair and a round, protruding stomach held a pod with one hand and a machete with the other. With swift, precise motions, he sliced the pod in half. The interior of the pod reminded me of brains and the smell made me think of fermented juice. A white, mucus-like membrane covered a string of cacao beans. He handed it to a man with a lengthy beard and longish hair who was kneeling by a metal bucket. With all that hair, he looked like someone who'd been stuck on an island for months. The man removed as much of the membrane as he could and dumped the beans inside the bucket. Once it was full, he carried it along a trail.

"Where is he taking them?" I asked.

"To the warehouse, for fermentation. We'll go there next."

I tried to follow Martin on the path, but apparently, Pacha had other plans. She darted through the woods, dodging tree trunks and branches, and picked up speed as the reins slipped from my hands.

I grasped her mane, kicking her sides to stop her, but she was immune to every attempt to dominate her. A branch hit my face and knocked Cristóbal's spectacles to the ground. I brought a hand to my beard to protect it.

"Pacha! Stop!" My voice came out high and screechy—good thing Martin wasn't around.

I got hold of the reins with one hand, still pressing on her sides. In the distance, I heard the hooves of another horse.

Martin!

Would he realize I was a woman without the glasses? And when was this damned horse going to stop? I could already taste the blood from a cut on my lower lip.

As we reached a stream, Pacha slowed her pace. She seemed to have forgotten that I was on her back as she approached the edge of the stream and ducked her head until it disappeared from view. *Jesús, María y José,* she was drinking, but all I wanted was to get down.

I managed to jump. The ground was moist and my shoes filled with mud. Rubbing my sore thighs, I retraced the steps Pacha had taken, trying to locate my glasses.

They must be around here. I took wide steps, my gaze on the crashing leaves. Out of the corner of my eye, something caught my attention. Something bright. I raised my head. Through the bushes, I could see a solid structure, a portion of a wall. I shoved the branches to the side and headed over.

It was a house and it had been destroyed by fire. There had been two stories once, but now the second floor was burned almost in its entirety. Parts of the charred walls remained standing and most of the windows on the first floor were broken. There were smoke stains all over the walls.

"Don Cristóbal!"

Martin's voice came from somewhere behind the bushes.

I didn't answer. I was afraid of how my voice would come out if I shouted. But his steps drew near nonetheless. He emerged on foot, pulling his horse by the reins.

"What happened to you?"

"Pacha decided to go for a drink," I said, pointing in the general direction of the stream.

"Well, she's not there anymore," he said, shaking his head. "But mares are finicky. Just like women." He chuckled.

I smiled unwillingly—it seemed like the proper reaction.

"You can ride Román back to the hacienda," he said.

I examined Martin's gray.

"That won't be necessary. I'll walk."

"Don't worry. I'll guide him."

"I said I'll walk."

Martin shrugged, then flashed my husband's spectacles. "Are these yours?"

"Yes." I extended my hand. "Thank you." I put the glasses on quickly before he could examine my features any further. "What happened there?" I lifted my chin toward the house.

He shrugged. "A fire. About a year ago. The foreman lived there with his family."

"Are they all right?"

"The father died. The mother and son survived, but they had third-degree burns, especially the son."

I swallowed. "A child?"

"Fortunately, no. He's all grown up, but the entire side of his face was burned."

CHAPTER 8

A burned man. I had to find out who he was and who in the family had hired him to kill me. Because I had no doubt that the man Martin mentioned, the one with the half-burnt face, was the bastard who had killed Cristóbal.

Alone in my room, I removed the check I'd found in the mysterious valise and examined it. The signature was illegible and it was postmarked May. In other words, the man couldn't cash the check until he was finished with me. The only other clue was the name of the bank in Vinces. Anyone in this house could've written the check and given it to the foreman's son. But who?

A stern knock on the door startled me. I needed to calm down. I was dressed like a man, I reasoned. My disguise made me less vulnerable. The house was filled with women; they would think twice before attacking me. In addition, I posed no threat, really, being that I supposedly inherited so little.

I shoved the check inside the night table drawer and searched for my beard and mustache on the surface.

Seeing my reflection in an oval mirror across the bed, I attached the hair to my face as quickly and precisely as possible. My chin itched. It was developing a rash from the adhesive.

"I'm sorry to interrupt your nap, Don Cristóbal," Julia, the maid, said from the other side of the door. "But Niña Angélica told me you'd had an incident with a horse and needed tending to."

I groaned. Everybody in this house seemed to follow Angél-ica's orders to the letter. Apparently, my sister was not satisfied with just sending me to rest, I needed a nurse, too.

The maid didn't wait for me to invite her in before she waltzed inside the chamber with a wicker basket in her hands. Poking out of the basket was a bottle of alcohol, a tin box, and rags.

"Oh, no, I'm fine," I said, even though I had a bad scrape on my arm and a large bruise on my outer thigh. "You don't need to bother."

"No bother. It's my job to serve you. Where are you hurt?"

There was no way I would remove my trousers in front of this woman, but the determination in Julia's eyes told me she wouldn't leave me alone unless she'd tended to at least one wound. I rolled my sleeve up to my elbow, revealing the fresh scrape. The blood had already dried but it was still tender and bright red. For the first time in my life, I was grateful for the fine hairs on my arms.

"It's nothing," I said.

Julia didn't answer. She was too busy setting the basket on my night table, removing a cotton ball from the tin box and moisten-ing it with alcohol.

If you looked at each of Julia's features with close attention, you wouldn't find anything particularly striking about any of them: her eyes were too distant from each other, her nose was rather common, and her eyebrows too thin, but all together they composed a harmonious, pleasant-looking face. Her one beauty lay perhaps in her soft, button mouth. She was thin, with no breasts to speak of, and wore tiny earrings—her only visible piece of jewelry.

"It's going to burn," she said before pressing the moist cotton against my elbow. I flinched at the sting and bit my lip.

Julia dressed the wound and, without a warning, pressed an-other cotton ball against my forehead. I froze. What if the beard and mustache fell down?

My hands dampened while she tended to my facial wound. Her warm breath tickled my nose. The aroma of sautéed onions and lavender lye wafted from her hair. As she parted her lips, I noticed her crooked front teeth, her overbite reminiscent of a rabbit. I've never been this close to a woman, except for my mother, and her proximity made me uncomfortable.

How would a man react to having a woman so close? Cristóbal would probably stare at my chest, but I couldn't bring myself to do that. I had an urge to push her away, but that would be suspicious.

After excruciating seconds bandaging my forehead, she leaned back. "There."

I stood up. "*Gracias.*"

"Dinner will be served in about twenty minutes. I will come and fetch you then."

"Don't bother. I can get there on my own," I said. I wasn't used to all these servants at my beck and call. Cristóbal and I had lived in a minuscule apartment in Sevilla with barely enough room for the two of us and our plants. I'd done all the cooking myself and Doña Candelaria, our landlady, sent her maid once a week to wash our clothes and tidy up the place.

Nodding, Julia collected the used cotton balls and placed them inside the basket.

"Julia?"

She lifted her eyes to meet mine.

"Have you worked here long?"

"It'll be four years in December," she said.

So, she'd met my father. And probably the burned man, too.

"Don Martin showed me a house today destroyed by a fire. Do you know who lived there?"

"The foreman and his family, but I vaguely remember them. I'm always at the house."

"You don't know their names?"

"Why?"

"I don't know. I was touched by what happened to them. Maybe something can be done for those poor people."

"They left after the fire."

She collected her things. I had to get more information from her before she left, like who else lived in this house.

"One last thing, Julia. Is Doña Catalina married?"

"No."

"But she's so pretty. She must have a lot of admirers."

"If she has any, I've never met them." She examined me in silence as if to determine if I was trustworthy or not. "You'd best stay away from her. La Niña Catalina is considered a saint around here."

I smiled, but Julia's frown left no doubt that she wasn't joking. I didn't know if I was more amused by the fact that she thought I had a romantic interest in my sister or by the saint comment.

"A saint? Why?"

"She saw the Virgin when she was a child."

I wasn't sure if I perceived contempt or admiration in her tone.

"Where did she see her?" I asked, swallowing the word "allegedly."

"She appeared in her room. She sent a message through her to all the villagers."

"What message?"

Julia finished collecting her things. "You'll have to ask her personally."

Without another word, she left the room. I'd only heard of Virgin apparitions in books and legends, never in real life. I wondered what my father thought of this saintly daughter of his. Did he, like Julia, believe this to be true? Or had he been a skeptic, like me?

CHAPTER 9

Catalina

Three months earlier

Angélica hadn't spoken to me in two days. This was not uncommon; she had one of those terrible tempers, just like our father—though she would never admit to it. This time, though, I didn't blame her for her anger. It must have been an abysmal blow to her ego to know that our father had left the majority of his assets to a sister we'd never met.

What I wasn't expecting was to see her poking her head inside my bedroom with that charming smile of hers. Angélica hadn't been to my room since we were little girls. Even then, I was always the one who followed her around the house.

"What is it?" I asked, ignoring my good manners.

She opened the door wider and stepped inside with Ramona on her shoulder. I was surprised not to see Laurent trailing behind Angélica like a shadow. His vocation in this world, it seemed, was to please my sister in every one of her whims.

"What? I can't stop by to say hello?" She slithered toward my bed and sat next to me. "What are you reading?"

I flipped my copy of *Fortunata y Jacinta* so she couldn't see the cover. Benito Pérez Galdós was on the Vatican's list of forbidden authors, but I was infatuated with this story. I'd waited years to get the book. What an odyssey it had been.

"Is there anything I can do for you, *hermana*?" I said.

"Actually, yes." Her delicate fingers traced the outline of my book, my favorite one, though Angélica had no idea. She didn't know a thing about me even though we'd spent every day of our lives under the same roof.

"Well, how do you feel about our father's will?"

I shrugged. I'd never had any expectations of inheriting. I supposed that was why I hadn't been too surprised with my father's last wishes.

"I know you're not an ambitious woman and you're more content with . . . spiritual matters. But don't you see that a big injustice has been committed on our behalf?"

"The world is not just. Look at what happened to our Lord, Jesus Christ."

"I agree." She stretched her arm in my direction with feline grace and rested her hand on mine. "But I worry about you, Catalina. What's going to happen to you when I'm gone? You know that as the oldest, I'll probably die before you. What are you going to do without the protection of a husband? We both know that our brother can't be of service to you. Who knows how much longer he'll stay in this parish. At any moment, they could send him away."

I didn't want to hear anything about husbands. The subject was one that hurt and embarrassed me—I was the only woman my age who hadn't married in all of París Chiquito.

"But things don't have to be that way," she said.

My patience was growing thin, but I couldn't bring myself to be rude to Angélica. It was a remnant of my childhood to always strive for her approval. To have my beloved, older sister in my room, paying me attention, had been my biggest desire as a child. She'd always been so sophisticated, so confident, the most popular girl in Vinces. At seventeen, there had not been a day when she didn't receive an admirer or at the very least, a gift. It had been maddening.

"And I think I have the solution," she said.

"What are you talking about?"

"*Hermana*, can't you see? With Purificación's part of the inheritance, we could have a meaningful dowry for you. You could finally get married!"

"At my age?"

Who would want to marry a twenty-three-year-old spinster?

Angélica let out a laugh, which reminded me of so many of those childhood years when she would beat me at cards.

"Catalina, dear, you're at your prime! You've never been more beautiful. The only reason men don't approach you is that they don't want to be damned for eternity. It can be intimidating for a man to be with a woman like you, the woman our Holy Mother has chosen as her messenger."

Heavens, I was so tired of hearing how saintly and pure I was!

"But how would a dowry change the fact that men, as you say, are intimidated by me?"

She stood. "Well, it would just *motivate* them to pursue you. They'll see that you're interested in having a family, a house of your own. Right now, people in town think you're perfectly content praying all day and communicating with the Virgin. They don't know there's a side of you who longs to be loved and have children." She squeezed my shoulder. "Don't let your life be just about that. You can have so much more, Catalina. You *deserve* more."

How could I explain the effect my sister's words had on me? I knew Angélica was slick as a cat—I'd always known—and yet, I couldn't resist her. I was simply one more pawn in the long list of people who couldn't deny Angélica any of her wishes.

CHAPTER 10

Puri

April 1920

The cedar floors creaked with every one of my steps down the staircase. I followed the voices coming from one of the rooms and opened the door. The entire family was seated around an oval table, a fine Italian Gobelin tapestry displayed across the wall. Martin was also there and a new face, a young priest (my brother?), at one end of the table. Even the cockatoo had a spot on the back of Angélica's chair.

"Don Cristóbal, I'm glad you could make it," said Angélica from the other end. She'd changed into a black sequin dress and a matching hat with a long feather, which held the bird's attention.

"Good evening," I said to all. I was getting better at lowering the range of my voice without having to clear my throat every two minutes.

It was a warm night, with mosquitoes being shooed away from a tray of crab legs and boiled shrimp. My sisters' fans followed the motions of their tireless wrists. I could already tell I wouldn't be able to sleep under this heat. The air was so dense I could almost touch it and Cristóbal's shirt was glued to my back. Good thing I'd cut my hair so short.

"Don Cristóbal," Angélica said. "This is my brother, Padre Alberto."

"Delighted," he said, setting his glass of water down.

I nodded in return. He stared at me. Too intently. He was a lean man with lengthy arms, like mine, and sunken hazel eyes. He gave an aura of ease that contrasted with Angélica's constant fidgeting.

I took a seat in an empty spot across from Catalina and Martin. To my left was Angélica's husband, Laurent, and to my right, the priest. Laurent served me a glass of wine. It seemed I had interrupted a conversation and the silence in the room was making me nervous. I inadvertently touched my chin to make sure my beard was still in place.

Martin was also staring—did he live here, too? I found his presence unnerving, knowing he carried a gun with him. The only one who didn't seem threatening was Catalina, who watched me with a kind smile as she dabbed her mouth with a napkin.

Maybe I should've stayed in Vinces. Or maybe I should have hired someone to protect me as I stormed into the hacienda to claim my inheritance. But where in this remote land would I find this someone? Certainly not in the newspaper.

"Quiere cacao, quiere cacao," the cockatoo recited.

It took me a minute to understand what she was saying.

"Here, Ramona, but be quiet, dear, we have guests." Angélica picked some kind of bean from a tiny bowl by her plate and fed it to the bird.

"Quiere cacao, quiere cacao."

Wants cacao? Yes, that's what she'd said. Angélica was feeding her cacao beans. As hard to find and expensive as they were in Spain and this woman wasted them on a bird.

"Angélica, honestly, does Ramona have to be with you even at dinnertime?" Catalina said.

Angélica frowned. "Nobody asked your opinion."

"Come on, *hermanas*, be nice. Our brother-in-law is here," the priest said.

Brother-in-law? Oh, yes. Me.

"Don Cristóbal," Alberto said, "I'm looking forward to learning about your country. I've always wanted to go to Spain. It must be so different."

"It is," I said, "Andalucía is a lot drier."

"Is it true there are fortress cities all around?"

"Some."

"And windmills, like in *Don Quijote*?" Alberto said.

"Yes, and rows and rows of olive trees."

"Fascinating," he said.

"If you like olives," Catalina said, grimacing.

"Father used to love them," Angélica said with a distant voice. "He always teased Catalina that it was better that she didn't like them because they were so expensive and hard to have shipped to this part of the world. We usually get them from Perú."

I didn't comment. Not that I didn't want to hear about my father, but to learn about these cozy moments between him and my sisters bothered me. It reminded me of everything I'd missed.

I pulled crab meat from one of the legs. Another advantage of being a man was that you could eat with your hands and nobody looked at you twice. My sisters, on the other hand, had to use forks and knives to remove what little meat they could from the carcass.

Martin brought up the subject of the city's celebrations coming up.

"You should stay, Don Cristóbal," Catalina said. "There are a lot of amusing activities during that week."

"What's the celebration for?" I asked.

"The foundation of Vinces," Martin said.

I wasn't in the mood for celebrations, honestly, but my husband would've probably enjoyed this colloquial tradition. Plus, it could buy me some time. "I suppose it could be inspirational for my book," I said.

"Don't get your hopes up," Laurent pitched in. "It's all very archaic if you ask me."

"Archaic or not," Martin said, "it would be a good opportunity to mingle with foreign buyers."

"I agree," I said, unable to suppress my opinion; this was going to be my business, too.

Martin gazed at me.

"You know what would bring some cachet to the festivities?" Laurent told his wife. "A regatta."

"A regatta?" Martin said. "How is that going to sell cacao beans?"

"Didn't you say you wanted to bring in foreign buyers? Regattas are the fad in Europe."

"Who said we wanted to be like Europeans?"

"Martin, please," Angélica said, then squeezed Laurent's hand. "I think that's a wonderful idea, *mon amour*."

"A regatta. I like the sound of that," my brother said. "Perhaps the Church should have its own team, too. The exercise would do a lot of good to some of its heavier members. Perhaps Father Telmo could be team captain." He winked at me, patting his flat stomach.

"Alberto!" Catalina said. "That's not a very Christian thing to say."

"Relax, *hermanita*. The Virgin likes jokes, too."

"*Quiere cacao, quiere cacao.*"

"Julia!" Angélica said. "More cacao for Ramona, please."

Julia entered carrying tiny cups of coffee for all. "There's no more cacao."

"Nonsense!" Angélica said, standing. "We live on a plantation. Of course there's cacao."

My sister darted through the kitchen door.

"*Quiere cacao, quiere cacao.*"

Alberto launched toward the cockatoo and covered her face with his long napkin.

"There, go to sleep, Ramona."

The cockatoo moved its feet up and down from the back of the chair, whistling.

As Julia placed a coffee in front of me, I longed for my cocoa. I hadn't had one since I left my country. "If Angélica manages to find some beans," I said, "I could prepare hot cocoa for all."

They all looked at one another. Had I said something wrong? Of course. Men did *not* prepare anything for others (unless it involved alcohol). They could barely cut the food on their own plates. What an idiot I was—I'd given myself away with my innate desire to serve.

"Hot cocoa?" Catalina said. "What is that?"

"Chocolate," I said. "Mixed with milk, sugar, and cinnamon. Served warm."

"You would think that with all this cacao around, we would've tried those delicacies," she said, "but we exporters don't ever get to see the other part of the cacao cycle."

I couldn't believe it—*they'd never tried chocolate.*

"I have," Laurent said. "My country practically invented chocolate."

"Actually," I said, "it was the Spanish who brought chocolate to Europe from the American continent, and we were the first ones to add milk and sugar to it."

"Don Cristóbal is right," Martin said. Of course, anything to contradict Laurent.

Ramona let out a loud screech, her body bouncing up and down.

"Ramona! What's happened to you?" Angélica was back, nestling some seeds in her hand. She removed the cloth from the bird's head. Ramona puffed, exposing the yellow plumage under her wings, and went on a tirade of indecipherable insults. "You're not funny, Alberto. Honestly, I don't know how people confess their sins to *you*," Angélica said.

"Well, they do. Happily," he said. "In fact, you should, too."

"Thank you." Angélica took her seat and calmed her bird with the seeds. "But I'm perfectly content with Father Telmo."

"That's because he falls asleep while you talk."

"Alberto!" Catalina said. "Enough blasphemy, please. What is Don Cristóbal going to think? That we mock our faith?"

I didn't know what to think of them, honestly. I forced myself to finish my coffee—it was so bitter in comparison to my cocoa.

After dinner, my sisters played their instruments. They made a great duet: Angélica with the harp and Catalina with the violin. It was obvious that they'd had formal musical training. Had my father sent for me years ago, I might have had my own instructor and could have become a proficient performer, too—I loved music so.

I refrained from humming or swaying, though I was moved by the beautiful sounds coming from my sisters' dextrous fingers. I wished I could accompany them with my singing, but it would be disastrous if I did. For one, I had no ability as a tenor or a baritone, so my singing would be an obvious giveaway. Then there was the fact that I'd become insecure about my voice ever since Cristóbal and La Cordobesa had gotten into the habit of shoving cotton balls into their ears every time I sang. The nerve of those two! I knew I wasn't La Caramba or one of those legendary *zarzuela* singers, but I liked to think I had some flair when I sang, which I did often, usually when roasting cacao beans at the shop. I sighed. How I missed my old life. But it was gone for good.

"Don Cristóbal?" Martin's voice interrupted my thoughts.

My sisters were done performing and stared at me expectantly.

"Yes?" I said.

"I was asking if you'd like to join me and Alberto for a drink in town?"

A drink with a priest? My first inclination was to decline. I didn't like to stay up late and I didn't particularly enjoy Martin's company, but I stopped myself. This might be a good opportunity to get some information from these men. Moreover, if I found a way to spend the night in town, I could take the check to the bank first thing in the morning and find out who had signed it. Otherwise, I would have to find a ride to Vinces in the morning or climb on one of those horses again and take myself to the bank. My sore bottom didn't like that idea one bit.

"Sure," I said.

While my brother said goodbye to my sisters, I rushed upstairs and collected the check.

HAPTER 11

It was apparent I knew little about males and their habits because I'd never heard of priests going to bars. Or maybe my brother was different from other men of God. But tonight, I had the rare opportunity to enter the male mind without any restrictions. To my surprise, I was growing excited to get to know this mysterious world of theirs.

I followed Martin and Alberto to a dim room, where the laughter and the clicking of bottles and glasses became louder. We walked past a long bar aligned with stools and two bartenders in pressed white aprons hustling behind the counter.

We settled in one of the back tables. As the first round of *aguardiente* was passed, I studied my two companions. There was a camaraderie between them that hadn't been apparent at the house, in a way I'd never experienced with women. With the women in my life—my mother, my friends, my assistant—I always had to choose my words carefully, lest I hurt their feelings. But these two men were completely at ease with each other. Martin explained that the two of them had known each other all their lives even though Alberto was three years younger than Martin.

"I tried to save this one from a life of celibacy, but he wouldn't listen," Martin said, rolling up his sleeves. "Now he has to pay the consequences with a sore wrist."

It took me a moment to understand the implication, but when

I did, I offered a chuckle of approval—not that this was my kind of humor—but it seemed to appeal to both of them.

Martin ran his fingers through his hair, laughing with gusto, while Alberto watched him with an amused smile. Martin refilled his glass and tried to add more *puro*, as he called it, to mine, but I shook my head.

Martin scoffed. "What? You're worried about this cassock?" He nodded at Alberto. "He's not going to hold it against you. He doesn't go around counting sins."

Well, if I was going to convince these men that I was one of them, then I had to act like them. If the priest was drinking, then I'd better do it too, even if I wasn't fond of alcohol. Oh, no, was I going to turn into a drunk by the end of this experience?

"All right, just one more," I said. "I'm trying to cut back."

Martin filled my glass. "Why? You're a free man now."

The callousness of this man! Alberto widened his eyes. I must have done the same because Martin seemed taken aback.

"I'm sorry, *hermano*," he told me. "It slipped out." Martin dipped his chin down.

Alberto leaned forward, his bony fingers crossed on the table. "Excuse him, Don Cristóbal. Martin hasn't had the best of luck with women so he thinks every man feels the same way he does." He then turned to Martin. "If you don't watch what you say, Don Cristóbal is going to think you're a misogynist like Aristotle."

"What does Aristotle have to do with anything?" Martin said.

"Incidentally, I was just reading today that he'd said women were biologically inferior to men. And you know how the Greeks had all those negative depictions of women, starting with Pandora."

"Well, I'm not Greek nor do I hate women, clergyman. On the contrary."

I wasn't so sure I believed Martin. He was cold with my sisters and that comment he'd just thrown didn't sound like he had a lot of respect for women. In fact, he seemed like the kind of man who wouldn't be thrilled with a woman for a boss.

As Alberto continued his exploration of Greek mythology and their idiosyncrasies, I examined both men, wishing I could read their thoughts and hearts. Alberto appeared incapable of killing a fly, much less his older sister, but there was something odd about him. The religious men I'd met in the past were neither friendly nor easygoing. They had a somberness about them, a permanent state of melancholy, but Alberto didn't appear to take himself too seriously. What could've prompted him to devote his life to the Church? I'd known a couple of families in Spain who forced their sons into the seminary when they were little. Some parents dreamt of having a religious son or daughter. Perhaps this had been the case with my brother.

Regardless, Alberto had no clear motive for killing me. He'd voluntarily given away his portion of the estate (or so Aquilino said). It made no sense that he would send someone to kill me after he'd renounced the money. Unless he was *pretending* to be humble and in reality, he had an evil plan to keep his portion *and* mine.

It didn't seem likely.

I then turned my attention to Martin Sabater with his disheveled hair, unfastened tie, and purple circles under his eyes. He'd removed his jacket a long time ago and seemed perfectly at ease in this dump. Now, there was a dark soul. He drank, he cursed (as I'd heard him do several times since we'd sat down), and he didn't seem to have much respect for women. In addition, he carried a gun.

But how would he benefit from my death? He still wouldn't inherit anything. Unless he'd reached an agreement with one of my sisters? I couldn't recall anything peculiar in his behavior toward either one of them. No strange looks or whispers. On the contrary, Angélica didn't seem to like him much, and Catalina had been indifferent to him. And yet, if someone in this place appeared capable of harming others, it was this man.

"What do you think, Don Cristóbal?" Martin said.

The two of them were staring at me.

"Sorry, you were saying?"

"Alberto here wanted to know whether you think goodness is innate or learned."

I gave this some thought. Someone like Cristóbal or my mother? Innately good. Me, I wasn't so sure. The fact that I'd persuaded my husband to leave everything behind to follow *my*

dream and that I was deceiving all these people—both the innocent and the guilty—didn't speak wonders about my inherent
moral virtues.

"Both." I turned to Martin. "And you?"

"I think the question is too simplistic—no offense, *hermano*,"
he told Alberto. "Goodness itself is subjective. What you consider good may not be the same thing I do. Is goodness behaving
according to societal norms or laws imposed by either a government or the clergy? Is goodness becoming self-sacrificial? Because there may be a conflict there between what you want and
what others do. But what makes other people's wants or needs
more important than yours? What happens if you're good to others, but not to yourself? Wouldn't motivation play a part, too?
What if you act like a good person, but inside, all you want is to
kill the world? What if you're doing it just so others *think* you're
good? So, the real question is what makes someone good, their
actions or their motivations?" Martin split the remains of the bottle between Alberto and me. "What do you say, Padre?"

"Actions."

"But isn't your God supposed to know what's in the heart of
every human?" Martin said.

"So what?" I said. "If you have evil thoughts, but don't act on
them, why should you be punished for them?"

"Who's talking about punishment? I'm talking about moral
theory here."

Alberto crossed his hands behind his head and watched us
with a tight-lipped smile. His pleased expression told me he'd
been a troublemaker as a child.

"Well," I said after giving his words some thought. "I think
good and evil lives inside every person. It's a struggle we all live
with. Whatever tendency one favors is what we are, I suppose." I
held his stare for a long moment. I was surprised that someone
like Martin, someone who seconds ago I'd judged as a brute and
a woman-hater, would have the mind and eloquence to speak
about a complex philosophical matter with such intensity.

"Well," Alberto said, standing. "I'm afraid it's time for me to
go back to my daily struggle with my own demons. Don Cristóbal, it has been an absolute pleasure to meet you." He extended

his hand toward me. Was I supposed to kiss it or shake it? I chose the latter.

"Likewise."

"What on earth? You introduce a thorny subject and then you leave us?" Martin said. "Don't go, *hermano*. It's still early. I'll drive you in fifteen minutes, I promise."

"Don't bother, Martin. It's a beautiful night to walk." He turned to me. "Next time we meet, I'd like to hear about my sister Purificación."

For reasons I couldn't describe, Alberto's comment gave me the urge to cry. I'd become so sensitive since Cristóbal's passing. Perhaps it was the *aguardiente*.

I stared after my brother as he left the bar, about to ask Martin if he lived in town—that might solve my imminent problem of where to spend the night and how to get to the bank early—when two women approached us. *What now?* I was so exhausted—all I wanted was to sleep. But men apparently had more energy than us. Martin opened his arms to one of the women, a lanky one with the lavender strap of her dress drooping over her arm and unruly charcoal hair, who promptly sat on his lap.

"*Christ on the cross!*" she said. "I thought that priest would never leave!"

Martin whispered into her ear. She looked at me, then turned to say something to her friend.

Oh, no, what awaited me? Swallowing, I glanced at the other woman, standing a step away from me. The woman watched me with a smile, twirling one of the loose tendrils by her ear. This one was heavier, short, and had applied at least a pound of rouge to her cheeks.

"Would you like some company?" she said.

"I'm fine, thank you." I looked at the front door, longingly. Perhaps I could still catch my brother and seek refuge at the monastery or wherever he lived.

Despite my response, she sat on my lap. *¡Madre mía!*, she was so heavy my legs were about to break.

"*Mi amor*, there's no reason to be lonely."

The woman, who said her name was Carmela, cupped my chin with her hands.

"You're adorable. Look at that dainty beard!"

Adorable and dainty weren't exactly manly compliments. I hoped Martin hadn't heard. I pulled back as much as I could but there was nowhere to go.

"But why are you so tense? You're with friends."

Through the space between her curls, I could see that Martin was kissing the other woman. For the love of everything holy, how did one politely dismiss a prostitute? As a woman, I'd never confronted such a dilemma.

"Excuse me, Carmela," I said. "It's late and I have to be some—Wait! What are you doing?"

The woman was kissing, yes, *kissing* my neck!

"You smell so good," she said, "like a real man."

A *real man?* Yes, good thing she reminded me. A real man wouldn't push a woman away from him in horror. As much as I wanted to escape her loving claws, I had an image to protect. I couldn't let Martin suspect anything.

Her hand cruised along my inner thigh to my groin. I yelped. Fortunately, Martin was so immersed in the heat of passion that he didn't seem to hear me.

"Where is it?" Carmela whispered.

How could I explain that "it" was nothing but a sock and it had moved from its proper spot?

"Wait," I said. "Isn't there a more private place where we could go?"

She pulled back. "I thought you'd never ask."

Collecting the skirt of her purple dress, she stood up and offered me a hand. In a pause between kisses, Martin winked at me.

Donning my bowler hat, I followed Carmela outside the bar. What a relief to be able to breathe fresh air again! I scouted every corner, trying to plan my escape, but the streets were so bright it wouldn't be so simple.

The city of Vinces had a different face at night. A cheerful energy surrounded us. Perhaps it was the electric lights illuminating roads and buildings. Or the music coming from a distant accordion and a set of drums. Or a choir of voices singing. I still couldn't believe there was electricity in this pocket of the world.

Cristóbal and I had speculated for days about what we would find in this rural town. Modern commodities were nowhere on our imaginary list topped by donkeys and barefoot peasants. It wasn't that París Chiquito was overly sophisticated or rich, but there had been careful consideration in its construction. During our ride into town, Alberto and Martin had told me that local carpenters had used all their creativity to craft in wood a similar aesthetic that was achieved with granite, marble, and stone in Europe.

Carmela and I turned into a narrow, paved street. And the magic of the plaza and the impressive architecture were gone. In their place stood the skeletons of what must have been a once-prosperous neighborhood. Carmela squeezed my hand and pulled me with determination into a weary building and up a narrow staircase.

"Listen, Carmela," I started as she unlocked a door in the hallway. But she wasn't listening. She pushed the door in and we entered a room, which was both tiny and cluttered. I hesitantly stood by a vanity table overflowing with bottles of castor and peppermint oil, powders, and earrings. Feathers and necklaces hung from an oval mirror and there were gowns scattered on the bed and on the floor.

"Forgive my mess," Carmela said, grabbing a handful of dresses from the bed and dumping them inside the armoire.

While she picked up, I made my way between shoes and scarves toward the window and moved the curtain to one side. Across the alley was a building with peeling paint and cracked windows that blocked the view. The alleyway was empty except for a scrawny cat treading along the street with hypnotic movements. There was music nearby, but I couldn't tell if it came from this building or a two-story house at the end of the block.

When I was done inspecting the neighborhood, I turned around. Carmela was already waiting for me on the bed.

Naked.

She patted the side of the bed. "Come here, *papi*."

As she moved her arm, one of her bare breasts spread on the sheet like a pile of raw dough. I looked away and paced the room.

"Carmela, *cariño*. I didn't come here for that."

"Don't tell me that you're one of those men who . . ." She sat up. "I thought that might be the case, but don't worry, I can find you someone else, but it's going to cost you double."

"No, no. I don't need anyone." I sat on the edge of the bed, trying to avoid the sight of her flaccid body. "Is there a hotel nearby where I could stay?"

I dug for my wallet in my back pocket. I removed some bills and placed them by her hand.

She stared at the money. "Are you in some kind of trouble, mister? Are you hiding from someone?"

"No, no. The truth is I recently lost my wife and I don't think I can touch another woman. *Ever*."

Her smile vanished.

"But do you mind keeping this between us?" I said. "I don't want people to start talking about me. You know how small towns can be and my reputation is important to me."

"You must have loved her a lot."

I nodded, without looking at her.

"You may keep this for your troubles," I said, setting the bills on her hand. "Now tell me, *mi alma*, where's the closest hotel?"

CHAPTER 12

The closest hotel, as it turned out, was across from the brothel and it wasn't a lot nicer than Carmela's room. I'd barely been able to get any sleep in that squeaky, old bed and discolored sheets. The only fortunate outcome from my insomnia was that the dark circles under my eyes had intensified, which made me look less feminine—I needed all the help I could get.

The receptionist gave me directions to Banco Agrícola y Ganadero and I left the hotel as soon as the sun rose.

"Don Cristóbal!"

¡Por los clavos de Cristo!

I looked over my shoulder. Tucking his striped shirt inside his trousers, Martin strode in my direction.

"Here you are!" He patted my back. "I was wondering where you went. Did you have a good time with Carmela last night?"

He was smiling like a child opening a present. I was about to tell him that I was in mourning and hadn't touched Carmela (and never, ever would), but why give him any explanations? It might just give him a reason to doubt my masculinity—if he wasn't suspicious of me already.

I nodded, nonchalant, and kept walking.

His perception of me seemed to have changed. He was more relaxed, friendlier. Apparently, I'd been accepted into the male clan after drinking and visiting prostitutes without any objections. How different expectations for men were. If a woman had spent the night outside her home, in a hotel such as this one, she would've been shunned by society. But a man received praise and approval from his peers.

He shoved his hands inside his pockets. "And here I thought you were, you know . . ."

"I was, what?"

He was silent for a moment. But I knew what he meant. This was the second person who thought I was an effeminate man, one who indulges in forbidden pleasures with other men.

I frowned.

"Never mind," he said. "Are you ready to go back to the hacienda?"

"You go on without me, Don Martin. I need to go to the bank to exchange some money."

I didn't wait for an answer. I crossed the street and followed the receptionist's instructions to the bank, which was five blocks away.

It was odd how as a woman, I'd always been considered slightly masculine. My mother never understood why I wasn't like other girls my age and she was cross at me for months after Cristóbal and I opened the chocolate shop. She always said women belonged in their homes, not in the workplace, and why couldn't I just be a little more feminine?

But now, disguised as a man, all my femininity—so eclipsed in my normal life—seemed to come through.

I asked to see the manager and a balding man with sweaty palms and enormous spectacles came to greet me. After I mentioned I had a delicate matter to discuss with him, he hesitantly led me to his office. He was the nervous kind, the type of person who doesn't seem to know what to do with his hands. One moment he was rolling a fountain pen on his desk and the next he was shuffling papers from one pile to another.

I introduced myself as Don Armand Lafont's son-in-law. The news in Vinces traveled more quickly than I thought as he'd already heard about me. He stuttered his condolences on my wife's passing.

"How c-c-can I help you, Señor Balboa?" Through the glasses, his eyes looked monumental.

"I trust this conversation will remain private, Señor Aguirre?" I said. It was remarkable how I was learning to control the low register of my voice.

"Of c-c-course."

How on earth had this nervous little man climbed to such an important position in the company?

I removed the check from my pocket and placed it on the surface of the desk. For a moment, I hesitated. What if this man was friends with whoever had tried to kill me?

He looked at the check.

"Mr. Aguirre, I found this check among my wife's belongings. I know it's postdated to May and I don't intend to cash it, but I'd like to know whose signature this is."

Aguirre removed a magnifying glass from his top drawer and examined the penmanship for a moment.

"Mr. Balboa, this is Mr. Lafont's signature."

"Mr. Lafont? As in Armand Lafont?"

"The very same one."

"Are you sure?"

"Sir, I would r-r-recognize his signature anywhere. He was one of our most important clients for over t-t-t-twenty years."

This made no sense. "Is there anyone else who can sign on this account?"

"I believe Don Martin Sabater has a power of attorney given to him by Mr. Lafont for when he could no longer make business decisions, but Mr. Sabater can sign with his own name."

So, he wouldn't need to sign under my father's name. Unless he didn't want anyone else to know he was the one signing. But this didn't make him any more suspicious than my sisters. The only thing this proved was that someone had either forged the signature or that my father himself had signed a blank check and this person had stolen it. In either case, someone else was behind all of this because it made no sense that my father would send someone to kill me after making me his heir.

Frustrated, I thanked Mr. Aguirre and left. So, my murderer was a skilled swindler or a good thief—that was all I'd gotten from this meeting. What now? Was I going to hold calligraphy tests on all my suspects to know who had the ability to forge my father's signature?

CHAPTER 13

I found a ride home on a carriage pulled by a donkey. His owner, a humble old man with scarce teeth and a straw hat, nodded repeatedly as I placed a handful of coins in his hand, flashing his gums without a hint of self-consciousness. Neither one of my sisters asked where I'd spent the night—one of the perks of being a man, I supposed.

Laurent and Angélica were playing cards in the parlor, while Catalina sat by herself with a book.

"Why don't you join us, Don Cristóbal?" Angélica said. "We need a fourth player for Cuarenta. Poor Catalina never gets to play."

Catalina raised her gaze from the book, expectant.

"Sure," I said in a low voice. "But I don't know the game."

"Oh, it's easy. Isn't it, *cher*? My Laurent learned it in five minutes."

Laurent nodded.

The four of us sat around the table and Angélica explained the rules. Cuarenta had a simple concept: the couple who reached forty points first won, hence the name. It was fast-paced and filled with colloquial terms. They said it was the most popular game in Ecuador, but Laurent reassured me that the aristocrats in the region called it a game for simpletons and drunks.

So odd to be playing cards in the middle of the day. I'd usually been frantic in the mornings: preparing chocolate for my customers, making sure the tables were set just right, paying my suppliers. Cristóbal often told me I worked too much. "At least take the weekends off," he would say. But I told him those were the best days for business. Besides, I couldn't stand the thought of going back to our empty apartment, void of children's laughter and toys scattered throughout the parlor.

How different my sisters were. This life of luxury, of leisure, seemed to appeal to them very much. They probably wouldn't give it up so easily.

After an hour of playing—Angélica and Laurent were the undisputed champions—Catalina excused herself and Laurent decided to go for a walk. I studied Angélica as she put the cards away.

Could she be the one who forged the check? Her husband? How to know what was in the heart and mind of someone else— what that person was capable of—other than by getting to know them.

"Have you ever traveled, Doña Angélica?"

"Me?" She scoffed. "I've been to Guayaquil a handful of times and once to Quito for a wedding, but I was a child then."

"What about outside the country?"

"Oh, no, never."

I was shocked that someone who seemed so sophisticated, so at ease in her own skin, had been locked in this hacienda her entire life.

"I've always wanted to go to France, though," she said.

"So do I."

"You haven't? But it's right next to Spain."

I shrugged.

"Why Don Cristóbal, I took you for a worldly man. Who knows? Maybe I'll go there before you." She winked.

"You should," I said. "A woman like yourself shouldn't be stuck in a small town all her life."

She stopped her shuffling and looked at me as if I'd spoken in Polish.

In the afternoon, I met Martin at the fermentation warehouse. I was nervous to climb on Pacha again, but she was the only horse

available and I had to get over my fear. If I was to run this plantation one day, I couldn't let a finicky mare stop me. It was a minor
accomplishment that she didn't throw me down again, but our
battle of wills made my ride much longer than it should've been.

Upon seeing me, Martin smiled. It was amazing how much a
face changed when someone smiled, how much his eyes bright-
ened. He was almost unrecognizable.

"So, you're becoming friends after all." He grabbed Pacha's
reins and brought her to a halt. "I didn't expect you to ride her
again so soon."

"There are many things you don't know about me, Don Martin." My voice sounded graver than I'd intended.

I descended, too roughly for my taste. The grass was so tall it
reached my knees. And sodden. I hadn't even realized it had
rained at the hacienda last night.

"Great timing, Don Cristóbal. Come on."

The warehouse was filled with wooden boxes set up on con-
crete bleachers with a row of windows flanking them on either
side. There were three levels of boxes. We climbed to the top
and Martin pointed at the inside of one of the wooden boxes.

"This is where the beans start fermenting. We used to dig a
small hole and place the beans inside, but Don Armand was told
that this is a superior method. It makes the beans ferment more
evenly."

Large banana leaves covered the beans. He lifted one of the
leaves, displaying the beans underneath, still white as coconut
meat. A mild scent of alcohol emanated. "The leaves warm up
the beans so they ferment. They stay here for two days and then
we move them to those other boxes." He pointed at the second
tier.

I dug my hand inside the box—I couldn't help myself. The
beans were warm and slimy.

"Try one," he said.

I pulled out one, my fingers wet and sticky, and tasted the
bean.

"Well?" he said.

"It tastes nothing like chocolate," I said, shocked. Bitter and syrupy at the same time, the only thing I could compare it to was a very sweet lemon.

"Well, I wouldn't know," he said.

I hadn't noticed before how his eyelashes curled all the way to his eyebrows.

"*Por la Virgen de los Reyes*, Don Martin. It's a shame that having access to all these beans, you've never eaten chocolate. You must try it one day."

"I wouldn't even know how to prepare it," he said.

Right then and there I made a promise to myself: if this man had nothing to do with Cristóbal's death, I would prepare him the best chocolate he would ever taste.

The second row of boxes held more beans. At this point, they were turning darker, a deep violet hue. Martin shuffled and scooped some beans to show me.

"What happens if they don't get fermented?" I asked.

"They turn bitter. Fermentation removes the acidity from the beans, gives cacao its aroma and concentrates the flavor, or so I've been told."

I grabbed a handful of beans and smelled them.

"After two days inside these boxes, we move them there." He pointed at the bottom row. "For one day."

"So, they ferment for five days."

"Correct. Then we move them to the drying shed."

"Can we go see?" I tried not to sound too eager—after all, I'd reassured the family I had no interest in the plantation—but I wasn't sure I could hide my excitement. Martin gave me an odd look but led the way to a solid structure a few meters away.

"So, Doña Carmela, huh?" he said. "I would've never imagined you liked such exuberant women."

I sighed. Just when I was starting to forget the embarrassing incident from the previous night, he had to bring it up again. Oh, no, Cristóbal's boots were filling up with mud (or was it horse's dung?). I tried to step on drier patches to avoid dirtying them further, but something stopped me. Martin was watching me as though there were spiders crawling down my face.

Of course. Men didn't care if their shoes got a little soiled or wet. I needed to step with confidence, no matter how disgusting it felt to bury my feet on this uneven ground.

I did just that. The earth made a slurping sound, as though it wanted to swallow me.

"Don Martin, how long did you work for my f . . . father-in-law?"

"Seven years."

Plenty of time to learn his signature.

"But I knew him most of my life." He picked up a stick and split it.

"You're from here then?" I asked.

"You could say that."

"And your family? Do you have any?"

Martin entered the drying shed. It was made out of *caña* and so bright inside—it had a skylight ceiling—and the floor was covered with cacao beans, which had now acquired that rich brown color I was so familiar with.

"The beans dry here for three or four days if it's sunny, a little longer if it's cool."

He strode up and down the shed with a rake to shuffle the beans from corner to corner. *I may have to give this man a drink for him to start talking.* As I stepped inside, I inhaled the beans and their scent made me falter. They brought back a memory—aboard the ship. It was the smell of the man who'd killed Cristóbal.

I held on to a wooden pole.

"Are you all right?" Martin asked me.

"Yes, yes. I was just thinking about the house we saw yesterday. The one that had been set on fire. You said that the son had survived. Did he work here?"

"Yes, why? Why are you so interested in him?"

I hesitated. "Well, I saw a man with a scar like the one you mentioned on the ship we took in Cuba."

I examined his reaction. Martin's jaw tightened. Had he sent him there to kill me?

"It must be a coincidence," he said.

"Why? Is the man still here?"

"No, he left a while ago, but he wouldn't have the means to go on a trip to Cuba. Or a purpose."

No purpose? Ha! A crooked, evil one, thank you very much.

"Why did he leave the plantation?" I asked.

"I don't know. After the accident, well, he and his mother moved to Vinces. We haven't seen much of them since."

"Is his mother still there?"

Martin shrugged. "I suppose."

I wanted to know their names badly, but it would be too suspicious if I asked, wouldn't it?

A clatter of hooves warned us that a horse was coming. I peeked outside the storehouse. A man in a white two-piece suit and a boater hat stopped by the entrance. Behind me, Martin groaned.

The man on the horse clapped.

"Martin Sabater! Come out so I can see you!"

"What the hell do you want?"

The dozen workers surrounding the area stopped whatever they were doing to watch.

The man on the horse flashed a piece of paper. "Doña Angélica is suing me? She lent ears to her father's nonsense?"

"I have nothing to do with this, Del Río. Talk to her!"

"Of course you have something to do with it. You run this damned plantation!"

"Doña Angélica has never asked anyone's permission to do anything. You should know that better than anyone."

"Oh, shut up, Sabater." He looked so arrogant with his chin slightly tilted up and his trim mustache. "If you don't have any answers, then I shall go talk to her myself."

He pulled on the reins and turned his palomino around.

"For Christ's sake!" Martin darted to where his own horse was and got on top in one swift move.

If I had the smallest percentage of his skill with horses, I would've followed, intrigued as I was by his argument with this stranger, but I didn't feel like breaking my neck this afternoon.

Instead, I meandered toward Pacha, dodging patches of manure and puddles of evening rain. I walked past a worker pushing a wagon—the one who looked like a caveman who had been removing beans from the cacao pods. They'd called him Don Pepe. I removed a few coins from my pocket and extended them to him.

"Who was that man on the horse?"

The man scratched his long beard, then took the money. "Fernando del Río. He owns the property next to this one."

"He didn't seem to get along with Don Martin."

"Oh, no. They hate each other. Nobody here likes Don Fernando. They are always fighting over some land by the creek."

"So, what is this about a lawsuit?"

Don Pepe shrugged and renewed his walk.

"Wait," I said. "What's the name of the family whose house got burned in the fire last year?"

"The foreman's?"

I nodded.

The man tilted his hat back and scratched his thinning crown. I groaned, then removed more coins to pay him.

"His name was Pedro Duarte."

"And the son's name?"

"Franco."

Franco Duarte. The name was foreign to me.

"And the mother?"

"Doña Soledad. She's the town's *curandera.* Just ask anybody in Vinces and they'll tell you how to find her."

"One more thing," I said.

The worker shot me another greedy look.

"How did the house burn?" I deposited more money on his callused palm.

"Nobody knows, but one thing is for sure, it wasn't an accident."

He picked up his wagon.

"Wait, why do you say that? How do you know?"

Don Pepe was about to say something else when another worker came near us.

"Good afternoon, señor," my informant told me, and dashed away.

*   *   *

That night, I woke up to a light tickle in my face. I rubbed my forehead, my eyes still shut, and felt something cold and smooth on my hand. I pushed it away and turned on the gas lantern on the bedside table. *Holy Mother!* There was a snake on my pillow! A real-life, long and curly snake with red, black, and white stripes.

And it had been slithering all over my face!

I covered my mouth to muffle a scream and jumped out of bed. How on earth had that thing found its way to my room *and* to my face? Had someone brought her? But how could that be when I lock my room every night?

Unless they had brought it earlier and I just noticed it now?

I was becoming paranoid. My window was open. Snakes abounded in the country. Besides, if someone had wanted to kill me, they would've found a more efficient method. The minute I thought this, the snake stuck its tongue out at me as though attempting to shoot poison. I shivered and rushed toward the door.

It could be a coincidence, but what better way to get rid of me than provoking an accident with a snake? No one would think it had been done on purpose.

I couldn't stand being here one more minute. In front of the mirror, I attached my facial hair, put on Cristóbal's spectacles and robe, and dashed out of the room.

There was someone coming toward me in the hall. I gripped the door handle. That someone was holding a candle.

"Don Cristóbal, what are you doing here? Is there something wrong?"

Julia.

I fought my impulse to scream. A man wouldn't do that. Instead, I let go of the doorknob and fixed the collar of Cristóbal's smoke jacket.

"There's a snake in my chamber," I said as calmly as I could muster.

"A snake? *Virgen Santa.* I'm so sorry, Don Cristóbal, that's very common here, especially on cooler nights, such as this one."

She called *this* a cool night?

"Allow me." She entered the room.

A few minutes later, she came out, snake in hand.

"Good thing you didn't touch it yourself," she said. "These snakes are poisonous, and they attack when they smell fear, but I have been around them all my life so I'm not afraid of them."

She walked past me as if she were carrying a tray of tea instead of a live snake.

"Good night," she said.

I stood there for a moment, hand on my chest. If someone wanted to persuade me to leave, they were on the right track.

CHAPTER 14

Angélica

Vinces, 1907

"Thanks for saving my life yesterday," I told Juan.

He was sitting under his favorite tree, holding a long bamboo stick.

When he looked up, my heart thumped against a shield of ribs and flesh. He was so handsome.

I had to pretend things hadn't changed between us in the last twenty-four hours when he'd held my hand for the first time. I had to treat him like I always had, like a good childhood friend, even though we weren't kids anymore. He'd turned fifteen last month and I was thirteen.

I shivered, remembering the feel of his hand tightening against mine as he saved me from falling from the bridge yesterday. There had been a loose board on the bridge that fell in the river when I stepped on it. I'd lost my balance and nearly fell into those deep brown waters.

"You don't need to thank me," he said. "Anyone would've done the same."

"I don't know about that. My brother might have let me fall," I said.

Juan chuckled. "Yeah, maybe."

Oh, how I loved his smile. In truth, I loved everything about him. He was the only boy in the region who paid me any attention. Other boys just wanted to play with Alberto since they didn't think I was capable of doing fun things, like climb trees or fish. But Juan was different. He always found ways to include me in his games with Alberto, and if my brother's mean friends would leave me alone, Juan would come find me or invent a game where I could partake. He even taught me how to swim. I was so lucky to have him as a neighbor. But I shouldn't fool myself— he'd only held my hand so I wouldn't fall and drown. He was just being a decent person.

"What do you have in there?" I asked, peeking into the box. It was filled with stones and leaves.

With his stick, he shuffled the stones exposing a long snake.

I cringed.

This topped it all. I'd known Juan to collect frogs and lizards. He even had a black widow spider once because he was fascinated by the fact that she would kill the male after mating.

I was so embarrassed every time he mentioned *mating*, even if it was between insects. Especially now with my unrequited devotion for him.

I never minded his collections before, but those animals never hurt anyone. They were just ugly to look at, but interesting. Snakes, on the other hand, scared me ever since I'd heard from one of the maids that the carpenter's son had died of a poisonous bite.

"Her name is Lola," he said, as if he was talking about a family friend.

The snake had a beautiful pattern in red and black. I was strangely attracted to this creature, more so than the black widow he'd already discarded.

"Is she friendly?" I said.

"As friendly as snakes can be." He shrugged. "Usually this type of snake doesn't like to be near humans, but Lola is different. She lets me touch her sometimes."

"Can I?"

He knelt beside the box, setting the stick on the ground. Very slowly, he reached out for her and rubbed her.

"It's me, Lola," he said. "Want to meet my friend?"

The snake remained still. Juan turned toward me and grabbed my hand. My heart did a flip.

I crouched beside him and he guided my fingers toward the snake's body, which was softer than I'd ever imagined. And so cold.

"I like her," I said.

"I think she likes you, too."

After a moment, Lola slid away from us and hid behind a rock in the corner of the box. Juan helped me stand and dropped my hand.

"You look different today," he said.

"Different, how?"

"I don't know. Older."

I refrained from smiling. I so wanted him to touch my hand again. Or even . . .

As if reading my mind, he leaned over and brushed his lips against mine. His kiss was so unexpected I remained stiff. I'd never had another face this close to mine before and I did my best not to bump my nose with his. Maybe I should close my eyes? That was what the heroines in those novels my mother hid under the mattress always did. When I closed my eyes, something weird happened. Juan inserted his tongue inside my mouth. It was warm and wet. I panicked and pushed him back. What kind of kiss was this? What did the tongue have to do with *anything*? The books didn't talk about tongues.

"Sorry," he said.

"No, don't apologize. I . . . I just wasn't expecting that."

"I have to go," he said. "My father wanted me to help him with something."

I knew he was lying. The entire town knew his father had only one obsession in life: chess. He'd given up on everything else a long time ago: his work, his family, or any activity outside staring at his chess board and studying every move and book on the subject he could get his hands on.

I didn't say this, of course, I would rather die than embarrass Juan—I loved him so. I wanted him to kiss me again. I would even take his tongue inside my mouth if it meant he wouldn't leave.

But the magic was over.

He was about to say something else, but instead, he picked up his box and walked away.

What was I supposed to do now with this grasshopper jumping up and down in my stomach? I could barely suppress my own desire to jump and scream myself. I never thought Juan liked me this way. From now on, I would always wear this dress. He said I looked older in it.

I stared after him as he walked away with the snake.

CHAPTER 15

Puri

April 1920

If you saw Soledad Duarte from a distance you wouldn't think there was anything wrong with her. She must have been beautiful once with that abundant, wavy mane. But up close, you would notice a thick scar starting on her throat, across her collarbone, and continuing into the neckline of her blouse. As you glanced up immediately—to avoid being rude—you might notice her angular eyebrows, which appeared to be painted with a fine brush, and you would also see that despite her confident stance, there was a frailty about her, as if the mere act of breathing took an extraordinary effort.

Her house, if you could call it that considering there was only one room, was made entirely out of reed. The place looked more like a storage room than a home, but after I'd knocked on her door and requested her professional services as a healer, she led me into a clear corner of the room with a table and two chairs.

I sat in front of the *curandera*. I didn't know exactly what I was going to tell her but figured that by offering to pay for her services, she would be more willing to talk to me. Now, how was I going to deceive a healer into believing I was a man? And how did I turn the subject to her son?

"You're not from here?" she asked in a kind voice.

"No," I said.

"What brings you to these lands?"

"Well," I said in a low pitch. "I'm a writer and I came here to do some research for my novel." I purposely spoke slowly in an effort to keep my voice at the bottom of my range.

She smiled. "And you need a *curandera* for that?"

"No," I said. "I came to see you for something else. A more personal reason." I'd once heard that the best way to deceive someone was to say a partial truth. "I've been suffering from melancholia. I don't have any enthusiasm to do the things I used to find enjoyable. Sometimes I have to force myself to get out of bed every morning."

She studied me carefully. "Yes, there is a sadness about you. I noticed it the minute you walked in. Did you lose someone close?"

Cristóbal's shocked face seconds before falling off the stern flashed through my mind.

"Yes."

She nodded, lighting a candle on the table.

Why did I have this sudden urge to cry? Right here, in front of this stranger? And the mother of Cristóbal's assassin, at that. Her soothing voice, her compassionate expression, her delicate hands—every part of her urged me to open up. It wasn't just about Cristóbal and his horrendous demise, it was also the fact that I was so far from my home, so lonely. If at least I'd had the child I'd always wanted, someone who would be with me always. Under different circumstances, I might have asked this woman to help me become a mother.

"Losing someone is not easy," she said. "Your feelings are normal, Señor . . ."

"Balboa." I shifted in my seat. Behind a halfway-opened curtain was a little altar with a hand-sized statue of the Virgin Mary. In front of it was a small photograph of a child in what looked like a First Communion outfit. He was dressed entirely in white and held a rosary and a Bible in his hands. Surrounding the portrait were lit candles and gardenias.

"Is there something you can give me?" I said. "Something that might help improve my mood?"

"The *plant of happiness*," she said, pensive. She stood up and turned toward a shelf filled with jars. She gathered a bunch of herbs from one of the jars and wrapped them in a sheet of newspaper. "It's called *Hierba de San Juan*. Make a tea with it and drink half a cup twice a day. Be careful with it because it's potent and hard to find." She set the package in front of me.

Oh, no, the visit was coming to an end.

I pointed at the boy in the altar. "Is that your son?"

"How do you know I have a son?"

"It was just a guess. He's a handsome child."

She glanced at the photograph. "He's not a child anymore."

This was my opportunity.

"Did . . . did something happen to him?"

"Why do you ask?"

"The altar."

She hesitated. "He's been missing for a few weeks, but the authorities aren't helping me. Nobody here cares."

"I understand you better than you think," I said honestly.

Her eyes filled with tears.

"Then maybe you can help me," she said, surprising me with the despair in her voice, with her sudden vulnerability. "You look like a refined man. You know how to talk to people with fancy words. And you look like you have money."

"But how can I possibly help you?"

"The authorities won't listen to me, they say my son must have moved somewhere else, they say he's too old for them to be wasting their time on someone who doesn't want to be found, but they'll listen to you. I know my Franco didn't move somewhere else. He left all his things here." She pointed at a cot behind me and an ajar armoire filled with clothes. "I don't have any money. I can't pay anyone to find him. Look at where I live. After our house burned, I was left with nothing." She shook her head. "All I know is that Franco wouldn't have left without that woman."

"What woman?" I asked, barely able to control the even tone in my voice.

"I don't know who she is, but I know that she drove him crazy. She made him do things he wouldn't have done otherwise."

"What things?"

She avoided my gaze. "He stopped working, he was gone all the time, he hardly ate, and then, he left without saying where. I'm sure she put a spell on him. I tried to fight it, but nothing worked."

"But if you never met her, how do you know there was a woman?"

"He told me about her. He said he loved her like no one else."

"How do you know she didn't leave with him?"

"He told me he would be back. He said he was going to do something for her and that he would return in a few days. But it's been three weeks already." She reached out for my hands. "Will you help me?"

I would've wanted to despise her like I did her son, but this woman seemed so fragile, so desperate. She clearly didn't know the evil in her son's heart. How could I not pity her? She'd lost everything, her husband, her house, and now her son. A part of me wanted to tell her the truth, but another part—the practical one—told me that this woman could be helpful in my investigation if I played along.

"I can try, but you have to be honest with me. What was he going to do for that woman and why?"

"I don't know. He didn't say."

"We need to find her. It's the only way to find him."

Doña Soledad removed a saffron handkerchief from her sleeve and wiped her tears with it. "I don't know how. I've already looked through his things and there's nothing." She blew her nose. "I know he was a good boy. He was always so obedient."

A good boy, all right.

"There are no letters?"

"Nothing."

"Could he have confided in a friend? Told someone about his girl?"

"He didn't have any friends."

She sniffed.

If Franco loved this mysterious woman and would do anything to please her, would he also take her money to kill me? Or was there someone else involved in this plan?

I spoke again. "You said your house burned in a fire, right?"

She watched me warily. "Yes."

"How did that happen?"

"What does the fire have to do with my son's disappearance?"

"Maybe there's a connection there. Tell me about it."

She sat down again. This was so surreal, me talking to the mother of the man who had killed my Cristóbal.

"It was a windy afternoon. And so dry. It hadn't rained in weeks. I'd gone to town to get rice and flour for my bread. Normally, my son would help me when I went to get provisions, but he'd said he had something important to do that afternoon. I assumed it had to do with work. When I saw the house in the distance, it was already in flames.

"It was surprisingly quiet and I wrongly assumed there was no one inside, so I just stood there, perplexed. I cried out for help, hoping some of the workers would hear me and come, but for a while nobody did." Her eyes watered. "If only I hadn't waited there like a ghost, things might have turned different. After a moment, I heard some coughing from inside, and Franco's voice calling out for my husband. I remember standing there, wondering if I'd heard right. Why would Pedro be at home at that time of the day? He usually worked until six. And Franco had said he had something to do. When I was certain that it was Franco, I barged inside. There were flames all over the living room and the ceiling. I wrapped myself with the tablecloth and went upstairs, calling out Franco's name."

Soledad's gaze was lost in a mysterious spot behind my head.

"I found Franco in the hallway. He was trying to put the fire out with a blanket. A beam had fallen and was blocking the way to my bedroom. I could see Pedro stuck underneath the beam. He was unconscious, probably dead already." Her voice cracked. "Franco kept calling his father, but there was nothing to do. I told him we needed to get out before the flames caught us. And that was when another beam fell on top of us. Fortunately, some workers had come to our rescue and dragged us out. But there was nothing anyone could do for Pedro." She dried the tears from her cheeks. "The workers told me later that he'd come home early because he'd been running a fever and said he was going to take a nap." She set her hand on her collarbone, right on her scar.

In a strange way, I felt sorry for Franco. I wondered if this tragedy shaped him into a harsh man capable of killing a stranger without a second thought. Or had he always been bad?

"Do you know what caused the fire?" I asked.

"Not for sure, but I think it had to do with Don Fernando."

"Don Fernando del Río?"

"You know him?"

"I met him briefly at La Puri. I'm a friend of the Lafont family."

"Well, Don Fernando wanted Pedro to do something for him." She rested her palms on the table's surface. There was a scar on one of her hands. "But it didn't work out."

"What did he want him to do?"

"Oh, I've said too much already. It has nothing to do with Franco anyway."

I wasn't so sure of this. I knew that Don Fernando had nothing to do with my father's will. But in his mind, I could've been one more obstacle, one more person to fight over this blessed creek. Perhaps he'd sent a woman to seduce Franco since he couldn't persuade him just with money?

No, it was too far-fetched. I was seeing conspiracies and murderers everywhere.

"Look, I will try to help you," I said, "but you must tell me everything you know, even if you don't see the connection. Tell me what Don Fernando wanted done."

She shook her head. "He paid Pedro to move some fence over so he could have that stupid piece of land the *patrón* and Don Fernando were always fighting about. Pedro shouldn't have done it. It cost him his life."

"But if he did it, why would Don Fernando try to hurt him? How do you know it wasn't your *patrón* who set the house on fire?"

I really hoped that my father wasn't involved in this fire. The last thing I needed was to learn that he'd been a murderer.

"Pedro was caught and he confessed that Don Fernando had threatened and paid him to do it, so Don Armand forgave him and let him come home, but then he sued Don Fernando. Don Fernando was so angry with my Pedro for talking. I'm certain he had one of his men burn our house."

Did this incident have something to do with Fernando's argument with Martin in the afternoon? Maybe Angélica was suing him for the very same thing.

"Are you staying in town, Don Cristóbal?" Soledad said, removing me from my speculations.

There was no point in lying. She would find out where I was staying anyway.

"No. At La Puri."

"Well, then you're lucky," she said. "You're staying with a saint."

"You mean Doña Catalina?"

"Who else? She's such a pure soul. Everybody in town knows she's favored by the Virgin. Ask her to intercede on your behalf and you'll see that with prayer and my remedy your soul will heal quickly."

I sighed. If only prayer could fix my problems.

There was a barely audible knock on the door. Doña Soledad rose. I grabbed the package of herbs and followed her to the front through a maze of boxes and chairs.

Nothing would've prepared me for the face on the other side of the threshold, the face of my sister Angélica.

CHAPTER 16

Neither Angélica nor I breathed a word about our encounter at the *curandera*'s house. During dinner, we avoided each other and barely spoke. Catalina didn't say much either. She was such an introvert.

The same couldn't be said for Laurent, who did all the talking. He mentioned a list of names that held little to no meaning to me: people he was planning to invite to an upcoming gathering; friends he'd run into at the café in Vinces; courtships and engagements he'd heard about. As usual, none of his chatter seemed to have any substance. He was fond of mixing languages. He might start a sentence in Spanish and then finish it in French. Angélica understood a lot but always answered in Spanish, whereas Catalina never said a word, either for lack of knowledge or lack of concern. I could understand Laurent, but I wasn't a confident speaker. What a shame, after having a French father. In my defense, my father had left Spain when I was tiny so I didn't have many opportunities to practice his native tongue. My knowledge of the language mainly came from books and from my correspondence with my father throughout the years.

My mother always said my father had had a talent for languages. Apparently, he'd learned Spanish during his travels to Spain, where his job as a merchant of *jerez* had taken him. My parents had met at the Feria de Sevilla after my mother became a widow and my father never wanted to go back to France after that. But after meeting my grandmother, his ambition took him farther away. Mamá accused her own mother of filling his head with ideas about chocolate and cacao beans and plantations across the ocean that she'd called the business of the future.

My mother never forgave her for that. Until the day she died, she blamed my grandmother for the loss of my father. Mamá said it hurt even more than losing her first husband to illness because there was no finality with my father, just waiting and longing.

As I glanced around the dining room, I asked where Martin was. Catalina informed me, in that angelic voice of hers, that he lived in a house between Vinces and the plantation, which he'd inherited from his father.

After finishing his meal, Laurent excused himself, saying he was due to play Corazones with the region's ranchers. "It's the only thing he likes about Vinces," Angélica said. "Cards, celebrations, and bird-watching."

Involuntarily, I glanced at Ramona, who was picking at the cacao beans on her plate.

Julia entered the room and asked Angélica if she could collect our plates. As usual, she only spoke to her. It was odd how Julia asked Angélica's permission for Every Single Thing. I knew Angélica was the oldest, but it appeared as if she was purposely ignoring Catalina.

What a relief when both of my sisters excused themselves, claiming exhaustion, and left me alone in the dining room. After the table was empty and the maids busied themselves washing dishes, I ventured into the house's lower level.

My mission? To find out connections, papers, signatures. Something to give me clarity about what had transpired after my father's death.

There were a few rooms surrounding the central patio. I peeked through the windows. One was a sewing room with a machine, a cutting table, and piles of fabric on top. There was a music room with a pianoforte and a phonograph, and the last room was a study.

My father's study?

I glanced over my shoulder and opened the door. The lantern in the hall cast light inside the room. I picked up an oil lamp from the desk and explored the space. There were two floor-to-ceiling bookshelves harboring what appeared to be an encyclopedia and several books in French.

On the cherrywood desk sat a wooden cigar box and a miniature sailboat. I opened the side drawers. There were several documents with my father's signature, which appeared to be the same from the check. There was also an accounting ledger from last year. The bottom drawer, which was larger than the top two, was locked. I opened the center drawer to find the key, but aside from fountain pens and other office supplies, there was nothing of interest except for a leather-bound notebook. I pulled it out and sifted through the pages. It was a journal, it seemed, dated years ago.

I glanced at the door. How long did I have? Nervously, I flipped to the beginning of the notebook.

My father must have started this journal when he first acquired the plantation as he'd written observations about the vegetation found on the hacienda, the plants' growth cycle during the seasons, a list of buyers, and other work-related information. As I turned the pages, I found charts, prices, and a variety of drawings of cacao pods and leaves. I was about to shut it when something caught my attention. Toward the end of the book, the writing was upside down. I shut the notebook and opened it from the back. Sure enough, he'd started another kind of journal from the back. On this one, there were long passages in French. I'd sat down to read when I heard a noise by the door.

I dropped the notebook inside the drawer as the door swung open.

"Don Cristóbal? What are you doing here?"

"Doña Angélica, you scared me! I apologize for my impertinence. I was just looking for some reading material as I suffer from chronic insomnia. I should have asked you."

She strolled into the room, looking at our father's desk.

"Please, help yourself. My father had some novels there." She pointed at the lower level of one of the bookshelves, which was nowhere near where I stood. "I have to tell you, though, my father was very particular about his things. He didn't let me or anybody else touch them. He was organized to a fault and one of his last dying wishes was that his encyclopedia and his book collection remained intact. He would've been cross if he found you here."

I headed for the bookshelf.

"Again, I apologize. This shall never happen again." Now how could I manage to take the notebook with me with Angélica's eyes scrutinizing my every move?

"Aha! *The Count of Monte Cristo*." I slid the book from the shelf. "I've always wanted to read it."

"You're welcome to it."

I refrained from turning toward my father's desk as I crept to the door. Angélica waited for me by the threshold, her hand on the knob. As soon as I walked out, she shut the door.

CHAPTER 17

Today I was going to prove my manhood to Don Martin.

I'd run into him in the morning after breakfast while taking a walk by the plantation. He'd disposed of his usual jacket and tie and had his shirt rolled up all the way to his elbows and long rubber boots over his pants.

"Want to come fishing?" he said.

"Right now?" I asked.

"It's what Sundays are for."

"Not church?" I said.

"This is my church," he said, pointing at the vegetation around us.

I couldn't say I disagreed. I accepted his invitation, mostly out of a desire to find out from him who was the mysterious woman dating Franco. I had a feeling that Martin knew a lot more than he let on about the foreman's son.

I wished I'd declined the offer to go fishing, though.

When Martin handed me a tin box and told me to collect worms for bait *with my bare hands*, I thought I would retch.

I'd always been squeamish but it was apparent that "other men" didn't feel this way. Martin had no qualms about digging into the soil by our feet and pulling out those wiggling creatures.

I stood in the middle of the field, paralyzed. Perhaps this was what Cristóbal had meant when he said we were city people. He was right about that. First, it had been the stubborn mare, then the snake, today worms. What tomorrow?

"Well, what are you waiting for?" he said.

I wanted to tell him that I couldn't touch a worm even if he paid me, but two things stopped me: my pride and the fear of being discovered.

I reached inside the mud and shut my eyes as I felt a squirmy worm between my thumb and index finger. I pulled it out, shivering and doing my best to ignore the nausea building up inside my throat. I dropped the thing immediately inside the tin box.

"You look like you've never touched a worm before," Martin said.

Swallowing, I forced my hand to dig inside the mud again.

"So Don Martin," I said, "this morning I walked past that house again, the one that got burned in the fire."

He was barely listening. He'd just picked up a colossal worm and flashed it dangerously close to my face so I would appreciate its size.

"I tell you what," he said, "I dare you to find a bigger worm than this."

What were we, ten years old?

I sighed.

No, we were men. Competitive. Daring. Not easily revolted men.

Despite my disgust, I wasn't about to let him win the challenge.

I dug with my full hand, letting the dirt build up under my nails and between my fingers. Among handfuls of soil, gray worms squirmed to the surface. As I collected a few of them and compared them in length to Martin's impressive catch, my revulsion diminished. Soon, I was finding worms at a faster speed than Martin and couldn't help but enjoy the race we'd immersed ourselves into. Much to my dismay, I giggled—it had been an unconscious reaction and now I was going to pay for it. Martin stopped his search and stared at me. For a moment, there was silence. I bet my cheeks were as red as a handful of cherries.

I returned to the task of finding the longest worm and felt a thick one between my fingers. It was as long as a cigarette holder.

I presented my catch. We stood too close for comfort—I could smell Martin's citric cologne masked under the unmistakable scent of moist soil. I took a step back.

"Fine, I concede. You win," he said. "Now let's go get some fish."

After casting our rods (mine took some effort to get in right) I sat on a rock next to Martin, our boots resting by the edge of the water. We sat there quietly for a moment, staring at the water's surface and its calming effect.

"You grew up here?" I asked after a few minutes.

"Yes, but I went to school in Colombia. I owe my education to Don Armand."

As his line stiffened, he reeled it in.

No catch.

He patiently cast his rod again.

"Don Armand paid for my boarding school and college after my father passed away," he said.

"You went to college?"

He didn't seem like the type. My husband fit my idea of what a university graduate ought to look like, not Martin. Then again, this trip seemed to be challenging all my preconceived notions about others.

"What did you study?" I said.

"Agronomy."

"That makes sense."

For a moment, the only sound was the gurgling of the brook.

"So, what happened to your father?" I finally said.

"He drowned."

His bluntness disconcerted me. Involuntarily, I faced the water. I regretted asking, but he didn't seem to mind the subject.

"He'd gotten drunk the night before and in the morning, he went for a swim. Some think that he got a cramp, but I think he was still drunk."

"Did he"—I lowered my tone—"did he get drunk often?"

"No. That's why he got so drunk this time. He couldn't handle his alcohol." He faced the pond, pensively. "I think it finally caught up with him."

"What?"

"His mistakes."

I wanted to know more, but I didn't think Cristóbal would've asked. Besides, after the giggling fiasco, I didn't want to call more attention to myself. Honestly, I was surprised Martin hadn't realized I was a woman yet. He seemed like an observant man.

"Well, that's all in the past. It doesn't change anything," he said with a hint of bitterness.

His fishing rod stiffened, then gave a small jerk. Martin stood up and pulled on the pole.

"It's a big one." He reeled and pulled the rod, exposing a bass that must have been at least six pounds.

As the fish wiggled, Martin removed the hook from its mouth, then inserted a needle with a long string through its mouth and gill, and tied it. He stuck the needle in the ground, letting the fish's body remain inside the water stream. "To keep fresh," he said. He didn't talk about his father anymore and I didn't dare ask. I had to strike a balance where I could earn his trust without overwhelming him with questions.

I had minimum luck with my own fishing, but at least I caught a couple of small bass. Then came the gory task of washing the fish and cutting them open to remove their insides. I marveled at Martin's skill, his precision for cutting, his speed. His hands were large, masculine, his fingernails soiled. It was fascinating to watch.

How come women never did amusing things like this? Well, at least I never did. I was too busy working.

I stared at his profile. What would he say if he knew who I was? Would he flirt with me, or be cold and distant? He would probably not use the kind of language that freely flew from his mouth now that he thought I was a man.

For the first time, I missed my long mane. It had been Cristóbal's weakness and I couldn't help but wish Martin could see me as a woman, too. Wait, what was I doing? My husband had just died and here I was wondering what another man thought of me.

Martin turned to me abruptly and asked if I'd like to come to his place to try the fish. I stuttered a yes, while I pinched my thigh on Cristóbal's behalf.

*   *   *

Martin's house was not far from the river, just outside my father's property. It was a two-story construction with a titian roof. As I walked in, I couldn't help but stare at the ceiling, speechless. Built in an A-shape, it alternated between thick beams and glass, letting in exorbitant amounts of light. Through the skylight, you could see the forest. It was so beautiful—it reminded me of those cabins in the fairy tales I used to read as a child. The stairs were part wood, part gray stones—sporadically covered in moss, like an old castle. It was a house that played with shapes and styles, a house with the power of making you question if you were inside or out.

I leaned on the kitchen counter while Martin chopped pieces of bass, covered them in flour, and sank them in hot oil. We were like two bachelors who'd known each other their entire lives and were completely comfortable with each other. Martin served me a beer called Pilsener while he told me stories about the women he'd had in that very same kitchen. I'd never heard such unrestrained talk before.

"How come there is no Mrs. Sabater?" I asked between blowing on a piece of fish to cool it down and taking cautious bites when I could no longer control my hunger.

"Because I'm not stupid." He chuckled.

I didn't get how this was funny or why getting married made you stupid, but I'd heard some of my clients joke about this to each other.

"And the real reason?" I said.

His smile vanished. He removed the rest of the fish from the pan and set it on a plate to cool down.

"I don't like the way many women treat their husbands," he said. "I've seen many of my friends—brilliant, capable men—being treated like children or like they're too dumb to know any better. Look at Angélica and Laurent. He can't make the smallest decisions without her consent. He has absolutely no say in day-to-day activities, much less business decisions, especially now that Don Armand is not around. I remember my mother doing that to my father, too." He shook his head. "I would hate to lose the ability to come and go as I please, or worse, to lose all confidence in myself."

I thought of my own relationship with Cristóbal. It was true that I directed the course of our lives in many ways. But I didn't think of my husband as stupid—I just thought he didn't care about the minute details of our lives, like the way we decorated our apartment or what friends we should invite for dinner, so I ended up making those decisions myself. Had he been unsatisfied with our arrangement? I recalled his words during our last quarrel.

I'm already doing what you wanted. Am I not?

"You make women sound like monsters," I told Martin.

"Oh, no. I love women. I just don't want one to run my life."

"But do you realize that most women never have had the freedoms you enjoy? They constantly have to explain their behaviors to their parents or to their husbands, and restrain their actions in a society that always judges them."

"Well, there are societal rules and laws for everybody. Just because I'm a man it doesn't mean I can kill someone. But perhaps you're right in that outside the home, women must show more restraint than men."

"That is a fact. Or can you imagine a woman paying a man to fornicate?"

He let out a boisterous laugh.

"I'd volunteer if they needed someone."

"I don't doubt it." I took a sip of beer. It was so bitter. How could people drink this *on purpose*? "So instead of running the risk of having a woman rule your life, you use all others?"

"You mean, the prostitutes?"

What else?

"It's a fair exchange," he said. "They need the money and I need their services. Or do you think I should be giving away money to every woman I meet just because they need it? Look, it's a rotten system, but I didn't create it and I don't know how to fix it. It's unfortunate that some women have to sell their bodies to survive, but life is not always pretty or clean. We're imperfect creatures. We're messy, we're flawed, we don't always have answers. I know I don't."

"And here I thought you were nursing a broken heart."

He turned around and grabbed a plate from an overhead cabinet.

"Enough of this dull talk," he said. "Let's eat."

It was dark when I returned to my father's house and my sisters had already gone to their rooms. My conversation with Martin was still on my mind as I climbed the staircase. He'd complained about husbands losing their freedoms to their wives. I could see how this thought deterred him against marriage—so far, the best part of being a man was having the freedom to do as I pleased without giving explanations to anybody. But this dynamic wasn't the same in all marriages. I can't imagine my father letting a woman dominate him. If he had, then he would've never left Spain.

Midway through the hall, something stopped my pondering.

The smell of smoke.

I froze by Catalina's room. Franco's house came to mind. Maybe she'd fallen asleep with a candle lit. I knocked on the door, but nobody answered. This close to the door the smell of smoke was stronger.

Politeness aside, I turned the knob.

I'd envisioned a dramatic scene of burning furniture and my sister passed out on the floor. Nothing would've prepared me for the sight of Catalina sitting on her bed with a long cigarette dangling between her fingers. The room smelled like the *cantina* in Vinces. The least she could've done was open the window.

She turned around as soon as she heard the door and looked at me with wide eyes. Her hand flew behind her back in a failed attempt to hide her cigarette.

So this was what Vinces's *Santa* did in her spare time: devote herself to a worldly, manly vice.

"Don Cristóbal! I didn't hear you!"

"I apologize for intruding on your privacy, but I smelled smoke and I worried about your well-being."

Her cheeks turned pink.

"Oh, this." She shook her head. "I know I shouldn't. It's not ladylike, but I'm afraid I'm hooked beyond repair."

I crossed the room toward the window. "Allow me."

I lifted the window open. "We don't want to cause an accident, right?"

She stood. "No, of course not."

She didn't seem to know what to do with the cigarette in her hand. I, for one, had never smoked and the one time I tried a cigar at Aquilino's house, I despised it, but somehow this little secret of hers humanized her and made me want to get to know her better.

"Did you have a good time with Don Martin today?" she asked. "Julia said you went fishing with him."

How did Julia know what I'd been doing?

"Yes."

"Julia washes our clothes nearby. She said she saw the two of you."

"I apologize for not letting you know. I hope you didn't wait on me for dinner?"

"No. It's quite all right."

The ashes in her cigarette grew long and thin. I was desperate for her to either take a drag or flip the ashes on the glass ashtray sitting on her night table. But she didn't do either. Instead, she squashed her cigarette against the ashtray's surface.

"Is that *Fortunata y Jacinta*?" I pointed at a book on the bed. I didn't say it, but I was astounded that she'd be reading such a scandalous novel.

Her cheeks flushed. "I found it among my mother's things." She shrugged. "It's just a silly love story."

I was familiar with the work of Benito Pérez Galdós. My Cristóbal breathed Spanish literature.

I sat next to her on the bed. "A tragic one."

"Yes. But there's beauty in tragedy," she said. "Don't you think?"

I remembered Cristóbal. Nothing beautiful about that.

"Not in real life."

"I'm sorry. That was insensitive of me with the recent passing of my . . . my sister." She picked up her fan from the table. Her embroidered collar was so high it must have choked her in this heat. "Tell me about her, about Purificación."

She was very personable, this sister of mine, her eyes looked at me with kindness and her voice carried concern and understanding. There was no possibility that she sent Franco to kill me, none whatsoever.

But I'd caught her smoking, which meant she hid things from others. She had flaws, just like the rest of us, except that nobody in town knew it.

Or maybe they did.

"Is it true that she had a chocolate store?"

"Yes." My voice cracked a little, thinking about the sunny salon where people enjoyed the delicacies La Cordobesa and I prepared. How simple my life was back then.

"My father was so proud of her."

"He was?"

"Yes, he always told Angélica and me that we should be more like her, but neither one of us ever showed any interest in the business."

Then why, oh why, did they want me gone? We could've all worked for a common goal, we could've continued with my father's legacy *together*. But it seemed like one of them was too greedy for that. Or maybe both were.

"I was so sorry about her passing. I wish I could've met her," she said.

Her words stung. They made me feel guilty, dirty about the way I was deceiving her. Catalina was a good person. She didn't deserve this. I wanted to tell her the truth so badly. Would she hate me if I did?

"I'm sure she would've liked to know you, too," I said.

"What did she look like? Anything like us?"

I hadn't thought of this. Angélica seemed to be a carbon copy of my father, but Catalina must have taken after her mother because she had olive skin and dark, Moorish eyes. People used to say I also looked like my mother, a big-boned, tall woman.

"In some ways," I said. "She had black hair like you, but your sister's nose. She was also very musical. She loved *zarzuelas*."

"Did she play any instruments, like Angélica and I?"

"Her voice was her instrument."

This might have been a stretch. If you asked Cristóbal or La

Cordobesa they would've said my "instrument" needed some tuning.

Catalina smiled. "How lucky you must have been to be married to a woman like her. She sounds exceptional."

I took a deep breath. My voice might crack if I spoke. I stood up.

"I should go," I finally said. "It isn't proper for me to be here."

"Of course."

"Good night, Doña Catalina."

I walked away without giving her the chance to answer. My sister's words had touched me deeply. No, Cristóbal hadn't been lucky to have me—the opposite was true. I wasn't the one who was buried in the depths of the ocean. And I couldn't believe how disloyal I'd been this afternoon by spending all that time with another man and what was even worse, enjoying myself. If there was a God in the Heavens, He would certainly punish me for such a callous betrayal.

CHAPTER 18

Catalina

Vinces, 1913

My mother's fingers squeezed my ear painfully. "Have you gone mad, Catalina?"

Startled, I dropped the cigarette in my hand. I didn't know what hurt more: my pride or my ear. I was already fifteen years old and yet my mother was treating me as though I were still a child.

"Pick it up!" she said, pointing at the cigarette I'd just dumped on the ground. I couldn't believe she'd found my hiding spot behind the palo santo tree. My mother never left the house. How did she find her way out here?

"Let me go!" I said, trying to push her away, but she had a good grip of my ear.

"I said, pick it up."

Twisting my body in an unnatural way, I picked up the cigarette. My mother dragged me toward the kitchen as if I were a sack of potatoes.

"How can you embarrass me like this?" she was saying. "Don't you know you have a reputation around here? What if one of your father's *peones* had seen you? You know that news travels faster than light in this town. What is wrong with you?"

Yes, what *was* wrong with me? I knew I had to be good, but I couldn't stop myself from sinning.

"If it isn't one thing, it's another," my mother said.

Things had been so challenging for us lately. It was nothing but lecturing. This was wrong, that was wrong. Follow your brother's example, look how he entered the seminary.

For my mother, Gloria Alvarez de Lafont, having one child in the service of the Lord wasn't enough. She would've only been satisfied if the three of us dedicated our lives to the noble cause, but Angélica was beyond hope with all those admirers, and me, well, my mother had made it her life's goal to set me on the right path—no matter what.

To think that she'd been so proud of me when I told her I'd seen the Virgin. It had been months of prayer, of pilgrimage, of the eyes of the entire town and its surroundings on me. People had wanted to come see me, they wanted me to tell them all about the Sweet Mother, they'd traveled from every corner of the country to hear my message.

But that had been six years ago and my mother seemed to have forgotten already about our sore legs from kneeling on the cold floor—side by side—in prayer, or how she would comb my hair until it was as smooth as silk while she asked all the particulars of the Apparition. After all, she had to report every detail to her friends at the *Cofradía* since the town's priest had forbidden me to share my experiences with anybody else.

Still gripping my ear, my mother hauled me across the kitchen and I did my best not to bump into counters and chairs.

"Armand! Armand!" she screeched.

But my father, thank God, was not home. He'd left for the warehouse early in the morning. I'd seen him from my bedroom window, from my prison.

I managed to set myself free once we reached the inner patio. But she got hold of my arm and dragged me all the way to the Saints Room.

This was my mother's favorite room. It was smaller than the rest. It had a spare bed that had never been used and an armoire filled with doll-sized saints. There was the Virgin, of course, Saint Paul, Saint Joseph, and the Christ child. When I was little, I'd asked to play with the saints. After all, they looked just like

dolls to me, but that had constituted the biggest sin and blasphemy of all time in my mother's world.

An assortment of candles could be found inside one of the
drawers with matches, rosaries, and the book of prayer.

"Right here, in front of all the saints, you're going to purge!"
my mother said in a roaring voice.

She handed me the cigarette, which I'd just started and had
several more drags in it, and sentenced me.

"You're going to eat this."

Have I heard right? "Eat it?"

"Yes!"

She couldn't possibly.

"Do it!"

"No!"

My mother slapped me with all her might. My cheek felt as if
one of the saints had fallen on it.

"You're not leaving this room until you eat this. Do you know
what kind of women smoke?"

I shook my head.

"The kinds of women who get paid to copulate with men: *the
women of the night!* That's who!"

I stared at the cigarette in my hand, which Franco had gotten
for me with much effort, and I took a bite—it was the only way I
could ever leave this place. Once my mother got her mind set on
something, there was no contradicting her.

The cigarette tasted as if I'd licked the bottom of a chimney
and then chewed a piece of paper. I spat tobacco pieces on the
floor. Ignoring my coughs, my mother pushed my hand toward
my mouth, making it clear that I had to take another bite. I did
just that, eyes shut, breath held. This time I swallowed the moist
pieces.

"Are you ever going to do this again?"

I shook my head, swallowing the last piece between coughs.
My throat itched. I wanted to throw everything up.

"Now you're going to take me to your room and give me your
entire stash."

*   *   *

I'd never thought I'd crave cigarettes so much. I never even knew what they were until Franco offered me one. For as long as I could remember, Franco had been around—a silent boy who alternatively followed his father around the plantation or hunted squirrels, birds, or rabbits with his slingshot. In many ways, he was like me, though, a loner. The other kids in the area always spent time together, including my brother and sister, but Franco and I were younger so we were left out of all the fun and games. Plus, there was the issue of class. Franco was the son of one of my father's workers, so my siblings didn't give him the time of day. It wasn't done on purpose. They just knew that there were implied rules to follow in our micro-society. But I didn't mind so much.

The first time he'd talked to me I was twelve and he was thirteen, I'd been taking a walk along the stream near my house. He asked me if it was true that I'd seen the Virgin in my room. I avoided the question—I hated talking about that—and asked him if it was true that his mother had magical powers and could see the future.

It seemed like he liked to talk about his mother as much as I liked to talk about the Virgin.

So we decided to talk about ourselves instead. I told him what my favorite activities were (in no particular order): climbing lemon trees, lying on the grass to make out animal shapes with clouds, looking for four-leaf clovers, playing the violin, and reading novels. His were: carving wood, swimming in the river, and playing dominoes. He said that from my list, the only thing that interested him was climbing trees for fruit and he might consider searching for four-leaf clovers, but he didn't have any interest in playing music (or listening to me play) and he didn't know how to read. Occasionally, he would look at clouds, he confessed, but then declared that such activity was for small children. On his end, he offered to let me play dominoes with him.

I accepted with a shrug but was shocked to hear that a boy his age couldn't read. I made a solemn vow that day: I would teach him.

CHAPTER 19

Puri

April 1920

I heard Angélica sobbing last night.

It happened after I left Catalina, on my way to my room. I could hear my sister clearly from what I assumed to be her bedroom, and Laurent seemed to be consoling her, calling her *ma chère* and telling her *calmes-toi*. I stood by their door for a few minutes but after a while, I couldn't hear them anymore.

This event, however minor, had propelled an interesting discovery: I now knew where Angélica's chamber was, and tonight might be my only opportunity to go inside and see if there was any evidence connecting her to Franco or the check in my possession.

During breakfast, I'd come up with the perfect plan. Tonight was Bingo Night and a few couples were coming. They did this every week, Angélica said while serving me a glass of papaya juice, and they rotated hosts and houses. I didn't care about bingo or my sister's friends. What this meant was that people would be so distracted they might not notice if I stepped out for a few minutes. And Julia, who seemed to have eyes everywhere, would be too busy tending to the guests. I might even be able to get a hold of my father's journal in the study.

I wore one of Cristóbal's better outfits: a three-piece suit with a striped waistcoat, wool trousers, and a matching jacket. The selection might be too thick for the weather, but this was one of Cristóbal's fanciest suits and Laurent was wearing a tuxedo. It was astonishing how much confidence—and power—an elegant suit could give a person. In it, I felt like a man. I put on my husband's gambler hat and stepped out of my room.

I could already hear the giggles and compliments downstairs. Interestingly, most of the conversations were in French. From the balustrade, I spotted men in white ties and ladies in long glittery dresses, minks, and feathers in their hair. Straightening my lapels, I descended the staircase. Angélica introduced me to all as her brother-in-law and we proceeded to the dining room, which was filled with appetizers: shrimp-stuffed avocados, *conchitas asadas*, corn tamales, *empanadas de verde*. There were also French favorites: chicken liver pâté, mushroom vol-au-vent, and caviar.

I was used to always being the hostess at my chocolate shop. I would wander from corner to corner making sure everyone was well tended to and satisfied and even cracked a joke or two. I'd always enjoyed feigning voices, especially telling *gallego* or old lady jokes. It was so foreign to see my sister Angélica taking on that role. It bothered me somewhat. (Was I turning into a jealous person? I'd never been one. This experience was certainly having strange effects on me.) But at the same time, I felt an odd sense of pride. It wasn't just her beauty, although people were always drawn to good-looking women, but she had an ease about her, a way to make everyone crave her attention. I could see it in the way her friends held her arm to call her attention or whispered into her ear. In return, she would reward them with a heartfelt laugh.

Laurent looked more vivacious than ever. He thrived telling stories about his travels, his many friends, his expensive purchases to enjoy his hobbies (he mentioned a Brownie camera brought from France and a pair of binoculars for bird-watching). After a while, I was ready to stuff one of those *conchitas asadas* into his mouth to see if that would keep him quiet for two minutes.

With her customary discretion, Julia made sure our drinks were always filled to the rim. The cook, Rosita, whom I'd just met, brought in a serving bowl of *cazuela de mariscos*—the main star of the evening—while her plump derrière wobbled from side to side.

I had no other choice but to continue shoving copious amounts of food in my mouth until I found the perfect moment to escape.

The time came after dinner, when Angélica invited the group to the patio. There, they'd set up three rows of tables. On each table were bingo cards and chips. I sat in the last row.

There was a lot of movement around me. Laughter, gossip, men flirting with women and women flirting with men. The only person who seemed as out of place as me was Catalina—I only hoped she stayed here and didn't decide to wander about the house, too.

As Laurent and Angélica called out numbers, I took advantage of the distraction and, making sure no one was watching, I stepped away from the group at the same time a woman yelled: "Bingo!"

I darted up the stairs, glancing behind me every few minutes, and headed straight to Angélica's bedroom. Hopefully, she didn't lock her door.

Drying my sweaty hands on my trousers, I turned the knob.

My sister's chamber consisted of two rooms: a sitting area and a sleeping area. I felt a little stupid standing there, not knowing where to look, playing detective. What could I possibly find here to tie my sister to Franco?

"Quiere cacao, quiere cacao."

¡Mierda!

Ramona flew toward me. I ducked.

"Quiere cacao, quiere cacao."

"Shhh," I told her, but she kept repeating the same mantra.

Before anyone else could hear her, I headed for one of the night tables and opened the top drawer. There didn't seem to be anything remotely incriminating unless you considered a French-Spanish dictionary and a jewelry box suspicious. Inside the second drawer was a pile of letters wrapped in a red ribbon. Upon inspection, there seemed to be letters to Angélica from different men. Admirers? I thought it strange that she would keep letters from other men in close proximity to her husband.

There didn't seem to be any correspondence from Franco, at

least not in the letters I checked. Underneath all the envelopes was a photograph of a little girl, her face vaguely familiar though I couldn't pinpoint why. I was only certain that this wasn't Angélica or Catalina because both of my sisters' coloring was much lighter than this child's. The girl, who couldn't have been older than ten, stared at the camera with a hardened expression, as though she couldn't stand the thought of having her picture taken. But there was more than anger here. Her expression revealed pain, too, as if she'd been crying minutes before the picture was taken. Her hair was fixed in two stiff braids and she wore a sailor dress she had outgrown.

As I circled the bed toward the other table, I noticed a glass box sitting under the window. A rectangular, large *cage*. A slight tremor took over my legs. I slowly made my way to the cage. Curled on the bottom, behind a large rock, was the red, black, and white snake I'd seen in my room. Ramona became more agitated. She flew over my head. This time she was saying something else, some kind of warning, but I couldn't understand her.

My hands turned sweaty.

Why would Angélica keep a snake in her room? Even worse, why was *her* venomous snake in my bed the other night? It would be too much of a coincidence that it had escaped its properly secured cage and found its way next to me, wouldn't it?

But I didn't have time to ponder any further because there was a noise in the hall. I looked around in despair, but before I could move a single muscle, I heard someone at the door, and that someone was turning the knob.

CHAPTER 20

Catalina

Vinces, 1907

Yesterday I saw that girl again. She waved at me from the other side of the pond. Part of her allure was that she didn't have to wear fancy clothes like Angélica and I did. I was tired of fluffy sleeves and long stockings. I wished I could just wear a slip all day and run along the stream like Elisa did. I waved back and circled the pond to meet her.

"I have something for you," she said. She was kneeling by the edge of the water, her fingers buried in the mud. One of her tight plaits fell on her shoulder.

"It's not a snail, is it?" I said, grimacing.

"No."

I jumped up and down. "Then, what is it? What is it?"

"I can't tell you." She turned around to make sure no one was behind us and whispered. "Tonight. At your house."

"But Mamita will be cross with me."

"She won't see me."

I hoped she was right. The last time Mamita had seen me talking to Elisa, she'd yelled and spanked my bottom. "I don't ever want to see you with that girl again! You hear?" she'd said.

I'd promised I wouldn't talk to her again, but Elisa was so much fun. Much more pleasant than Angélica, who never let me touch her dolls.

"You'll get them dirty," she would say, wiping Ursula's porcelain cheeks with a moist handkerchief. "Look at your hands! Don't you see that these dolls are ornaments? You're too young to understand now, but when you're thirteen, like me, you will." She smiled that awful, evil smile of hers. Her teeth in perfect alignment already, unlike mine which were just coming out, big and awkward in a foreign mouth. "Well? Don't you have something better to do? Why don't you go practice your violin or play with Alberto?"

Oh, if I could just pull those blond ringlets out of her stiff head!

I couldn't imagine on what planet it would be fun to play with Alberto. All he ever did was pretend his corks were soldiers immersed in gruesome battles, which involved spitting sounds and rolling around on the ground. You would think Angélica would want to play with me. I was her only sister and nearly ten. But Angélica would rather sit in the presence of adults, looking as stiff as one of her precious dolls, while they engaged in those boring, never-ending conversations. I'd rather watch hair grow than listen to them. The only sign that Angélica was still alive was that every few minutes she would stand and offer roasted peanuts and olives to my father.

Elisa, on the other hand, was like a fireball. She always knew where the fun was (it usually involved an activity that was forbidden to us kids) like climbing on rooftops blindfolded (it was a test of trust, she would say, as you were supposed to let the other person guide you when you were on top), jumping off the highest branch of a tree (and not crying, even if you had a painful landing with scrapes and blood), or standing on the back of a horse while he strolled. The one time Alberto had joined us, Elisa had insisted we play the *hold your breath under the water* game, but there was a twist. She was the one who decided how long my brother's head would remain inside the pond. She held him down for almost a minute, even though he was flapping his arms and kicking the ground. When she finally let him go, he cursed her ("*¡Maldita!*"). I'd never heard him say the Forbidden Word before, my mother would've been aghast if she knew. Alberto had darted off swearing that he would never play with her (or me) again. In response, Elisa had laughed and called him a baby.

The other thing that was fascinating about Elisa was that nobody knew where she lived or how she'd arrived at the hacienda. One day, she was just sitting there on a rock by the pond and no explanations were given. When I asked her who her parents were or where her house was, she pointed at the sky and said she lived on one of the clouds.

"Which one? That one?" I said pointing at the fattest one.

"No! The one behind it!"

"The grayish one with the shape of a pear?"

"No, silly! The one *next* to it."

"Oh," I said, though I couldn't be exactly sure of which one she meant—they were all moving. "Are you an angel then?" I asked, but honestly, I doubted it—she seemed a little too dirty to be one, but I had to ask.

Her sole answer was a smirk.

She kept coming every other day, and our games became bolder. When my mother saw us hanging from the railing of a bridge, she yelled until her ears turned red. She forbade me from ever speaking to that *niñita machona* again. After the mother incident, Elisa disappeared for over a month, which is why I couldn't say no to her when she offered to bring me a gift. Besides, who rejects a gift?

Lying under my sateen sheets, I heard the tap on the window.

The moon was bright and full behind Elisa. She was carrying a package wrapped in newspaper. I was so excited I could barely unlock the window.

When she stepped in, she studied my room as though it were a museum. She walked in circles, exploring every one of my possessions. Once she'd concluded her inspection, she handed the package to me.

"Here."

I unwrapped it with trembling hands. *Virgencita del Cisne*, it was a doll! A dancer! But the strangest one I'd ever seen. From the waist up, she was a regular girl, but her bottom was made out of a round pillow covered with a red skirt. She was beautiful, even if her face was soiled and she was half-bald, which told me that this doll had been played with, unlike my sister's.

"She's so pretty," I said. "Are you sure you don't want it?"

"It's yours." She'd found my book of prayers and was sifting through it. "With one condition."

"Whatever you want!"

A knock on the door startled us. "Who's in there, Catalina? Who are you talking to?"

"Nobody, Mamita."

"Don't lie to me! I heard another voice. Is it that girl?" She banged the door. "Open!"

If my mother saw Elisa she would take the doll from me and I so wanted to keep it.

"No! It's not her!"

As my mother twisted the door open, Elisa dashed toward the window and hid behind the curtain.

My mother was carrying a candle in one hand and her rosary in the other. She paced the room, examining every corner. It was a miracle that she didn't see Elisa behind the flowing curtain. It was an especially bright night. The moon was so wide outside my window I might be able to touch it.

"Where is she?" my mother said.

"Who?"

"I heard a voice!"

"I was talking to myself!"

"Don't take me for a fool, Catalina, I clearly heard two female voices."

I didn't know if it was the rosary in her hand, my prayers to the Virgin, or the bright light outside my window, but before I knew it, I came up with the perfect answer.

"It was the Virgin Mary."

I thought my mother would start laughing, but she didn't. "Are you lying to me, Catalina?"

I shook my head, glancing at the flash of red under my bed— the doll's skirt.

"Don't joke about this, Catalina."

I avoided her eyes. "I'm not. It was truly her."

She looked around the room. "Where is she?"

"She disappeared as soon as you knocked."

"You know that lying about this is a mortal sin."

I swallowed hard, unable to produce another word.

"But the Virgin is well known to show herself to the most in-nocent," my mother said in a whisper. "If what you're telling me is true, Catalina, then this is a miracle."

I nodded. I would confess the truth later, but I was so afraid that she would see Elisa or the doll that I would've said anything to make her leave the room.

As if waking, my mother made the sign of the cross. "*¡Cristo Bendito!* The Holy Mother here?" She groped me by the shoulders. "Are you sure? What did she say?"

I shrugged.

"She must have said something. She always presents herself with a message."

"She said to love one another," I guessed.

My mother fell to her knees, weeping. After a moment—as long as a full day and night—my mother stood up, almost vio-lently.

"I must tell your father. I must tell Padre Elodio. The Church must learn about this! Everybody must."

"No!" I grabbed her by the sleeve. "I mean, I don't know if the Virgin would like that."

"Dear child, why else would she have made an appearance if it wasn't to transmit a message to all the children of God?"

She caressed my chin. "You wait here, in case she appears again."

She dashed out of the room, leaving me all alone with Elisa.

The girl shoved the curtain aside, a wide smile on her face. "The Virgin?"

"I couldn't think of anything else." I glanced at the open door. "You'd better leave before they come back. What was your con-dition for me to keep the doll?"

Elisa climbed onto the window ledge.

"Make sure you show it to your father."

After she jumped down, the curtain flowed with the wind after her.

CHAPTER 21

Puri

April 1920

There had to be a more dignified way to find my potential assassin than this. From under Angélica's bed, I could see two pairs of men's legs approaching. I hoped the flower quilt on the bed would cover me completely. The men were laughing about something said downstairs, but I couldn't understand what. They were speaking in French way too fast. One of them was Laurent.

Come on, Laurent, grab whatever it is that you came for and get out already. But the men were in no hurry. They kept talking and laughing. Ramona screeched and her wings flapped.

"*Tais-toi!*" Laurent said, slamming the cage door. And Ramona inside of it. He'd never been so rough with her in front of Angélica.

The men turned suddenly quiet, their feet in close proximity to each other. Had they heard me? I held my breath.

What were they doing? Didn't they have a bingo game to go to? Sweat peppered my back and armpits. If I stretched out my arm, I could touch their shoes—that was how close they stood from me. I remembered to breathe, hoping they couldn't hear me. What was taking so long? I glanced at their feet again.

There was something strange about the way they were standing. They were facing each other. If they'd been a man and a woman, I would've sworn they were kissing, close as they were.

What else could they be doing? But no, they wouldn't, would they?

One of them was probably helping the other with his tie or something like that. My mother used to say I had an overactive imagination. There was probably a reasonable explanation for this. Laurent wasn't that kind of man. He was married to Angél- ica and he was very flirtatious.

Wait.

He was flirtatious with *me,* someone he thought to be a man.

And besides, if one of them was fixing the other one's tie, he would've been done already, or they could've continued talking. Was I imagining kissing sounds?

After what seemed like hours under the bed, one of the men took a step back.

"We should go back," he said, this time in Spanish. His voice was low and hoarse and he didn't have as much of an accent as Laurent.

The two pairs of legs ambled to the door and left the room.

I slid from beneath the bed in a state of shock. What had I just witnessed? Had I imagined things or did Angélica's husband have a taste for men?

CHAPTER 22

Angélica

Vinces, 1913

"I think you should wear royal blue," Silvia said. "You can never go wrong with blue. It's very becoming. More so than pink. Pink is for young girls or people like Catalina."

I resented my best friend's disdain when mentioning my sister. I knew Catalina was awkward and not popular among the girls in París Chiquito, but that didn't mean Silvia had to mock her.

Only I could do that.

"It's not every day that one turns eighteen," she said. "You have to do something memorable, something this town has never seen."

Every time I tried to say something, she would speak again. But that was how Silvia was. Difficult to talk to. She never listened to anyone but herself. And yet, I enjoyed her company more than anybody else's.

She strolled by my side along my favorite trail. The ground was plastered with torn twigs and fallen leaves, which crunched with every one of my steps. I'd always loved the crisp sounds of the morning: the wind ruffling the towering tree branches, blackbirds and white-tail jays singing, and, if you were lucky enough, you might hear monkey howls coming from the forest. Above my head, a canopy of foliage shrouded the rising sunlight. The familiar scent of moist earth and decomposing vegetation was somewhat placating. I loved this place, particularly these majestic trees flanking the road. In the distance, I could see the hacienda standing proudly among my green Eden. Even though I lived here and took this walk every morning, I never grew tired of looking at my father's impressive construction.

"Actually," I said, lifting up my skirt to avoid soiling the hem, "I was thinking about red."

Silvia stopped sharp and dropped my arm. "You're joking, right?"

I smiled. I knew all about the Indecency of Red. Even if I wanted a red gown, my mother would've never allowed me to wear it. It was *scandalous*, she would say, and would cancel the party at once. "I'm thinking about white."

"No. Too chaste."

"What's wrong with that?"

"Do you want to be the center of attention or not? If you wear white, you'll look muted. That only works for brides."

"How come you always have an opinion about everything?"

"Because I do. Now, listen to me and have your seamstress make you a blue dress."

"Fine!"

I was not thrilled with "our" decision but at this point, I would've said anything to quiet her. The only reason I let Silvia be so overbearing was because I was grateful that she'd moved to Vinces two years ago. She'd energized the entire town. She came from one of the most affluent families in Guayaquil and was full of opinions about fashion and boys. All the girls had wanted to befriend her and dress like her, but she picked me.

"Now, we have to decide on the flowers."

Santa María, please make her stop. I quickened my pace as she continued weighing all the pros and cons of every flower in the region. What a relief it was to arrive home! I opened the front door and removed my hat, while Silvia's incessant chatter buzzed behind me.

"Would you like some lemonade?" I interrupted.

Silvia barely dropped a yes between run-on sentences. "I do favor hyacinths over orchids, but orchids would create such a lovely contrast with your blue dress."

Halfway through the foyer, I nearly lost my footing when I saw who was sitting on the parlor sofa.

I couldn't believe he was back, after all these years. And he was more attractive than ever with those sideburns. He'd gained weight, too, he was no longer the lanky teenager I'd last seen.

Juan stood up while I froze, like a statue, in front of him.

"Hello," he said as if he'd seen me a few hours ago. No kisses or hugs. "I'm waiting for your father."

Silvia was still talking behind me, but her last thought died mid-sentence when she spotted Juan.

My Juan.

I felt oddly possessive of him when I saw the way Silvia curled a strand of hair around her fingers.

"Does he know you're here?" I said, equally cold as him.

He eyed Silvia. Men often liked her. She wasn't beautiful—not in the classical sense—but she had a way of swaying her hips when she walked and slightly touching men's arms in conversation that simply drew them in, as if casting a spell.

"No. The cook—Rosita?—said he went horseback riding."

I couldn't believe it. He'd almost forgotten Rosita's name even though she'd been around since the beginning of humanity. Had he forgotten my name, too?

The *arrogance*!

Silvia turned her head toward me and one of her eyebrows arched up, questioning me. Was I this obvious? I had to get a hold of myself. Yes, Juan was better looking than most men in our circle and I'd loved him since we were kids, but look at him. His clothes were ancient. The fabric of his collar and sleeves was falling apart from all the washing and his tie was at least three seasons old.

The hostess in me was telling me to offer him a drink, but Silvia's stern eye warned me not to dare.

"Well, why don't you wait for him in the kitchen?" I said, dismissive. *With that maid whose name nearly escapes you.* "Come on, *querida*," I told Silvia, and guided her to the dining room without another glance at Juan.

With every one of my steps, I felt more ashamed of myself. I couldn't believe I'd spoken to him that way when all these years I'd been eager to see him again and feel his arms around me.

But he'd been so cold.

My throat was scratchy. I'd ruined everything.

"Who was *that*?" Silvia said, and I wasn't sure if *that* was good or bad.

I shrugged, horrified to feel my eyes watery and burning. I would *not* cry in front of Silvia.

"Just one of our neighbors." Speaking hurt my throat more.

"Why haven't I met him?"

"He was gone for a while, traveling I think." I didn't want to get into details, not with her. Not when I saw the way she'd looked at him, even if now she was pretending to be uninterested.

"Well, he seemed a little rude."

Even Silvia had noticed.

"He's not very polished," I said. "His mother died when he was young and . . ." Why was I justifying Juan to her? Juan was not Silvia's business. I did *not* want to make him her business so she could have an opinion of him, just like she had about everything else. "Anyway, what were you saying about the flowers? Personally, I love daisies."

She twitched her nose. "Daisies? But they're so plain."

Good, I'd diverted her attention. Now, what was I going to do about Juan? I had to make it up to him. Later. After Silvia left, I would talk to him. I grabbed the pitcher of lemonade sitting in the cupboard and removed a couple of glasses from the cabinet. I should have offered Juan a drink. Maybe I still could? I had to get rid of Silvia so I could go back to him. What if this was just a quick stop and he wasn't staying in town?

Oh, why couldn't Silvia *stop talking*? I handed her a glass. Then filled my own and took a long drink. I peeked at the door behind her, calling Juan in my mind. I wanted to see him again. In fact, I could feel my legs tingling to go back to the parlor.

Silvia took a small sip.

"Maybe we should take a drink to Juan?" I said.

"Who?"

Oh, yes, I'd failed to introduce them. What was wrong with me? One glance at Juan and I'd turned into custard.

"The neighbor."

"Oh, *him*. No, don't bother, he didn't even introduce himself."

Silvia was right. Juan hadn't even made an effort to greet us properly, but what could be expected of him? He'd never been conventional and his father had been a madman. But he sure was handsome. Had he gotten married? I'd forgotten to look for a ring. That would explain his indifference, though.

The door burst open and my father entered the room. I expected to see Juan behind him, but Papá was alone.

"Silvia, what a pleasure to see you here, *ma belle*!"

"Don Armand!"

"You will join us for Angelique's party?" my dad said in his thick French accent. Over twenty years in Ecuador and he still sounded like he'd just stepped off of the ship.

"Of course, Don Armand. I will be delighted! In fact, your daughter and I were just planning all the details."

"Papá, did you see Juan? He was waiting for you in the parlor." Could he possibly have gone to the kitchen, like I'd suggested? Oh, why had I said such a stupid thing?

"What Juan?"

"The only Juan we know. Our neighbor."

"Oh, he's back?" He turned his attention back to Silvia and complimented her on how the olive of her dress matched her eyes so well.

I excused myself and headed for the kitchen. Rosita was alone in there, preparing the dough for *empanadas*.

"Have you seen Juan?"

"Last I saw he was in the living room."

I darted outside but there was no sign of him. I *could* go to his place, but that would be too undignified and besides, what would I say? *Why didn't you wait in the kitchen, like I told you?* He would think I was insane. And maybe I was losing my mind a little. I couldn't even understand what I was feeling. All I knew is that I hadn't expected to see Juan again. Not today, anyway.

I stared down the road that led to his house, wishing things could be as simple as they were before he'd left.

The guests were gathering downstairs already. My hands trembled as I put my sapphire earrings on. Silvia had been right. Blue suited me. My mother had agreed blindly with all of Silvia's suggestions, not caring much for terrestrial affairs herself.

My mother came from humble origins. She was one of eight siblings, and all of them considered her the luckiest girl in El Milagro, her hometown, to have found a rich foreigner to marry her—that was the lie they told everybody. The truth was my father already had a wife in Europe, but both of my parents acted as if his real wife was nothing but a long-lost relative.

I couldn't understand what my father saw in my mother. She was plain looking and not too bright, but she treated him like a god. She never argued, but simply joined her hands in prayer when he said something offensive. Such servitude, such blind loyalty was not easy to find. My father liked that she forgave easily, that she wasn't demanding. There had been only one instance that I knew of, one offense in their lukewarm life that my mother didn't tolerate. And he'd suffered for his extramarital indiscretion with one month of silence from my mother. Eventually, they'd reached a truce.

A few months after that, my father had gotten drunk and mentioned his Spanish wife for the first time. He said it was her birthday and he was drinking in her honor. He said her name was Maribel and she could dance flamenco like a goddess. He also said she had gorgeous hair, all the way to her waist, and skin as soft as the petal of a flower, but she had a rotten temper and held grudges for years. She was like a matchstick, he'd said, quickly incensed.

"What a foul mouth she had," he told me after finishing a bottle of wine, "but she sure knew how to love a man."

To say I was uncomfortable to hear my father speak like that about a woman was an understatement. The fact that it wasn't my mother made it even worse. I stood up and left him alone in his study with his bottles and his memories.

I'd always suspected that my mother's attempts to be the perfect wife had to do with that fiery woman my father could never forget.

I looked at my reflection one last time before joining the guests downstairs. Hopefully, my father had invited Juan. I hadn't seen him since the incident with Silvia and I was hoping for an opportunity to apologize for my rudeness. If he liked the way I looked tonight, I might be able to earn his forgiveness more easily.

There were about a hundred guests scattered throughout the foyer and the inside patio of the house. My father took my hand at the bottom of the stairs. He looked jubilant. I hadn't seen that proud look in his eyes before and having his attention was intoxicating.

"*Ma chère*, there's someone I want you to meet," Papá said into my ear as I waved to Silvia at a distance and searched for Juan among the faces. "*Laurent, je présente ma fille, Angélique.*"

"*Enchanté,*" the man said.

Good thing I was holding on to my father's forearm. In front of me stood a monument of a man and a true aristocrat. He kissed my hand, making my stomach float.

"Laurent has just arrived from France. He's a novelist."

A novelist? How sophisticated!

"I've never met an author before," I said in my botched French. I didn't speak it as fluently as I should have, considering my father was French. But it was his fault because he spoke in Spanish most of the time. "What is your novel about?"

"Oh, many things," he said, "love, lust, starvation, war."

I'd always had a gift with people. I knew exactly how to engage them in conversation. All I had to do was ask them about themselves. It hadn't failed once. I used my gift with Laurent.

It only took a few questions before the Frenchman told me all about himself. He was an artist, he explained, and the medium was irrelevant as long as he could express himself. He was a big fan of an innovative (fancy word!) new painter named Henri Émile

Benoît Matisse. According to Laurent, there were exciting artistic movements emerging all over Europe.

I'd always wanted to go to Europe, particularly to my father's homeland, but I doubted I would ever go. Not unless I married a native. Where had my father gone anyway? I spotted him sitting in his favorite chair, his throne, with a glass of *jerez*, surrounded by friends. But he was staring at me. Excluding his botched attempt to marry me to Don Fernando del Río and form some kind of medieval alliance with that arrogant rancher, my father had never been interested in my social life. He certainly hadn't introduced me to a man before, nor had he looked so pleased with me or attentive to my every move.

And now he was smiling at me. The evening couldn't be more perfect.

Someone greeted him. Someone wearing an old brown jacket. *Juan.*

Self-consciously, I shifted in my seat. Laurent and I shared the same settee as we waited for dinner to be served. He'd been discussing modern art for at least twenty minutes and I could barely get a word in. Not that I would even know what to say, I'd only studied until the sixth grade and then concentrated on my harp studies with a private tutor.

My father turned his attention to an elegant couple who approached him. Juan looked as out of place as a polar bear in the middle of the desert. He stood by himself, nestling a glass of champagne between his hands. I averted my gaze before he could see me. What had I been thinking when I considered it a good idea to apologize to him at my party? To even be *seen* around him by all my friends? Juan was badly underdressed—his outfit would belong in a government office better than a dinner party such as this one—and he didn't seem to fit in with anyone here. People kept bumping into him and excusing themselves. For a moment, I felt sorry for him. It wasn't his fault that he didn't have the money to afford newer clothes. It was odd how years ago he'd been so popular among the kids in the area, but tonight nobody gave him the time of day.

I ought to approach him and introduce him to some of my friends. He never let me stand by myself when we were children. Too bad Alberto had entered the seminary; otherwise, he could've kept Juan company right now.

A cold hand touched mine. I unglued my eyes from Juan.

"*Angélique*, are you listening?" Laurent glanced casually at Juan. "Do you want to go talk to him?"

"Oh, no." My father would've disowned me if I'd chosen to converse with the poor neighbor rather than his refined compatriot.

The quartet of violinists stopped playing and my father made a toast in my honor. For the first time in the evening, Juan looked directly at me. My ears burned.

Staring at his mouth as he drank from his champagne glass, I couldn't help but remember the first kiss he'd given me, under the shade of the evergreen. There had been more hurried kisses and caresses after that one. Back then, I'd lived in a permanent state of elation. I could've never pictured a scenario like this one—a time when I wouldn't want to run to him and kiss him.

I couldn't hold his gaze for much longer. How could I possibly explain to my younger self this change of heart? This disenchantment with reality when for so long, I'd relied on clouded, idealized memories when thinking about him?

I still remembered the day Juan left. I couldn't stand the thought of my life without him. I'd wanted to go after him or hibernate like a bear until it was all over and he would return. But time had run its course and little by little, I'd become interested in other people—new friends—and other activities until there came a time when I wouldn't think of him at all.

"Please join us for dinner," my mother announced to all, entering the room, her long gold skirt swishing around her legs.

The guests entered the dining area where several tables had been brought in for the occasion. The meal would certainly be exquisite. That was where my mother put all her efforts when tending to guests.

Juan didn't move from his spot. Laurent offered his hand to me and I took it immediately. Obviously, there was no comparison between the Frenchman and Juan—not only in looks, but Laurent was so refined, so knowledgeable that Juan seemed like a caveman in contrast. I glanced back at him nonetheless. Juan set his glass on the coffee table, but instead of following us to the dining room, he turned toward the front door.

"Excuse me for a moment, Laurent," I said, disentangling my arm from his.

I wasn't thinking straight. I just had a sudden urge to talk to Juan.

"Juan!" I said, as he opened the door to leave. "Wait!"

I followed him to the porch. He continued down the steps.

"Where are you going?"

"Home," he said, without turning.

"But you haven't had dinner yet."

"So what? I'd rather eat a plant than stand another minute in the midst of so much arrogance."

"That's such an unkind thing to say!"

He finally turned, but I could barely see his features under the dim light.

"And it's not unkind to ignore a guest, a . . . friend you haven't seen in seven years?"

"I was busy!"

"Yes." He raised his arms as he spoke. "I saw."

Somewhere in the hardened features of the man standing in front of me, I could see the softness of the teenager I'd once loved. But I couldn't recognize him anymore. It was the saddest feeling I'd ever had, a sense of loss that was indescribable.

"It's been too long," I said. "You were gone for too long."

"I had to." His voice softened a notch. "But I never forgot you."

A couple of years ago I would've said the same thing to him, but I couldn't now. Not when I was standing in front of a stranger. Oh, why did he have to come back now when I'd already forgotten him?

"Go back to your rich friends, to your fancy new beau." He turned to leave. "I won't bother you anymore."

CHAPTER 23

Puri

April 1920

My father's grave was exactly where Don Pepe, the caveman, had told me—in the heart of the plantation, where he'd asked to be buried. I hadn't been this close to my father's body since I was two years old. And yet, I'd never been more distant.

"*Hola, Papá,*" I said aloud, not finding a better place to sit than on top of the grave where he rested. "I hope I'm not squashing you."

Someone had brought him hyacinths, but it must have been weeks or months ago because they'd dried completely and drooped hopelessly into a sea of dead petals.

Strange. The grave was so close to the house. Why wouldn't anybody visit? Were they this resentful about the will?

I brushed the petals onto the ground.

"Well, I'm finally here," I said, "trying to sort out the mess you left." I looked around me. The tree branches seem to lean over me to listen. "I wish you wouldn't have raised such greedy children. Well, *one* greedy child."

I ran my fingers over my father's engraved name.

"Not only greedy, but evil." That was the only adjective I could use to describe what they'd done to Cristóbal.

I'd been thinking about my siblings last night. Catalina

seemed incapable of any bad deeds. So she smoked. That only meant she wasn't perfect, or the town's saint, like everybody claimed, but simply human and as such, flawed. Alberto, well, why would he want to kill me when he'd renounced his fortune? And besides, why would he need money in the seminary? Unless he was planning to get out. I couldn't help but remember our conversation about good vs. evil. Was there something I wasn't seeing? So far, the only person who seemed capable of harm was Angélica. After all, she had a snake in her room; a snake who happened to find its way to my bed.

But there was a hole in this theory. Nothing seemed to link Angélica to Franco or the check. The only thing remotely interesting in her drawer had been the photograph of an unknown girl.

"*Ay, Papá*. Your Angélica is something else, isn't she?"

I stood up, dusting the dirt from my trousers. I was not far from Franco's house. It would probably take me about five minutes to get there. I plucked a daisy from the ground and set it on my father's grave.

The burned-out house was larger than I remembered. There was no front door so I just stepped inside. It was hard to determine what I was looking at. Pieces of wood that must have belonged to the ceiling or a wall had collapsed on the floor and were now charred. Mountains of rubble filled what might have been, at one point, a parlor. The staircase was mostly gone, but surprisingly, the dining room was intact—an oval table with four chairs sat in the center of the room. It was incredible that among this destruction there were still discernable objects. Why hadn't Soledad and her son claimed some of these things? Scattered across the kitchen floor were broken ceramic cups, tarnished pots, and silverware. The wall next to the stove was stained with smoke and there was a hole carved out of the wood.

I spotted the corner of a golden tin box inside the hole. It was stuck with a piece of brick that had fallen on top, but with some effort, I slid it out. The lid was somewhat mangled. I removed it. Inside was a notebook and some pencils. I looked through the pages. It seemed to be a calligraphy or spelling notebook, as there were simple words and phrases repeated throughout. I skimmed through the pages until something caught my attention: a name written with clear penmanship.

Catalina is my best friend.

The sentence was repeated several times across the page. Catalina? Franco's friend? I couldn't imagine a friendship between two more discordant people. She was so pretty and sweet, a lady. And Franco, a brute, a man with no morals willing to kill a stranger for money.

And yet, I was holding the evidence that there had been, at least at one time, a friendship between them—the *only* evidence connecting one of my sisters to Franco. I couldn't just ignore it because it seemed improbable or ludicrous to me.

Could their friendship have evolved into something else— into a romance? Was she the woman who drove him crazy? I couldn't picture her asking him to kill me. I couldn't imagine her in a relationship with this man. What would she have seen in him? Unless she just used him to get rid of me.

No, this relationship must have started years ago. His handwriting seemed childish and so did the sentence.

I sifted through the pages, but couldn't find her name anywhere else. I shoved the notebook inside my trousers and covered it with my waistcoat while I continued to look for further proof of her presence in his life. I walked to the other side of the house.

"Don Cristóbal?"

Startled, I turned around.

"Don Martin! You nearly gave me a heart attack!"

"I thought it was you in here."

"I was just taking a walk and got curious about this place."

Martin looked puzzled.

"For inspiration," I said. "Did I tell you I'm writing a novel?"

"Many times."

He looked around, resting his hands on his hips.

"Well, it doesn't seem like you're going to find a lot of inspiration here. Not a lot is left."

"Yes. Poor family," I said, studying Martin as he glanced around the debris. If he'd lived here so many years, he might know if Catalina and Franco were in a relationship. "I met Doña Soledad, by coincidence, the other day. She's desperate because her son has disappeared."

He picked up a square object—it was virtually impossible to recognize what it had been. An ornament, a sewing kit, a jewelry box?

"Is she really?"

"Yes. She said that he was madly in love with a woman and she asked him to do something for him. After that, he never came back."

Martin placed the strange object on his head, and took a step with his arms widespread, trying to balance it.

I laughed. What was it about this man that was so distracting? I could never get any information from him. After he was done parading around with the box on his head, I spoke again.

"Do you have any idea of who that woman might have been?"

He ducked his head forward, making the object land in his hands. Then he bowed down as if he were a grand magician.

"No."

"You were not friends with him?"

"Why would I be? He worked for me."

He had a point.

"Careful with that glass," he told me before I stepped on a dozen pieces of broken glass. It could've been a bottle or part of a window. "Why do you care so much about this family?"

"Doña Soledad asked for my help finding her son." I averted my gaze. "I didn't see you at the bingo last night."

Martin waved his hand in dismissal. "Oh, Los Gran Cacao never invite me to those things. Not that I would go anyway."

"Los Gran Cacao?"

He shrugged. "It's what people around here call families with cacao money."

I had to admit that I would've rather not attended, either. Angélica's friends were a close-knit, arrogant crowd and they weren't too welcoming. The good thing about them ignoring me the entire evening had been that I didn't have to speak at all.

"Hey, what do you say we go to town and visit our friends tonight?" He winked at me.

Oh, not the prostitutes again!

I placed my hand on my stomach. "No, Don Martin, I can't. I felt terrible doing that to my wife so soon after her passing."

He stared at me with a mystified expression. Was I the only man ever to decline such an offer? The experience of going to the brothel had saddened me more than anything. Even though Carmela had seemed enthusiastic to offer her services to me, there had been a void in her eyes I couldn't ignore. A painful resignation, if you will, that had broken my heart.

"I understand," he said.

He did?

"Let's go to town anyway." He patted my arm. "There's a place I think you might like."

Thirty minutes later, we were in downtown Vinces driving toward the Malecón. From this angle, the turquoise walls of the Palacio Municipal stood out, like an overdecorated cake. We turned toward a park surrounded by a metal fence, palm trees, and various shrubs attempting to escape their metal captors. We drove slowly—we happened to be the only car in the area—and stopped for a group to cross the street. What struck me the most were the women's short, stylized haircuts, so similar to Angélica's, and their fancy stoles. Among the crowd was Alberto in a starched, white linen suit and a toquilla straw hat. This was the first time I'd seen him wearing something other than a cassock.

Martin rolled down his window. "Alberto!"

My brother kept shambling, pale, with his gaze straight ahead, as if sleepwalking. *In the middle of the afternoon?*

Martin called him again. He must have heard him—we weren't far at all. But Alberto didn't turn. Instead, he reached the steps of San Lorenzo church and went inside.

"What the hell's wrong with that idiot?" Martin said.

We continued down the street and I recognized Soledad's house. Her teal door opened and a young woman stepped outside. I'd seen her before, but where? I leaned toward the window to get a better look at her face. She removed a handkerchief from her purse and blew her nose. She seemed to be crying.

Martin was facing the road. I was going to ask him if he knew her, but we drove too fast and I lost my chance.

We parked next to a cafeteria across from the miniature Eiffel Tower. It was bizarre to see such a precise replica in this small South American town. To think that I'd always dreamt of seeing the real one. Strange that after having a French father, I would be exposed to this monument first.

We sat on a patio facing the Vinces River and Martin told me this place had the best coffee in town, known as *café arábigo*. I couldn't help but imagine myself selling truffles in a restaurant like this one, overlooking this spectacular river—I missed my chocolate shop so much, my Cordobesa, and most of all, Cristóbal. But my past seemed like it had belonged to someone else, especially because all those dear things were gone and would never be mine again. What I wasn't counting on was missing the chocolate-making process so much. It had always been predictable, reliable, and gratifying. I looked forward to it every morning. It offered me a relaxation and ease that no other activity did (except when La Cordobesa burned my beans). I loved to see the beans transform into a liquid blend—it was almost magical. The memories made me remember why I'd come here in the first place. It wasn't a need for revenge, it was a need to find the primary source of my passion.

"This coffee would go well with a piece of chocolate," I said.

Martin took a sip. "I've always wanted to taste it, but nobody here knows how to make it."

"So, in the meantime you chew cacao beans, like Ramona?"

He chuckled.

"The process is long, but not too complicated," I said. "I learned from watching my wife."

"And who taught her?"

"Her grandmother, Doña María Purificación García. She was the first one in the family to discover chocolate and she passed on her passion to her son-in-law, Don Armand."

"I'd love to try it one day, if you say it's so fantastic."

"It is."

"Well, I'm afraid we can't offer you anything so exquisite. So, until chocolate reaches this humble region, you must settle for our simple *humitas*," he said. "It's the closest thing to heaven you'll find here."

"What are those?"

"Don't ask me how to make them. All I know is that the dough is made out of corn and they wrap them in cornhusks and steam them. Oh, and I think they throw in some *ants*. Trust me, you'll like them. I haven't met a single person who hasn't."

Martin was right. *Humitas* were an unexpected delicacy—moist and fluffy and with a slight sweetness to them, but Martin said they also made them savory.

"These are delicious, Martin," I said.

He barely smiled. He seemed preoccupied, not the usual easygoing man I'd come to know.

"I have a business proposition for you," he said finally. "I trust this will stay between the two of us?"

Was he going to propose that we open a café like this one together?

"I know that you will soon inherit a portion of your wife's land and I'd like to buy it from you."

I would've rather he slapped me.

"I know it's a lot of money, but I have my life's savings, plus I think I may be able to get a loan from Banco Territorial or Banco Agrícola y Ganadero."

I pictured the bug-eyed manager who had told me that the signature in the check was my father's.

"You don't have to answer right now," he said. "I suppose Angélica or Catalina might want to buy your portion, too, but listen, nobody knows that plantation like I do. I worked with Don Armand for seven years and I love the land. Besides . . ."

He shook his head, setting his napkin on the table.

Was that why he'd been so nice to me all this time? Taking me out for drinks, teaching me how to fish, bringing me to this café. Because he had ambitions about owning the plantation, too? And here I thought he'd genuinely liked me. But he may have befriended me just to get his hands on my father's plantation.

A more disturbing thought came to mind. If he'd had dreams of owning the plantation for some time, then it would've been convenient to him if I'd perished aboard the ship. It would be one less person he would have to deal with. If he was, in fact, the one who'd hired Franco, it would make sense that he didn't sign the check with his own name. Without his signature, there would be no evidence that he'd hired Soledad's son, no way to track the check back to Martin.

This man had been my father's closest worker for almost a decade. He had plenty of time to learn my father's signature. How disappointing it must have been for him not to inherit anything. Was this why he never answered my questions about Franco? But Martin's possible involvement didn't answer the question about the woman Franco had been in love with.

"I don't know, Martin," I said curtly. "I haven't thought about what I'm going to do with the land yet."

"You told Tomás Aquilino that you had no interest in staying in Vinces, that you hated the country and had only come here to please your wife."

As soon as I heard the lawyer's name, I knew where I'd seen the girl leaving Soledad's house. She was Aquilino's maid. *Mayra?* She'd served us that mouth-watering fish the day I arrived in Guayaquil. But what was she doing all the way here?

I stopped swirling my spoon inside the coffee.

"Cristóbal? Are you all right?"

"Yes. Let me think about it, Martin. I promise you will be the first one to know my decision."

HAPTER 24

Catalina

Vinces, 1907

I never thought a small lie would turn into an avalanche, but that was precisely what this was, an avalanche of people following me uphill for a pilgrimage. I'd tried to stop this sham weeks ago by telling my mom that I wasn't really sure it had been a real apparition or a dream, but Mamita argued that it couldn't have been a dream because I was wide awake when she came into the room, and I'd never been a sleepwalker.

"Besides," she said, filling her hair with pins to curl it, "everyone knows the Virgin transmits her message only through those with a pure soul. You just have to be receptive to it. Don't be afraid. This is the best thing that will ever happen to you. Moreover, I already told Padre Elodio and all my friends at the *Cofradía*. The entire town has been elated thanks to this miracle. It's too late to change our story."

A story. That was exactly what this was, a pathetic story meant to cover up a forbidden friendship. But I was shocked to see that my mother went along with it with such enthusiasm, that she didn't care at all about the truth. Or did she think that if she believed my lie and shared it enough times it would become true? This may very well be the most exciting event of her life. I'd never seen her so happy—whistling in every corner of the house—busy with friends and activities. It had been a boost to her social life. For once, she wasn't walking behind my father, but in front of him. At parties or outside of church, people would stop her and ask to meet me. I lowered my face, such was my shame, but they all took it as humility. My father, at first, ignored the whole thing. But as the story grew and Father Elodio paid us an official visit, my father started to believe the lie, too. He would stare at me from across the dining table questioningly. Even though he'd always called himself an *agnostic* (a word that, according to my mother, meant that Satan himself had managed to convince the person that God didn't exist), I saw him picking up the Bible a couple of times after the priest's visit.

For the first time in years, Angélica showed interest in me again. She let me comb her dolls' tresses and lent me her favorite bows to wear to church. Sometimes I caught her staring at me with near reverence. My brother, Alberto, wasn't too delighted about our family's sudden notoriety and even attempted to get a confession out of me, but I didn't dare tell him the truth. Honestly, I was more nervous at my mother's reaction than the Roman Catholic Church's and all its congregation.

So here we were, walking up the hill, where the Virgin was meant to deliver another message. Behind my mother and me were my father and siblings, and of course, Padre Elodio. I really needed a miracle now! What would people do to me if nothing happened? What would I say? But I wasn't only afraid of human reactions. I also feared what the Almighty (and the Real Virgin) would think about all of this. Would they punish me in the afterlife? I'd already asked for their forgiveness in my daily prayers, but as the deceit grew so disproportionately, I wasn't sure if Ave Marías and Padres Nuestros would be enough to earn me a spot in Heaven.

The group became larger and larger the more we walked. It reminded me of a long line of ants. I didn't even know there were so many people in this area. But my father had said that parishioners were coming from nearby populations, too, like Quevedo and Palenque.

Dios Santo, what was I going to do now?

Once we reached a clearing among the abundant vegetation, my mother stopped.

"Here," she determined, and pushed me into a kneeling position. Not far from us was a thin creek. "*Hermanos*," my mother said in a loud voice. I'd never heard her talk so loud before; it was as though she'd been the one taken by the Virgin's spirit. "Please. My daughter needs silence and concentration to receive the Message."

One by one, people started to kneel and hold their hands in prayer. Others waved white handkerchiefs. As we started praying the rosary, people surrounded us. My father hugged me protectively as I faced the ground, still on my knees. When I looked up, briefly, I spotted someone across from me in a blue cloak. She moved it slightly from her face and I recognized her immediately.

Elisa.

She winked at me.

My mother, who was leading the prayer, helped me lean back, as in a trance. I looked at the vast sky and asked for forgiveness. At that precise moment, two things happened simultaneously: I discerned a bright light beneath the clouds, which seemed to be opening up to make room for it, and Elisa screamed.

"There she is!" she said.

"Yes!" a male voice responded. "Right there. Behind the clouds!"

"Hallelujah!"

"Praise the Lord!"

The prayer became a loud rumble, like a machine that had been turned on. People recited the Hail Mary with a devotion that hadn't been there a few minutes ago. They screamed it.

It was hard to explain what came over me. I didn't know if it was my posture, still leaning back over my mother's hand with my legs folded and my knees on the ground, or that I'd entered some sort of *ecstasy* like my mother called it later. But the truth was that my legs had turned numb and I was so lightheaded that everything started to move in rapid circles around me: Papá's concerned face, Mamita's teary eyes, the clouds above my head. Everything was spinning faster and faster and the voices—the prayers—became distant and muffled, as though I heard them through a tunnel. And then, everything turned black.

When I woke up, lying down on the grass, surrounded by my parents and the priest, something had changed. People looked at me with what I could only define as reverence. My mother was pressing a handkerchief with smelling salts against my nose.

"Out of the way," my father was saying. "She needs to breathe."

My brother helped me up and as soon as I stood, people made room for me to go through, as though I were some sort of queen. My father helped me down the trail and as I walked by, people touched my arms and shoulders. A woman even cut a piece of my hair.

"She smells like flowers," someone said.

I searched for Elisa among the crowd, but I couldn't find her. People crossed themselves as I walked past them, as though I'd turned into some kind of deity. I felt exhausted, physically and emotionally, and it was a relief to arrive back at the plantation. My father had to threaten those who attempted to enter his property. He'd already foreseen a scenario like this one and so his men stood in front of the gates by the dozens, some holding their machetes, others looking majestic on top of their horses.

My mother, with trembling hands, asked me if I wanted dinner. I declined; all I wanted was to lock myself in my room and sleep for hours.

In my room, I experience a deep sense of relief. I locked my door and headed for the bed.

"Hello, Catalina.

I screeched.

"Shhh, it's me, Elisa."

She emerged from behind the curtains, still wearing the blue cloak.

"What are you doing here?" I said, petrified. "My mom can't see you here!"

"I know, I know, I just came to say goodbye."

"Goodbye?"

"Yes, we're leaving. For good."

I wasn't sure who "we" were. I knew so little about her.

"Did you show your dad the doll?"

With all the excitement of the Apparition and the Virgin, I'd completely forgotten about the doll request. I could've lied, but lying was exhausting. I shook my head.

"Then I'm going to have to take it back."

"No, please. I promise I'll show him. Tomorrow. First thing in the morning."

She sighed. "It will be too late then."

Too late? What was she talking about?

"One day you'll understand," she said. "I have to go now."

She turned to the window and disappeared into the night. That was the last time I ever saw her.

I kept my promise. I showed my father the doll the next day. His reaction was not what I expected.

"Who gave you this?"

"A girl."

"Where is she?"

He seemed desperate, his eyes wide, his fingers pressing on my shoulders as he squeezed me to get an answer. Normally, he didn't care about anything other than his precious *Pepa de Oro*, which was why his reaction surprised me so much.

"I don't know, Papá, you're hurting me."

He let go.

"She said she was leaving forever."

"Do you know where she was staying?"

"No." I collected the doll before he would take it. "Who is she? Why did she want me to show you the doll?"

"Because I gave it to her. When she was small."

"Why?"

He was about to say something but seemed to change his mind.

"Tell me!"

"I will, but only if you tell me the truth. Is it true that the Virgin came to your room?"

I squeezed the doll's cushioned skirt. We were in his study, where I rarely came—we kids were not allowed in here. My father was sitting behind his desk where he'd been writing in a leather-bound notebook.

He rubbed my arm. "Come on, *ma petite poupée*, it will be our secret."

"If I tell you, will you make it stop?"

"Make what stop?"

"The pilgrimages, the praying."

"I promise. Now tell me. Did you see her?"

I bit my lower lip, then shook my head. There was a strange flicker in my father's eyes. For a moment, I thought he was going to strike me, but instead, he started laughing. It was a hoarse laugh; one I hadn't heard in years.

"But why would you make up such a thing?" he said, tears in the corner of his eyes from laughing so hard.

"It wasn't intentional, Papá, I never wanted this to happen. Elisa came to my room once and Mamita heard us. It was the only thing I could think of so she wouldn't find her there. She doesn't like her."

My father leaned back in his chair and crossed his arms.

"Yes, I know."

"Now it's your turn."

"My turn?"

"To tell me why you gave that doll to Elisa."

He cleared his throat. "Not a word to your brother or your sister. Understood?"

I nodded.

"Elisa is your sister."

"What? Why doesn't she live with us? Why does Mamita hate her?"

"Because she has a different mother than you. She lives with her."

"Like Purificación, your daughter in Spain?"

"Something like that." He lowered his voice. "When she was little, she lived here on the plantation, but when your mom found out who she really was, she sent her and her mother away. I don't know why they returned and didn't come to see me."

I remembered something Elisa had once said, weeks ago.

"Elisa said her grandmother was sick. Maybe that's why they came."

"Yes. Maybe." He patted my back. "Now go play, will you? I need to get some work done."

"But Papá, you're going to help me with Mamita, to make all of this stop?"

"I'll try."

I walked away, both relieved and disturbed by my conversation with my father. I couldn't believe Elisa was my sister! In a strange way, I was delighted with the news. I had another sister, one that I liked very much, and one who played with me. She even helped me up there, on that hill, where all those people surrounded me expecting to see the Virgin. But what good was it to have another sister when she was gone and might never come back? On the other hand, it felt good to tell someone the truth about the Virgin situation, but somehow that didn't stop the fear that crept through me ever since this big lie had begun.

CHAPTER 25

Puri

April 1920

I shut my father's journal, stunned by what I'd just read. It was after midnight, and I'd snuck out of my room and into the study after everyone had gone to bed. What a relief it had been to find that the door was unlocked.

I put away the notebook where my father had confessed that he'd had another child out of wedlock, a daughter named Elisa, whom he'd only met as a young child. She was the daughter of one of the housemaids, a *campesina* who had seduced him—that was the word he used: "seduced." *Séduit* in French.

When his wife, Gloria, had found out he was the father of the maid's child, she'd demanded that the woman leave. "It's me or her," she'd told him. At first, he'd denied everything, saying people loved to gossip around here and she shouldn't listen to that nonsense. He'd laughed the whole thing off. But Gloria didn't speak to him in four weeks, and that drove him crazy, he wrote, so he'd acquiesced to her demands.

My father gave the maid a big sum of money and she left. Once in a while, he would receive letters, reports if you will, about Elisa's well-being. What she was like, what was she doing. But these letters were sporadic, he said, because the maid didn't know how to read and write and had to rely on others to write the letters for her. And then one day, the letters stopped coming.

Oh, Papá, what a mess you created!

Another sister. As if I didn't have enough with three siblings. My mother must be turning over in her grave. I tried to recall the details of my father's will. Nowhere in there had my father mentioned this Elisa. Neither did Aquilino. Did that mean that he'd forgotten her? Had she died? But if she was still alive, where was she?

The photograph of the little girl in Angélica's room came to mind. Could she be Elisa?

The room had become stuffy and hot and I didn't know if it was the climate or my father's confession. All I knew was that I had to get out.

I stepped out of the study, crossed the patio, and left the hacienda through the kitchen door. It was such a relief to be outside, away from that confined space. My shirt was drenched in sweat and my arms covered with mosquito bites. I couldn't stop scratching. I undid my tie, thinking about my father. Were all men like him? I didn't think Cristóbal had ever been unfaithful to me. Had he? At this point, I wouldn't be surprised if some random child would show up claiming he was Cristóbal's long-lost son.

Oddly, the thought didn't horrify me. In fact, it might be good if he did have a child, being that I could never give him one. There would be something left of him in this world, something other than his old typewriter.

The moon looked sublime and it was so bright, it partially illuminated my path. I hiked for a long time, and the more I walked, the hotter I became. I could already hear the gurgle of the creek. I anticipated the cool water engulfing my feet and that vision gave me the strength to keep going.

When I arrived, I sat on one of the rocks, undid my shoelaces, and removed my shoes and socks. Under my bare feet, the heat appeared to be rising from the ground, like a coal stove. How could it be so hot at night? So hot and so humid? I submerged my feet in the water and my body temperature finally lowered down a few degrees.

Crickets chirped around me and an owl hooted. I was so uncomfortable with my back covered in sweat. I removed my tie and jacket.

In all this time, I hadn't been outside my room without a jacket. What a relief! I longed for the cool water against my skin. Without giving it much thought, I shrugged off my vest and removed my trousers, too. Looking around, I unbuttoned my shirt. Who would be here at this time of the night anyway? It seemed safe enough and I desperately needed a fresh bath.

Before long, I'd removed all my clothes, my spectacles, and my beard and entered the water. It was the most pleasant sensation I'd had in weeks. Without the corset pressing against my chest, I was free. I wished I could stay here all night, swimming, relaxing, not having to think about who was hiding what and whom I could and couldn't trust in this town.

It was exhausting.

Worse yet, the guilt of my deception grew exponentially as I got to know these people more intimately. Only one of them had most likely paid Franco to kill me, and yet, I was deceiving all of them. That, and the constant fear of getting caught, added to my distress, to my long nights of restlessness.

I must have spent an hour there, imagining what could've been had my father done things differently. By the time I got out of the water, my fingers had turned into prunes. I gathered all my clothes and got dressed. Obviously, my goatee wouldn't attach itself to my wet chin, so I would have to run the risk of going home without facial hair. If needed, I could always say I'd shaved it off. But I really hoped it wouldn't come to that; I was exposed without the beard.

The house was as still and dark as I'd left it and all the bedroom doors were shut. I quietly entered my room and locked the door. Nobody seemed to have noticed my absence.

In the morning, I joined the family for breakfast. I hadn't seen Laurent since Bingo Night. I tried not to stare while he cut his cantaloupe, but I was drawn to him. He wasn't feminine; just sophisticated. The details from the other night were fuzzy and I couldn't recall what I'd heard in that room and what I'd imagined.

He wasn't too attentive to Angélica, but there was a kinship between them. She always anticipated his desires—she would hand him the tray of bread without asking and added more juice to his glass. Laurent finished her sentences without lifting his gaze from the weekly news and patiently corrected her pronunciation when she said "croissants" or "confiture" as if this were his daily duty.

Although Angélica seemed less tense around me now, she wasn't as relaxed as she'd been with her guests on Bingo Night. Catalina, on the other hand, had warmed up to me and wanted to make sure I was satisfied with the meal and had slept well.

I assured her I had a splendid night. After the swim, I'd rested like I hadn't in weeks.

"Don Cristóbal," Angélica said, addressing me for the first time since I sat down. "Have you received any news about María Purificación's death certificate yet?" She absently fed Ramona breadcrumbs, which the bird didn't seem to appreciate as much as the cacao beans. "It's been a week already."

"No, I'm sorry to say." I wiped my mouth. "I hope I'm not inconveniencing you. I'd be happy to make arrangements elsewhere."

Even if I was making progress with my investigation, I didn't want to be in a place where they didn't want me. My pride wouldn't let me.

Catalina placed her hand on mine. "Of course you're not an inconvenience, Don Cristóbal. Angélica and I are pleased to have you here. It's the least we can do for our sister."

Catalina caressed my hand with her thumb—for too long, it seemed—and then smiled. How different my two sisters were. I couldn't imagine Catalina, with that sweet demeanor and kindness, plotting against me. Even if Franco was her "best friend," according to the notebook now hidden under my mattress. Then again, my mother used to say that we had to fear more those who came shrouded in sheep's skin.

"Catalina is right, Don Cristóbal. You may stay as long as you need to." Angélica set her napkin on the table. "Would you excuse us? We must practice our number for the festivities. Vinces's foundation is coming up."

I stood up. "Of course."

As my sisters left the room, Ramona flew behind Angélica. Once the muffled sounds of the violin and the harp began, I sat and turned to Angélica's husband.

"What brought you to these lands, Laurent?"

"Adventure." He took a bite of his baguette. One of his slick locks fell across his forehead. "A friend of mine mentioned there was a significant French community here so I thought, why not? If I don't travel while I'm young, then when? Besides, I was tired of those long European winters. It turned out to be the best decision I could ever make because I avoided that awful war. *Mon Dieu*, what a disaster that was."

"Do you plan to go back to Europe one day?"

He set the bread on his plate, then crossed his arms on the table. "Do *you*?"

I looked out the window. Cacao pods hung from a nearby tree branch. There were so many of them they seemed to multiply like bees in a hive.

"Of course," I said. "I'm not cut out for the country."

Nothing was further from the truth. I'd enjoyed my fishing expedition with Martin more than I could've ever imagined and those walks in the forest in the early morning were invigorating. Last night at the creek had been like adding *crème chantilly* to a chocolate mousse. No, I didn't see myself leaving any time soon.

"I don't blame you," he said. "It has taken me a while to get used to this place." He leaned over, lowering his voice. "People here can be so provincial. Cacao has given them more money than they know what to do with, but you can't buy refinement or class. They all smell of new money. Fortunately, there are many compatriots of mine, but other than them, I can count on one hand the number of people that are worth having a conversation with around here."

"I certainly hope Doña Angélica is one of them."

He smirked, but other than that, his expression was unreadable. He was about to say something else, but instead, he squinted through the window.

"What is she doing here?" Laurent said, almost to himself.

I followed his gaze toward a woman walking by. She wore a

beige skirt that nearly touched the ground and a high-collared white shirt. I couldn't make out her face from afar, but I recognized her unruly waves loosely held in a high bun.

"Do you know her?"

"*Oui*," he said, "it's Aquilino's maid. God knows what her name is."

"Mayra," I said automatically.

He seemed to lose interest. "Something like that. I think she's Julia's cousin."

They were cousins? I had no idea.

He took a last sip of coffee and set the cup down. "Would you like to take a walk by the river, Don Cristóbal?"

I wouldn't mind getting to know Laurent better to see if he had any connection with Franco, but I could do that any other day, whereas I might not get another opportunity to find out what Mayra was doing here and why she was crying the other day—anything that had to do with my father's attorney was of interest to me. As the first person to know of my traveling arrangements, Aquilino was still under suspicion. Perhaps Mayra had seen someone or something relevant at the lawyer's house and could provide valuable information.

"Maybe another day, Laurent. I think I'm going to have another coffee."

"As you wish."

He strolled away with his head raised high and a straight back. I couldn't fathom how a man this young could only live off his hobbies and social events and nothing else. I was a woman, and yet, I missed my daily routine at the chocolate store. I wasn't convinced either that he loved adventure as much as he said. If he did, he would've gotten tired of being idle here for so many years already. What was obvious to me was that he wouldn't give up this comfort so easily. He seemed to be too satisfied with his current living arrangement.

What if he hired Franco, but didn't tell Angélica about it?

It could be a mistake to assume that they were a team.

I stood up and headed for the kitchen. Rosita was standing by the stove, eating a hard-boiled egg. She nearly choked when she saw me.

"Don Cristóbal, do you need anything?"

"No, *cariño*, don't you worry about me. I just wanted a piece of fruit."

I grabbed the first thing I could find, a banana, while searching for Mayra outside the window. She must be talking to Julia.

I stepped out and walked toward the servants' quarters.

Sure enough, Julia and Mayra were immersed in conversation. Mayra covered her eyes with her hands while Julia stood in front of her, arms folded over her chest.

I hid behind the foliage. I couldn't hear a word they were saying, just the way Julia's voice rose once in a while in an accusatory tone. Her finger pointing at Mayra as she scolded her. One of my legs got numb from my unnatural position and I had to gently shake it to get the circulation moving again. Finally, Julia turned around and went back into the house.

This was my chance.

After Julia entered the kitchen through the back door, I approached Mayra, who was leaning against a rock.

She wiped her tears as soon as she saw me and stood up straight. Up close, I could see that her clothes were discolored and shabby as if she'd washed them too many times. Her skirt was wrinkled and the lace of her sleeves and collar looked stained.

"Don Cristóbal!"

"Mayra, are you all right?"

She nodded, her eyes puffy.

"What are you doing here? Shouldn't you be in Guayaquil?"

She renewed her sobbing, hiccups included. I didn't know what the proper course of action would be. Patting her back? Talking in a soothing voice? As a man, I couldn't take the same liberties as I normally would. Touching her would be highly inappropriate. I ended up handing her the banana.

"Here, have something to eat. You look pale."

Surprisingly, she grabbed the fruit. "Thank you. I haven't eaten since yesterday."

She peeled the banana and took a bite. I sat on the rock and invited her to do the same. As she ate, her crying stopped. I removed Cristóbal's handkerchief from my back pocket and handed it to her.

"Do you want to tell me what's wrong? Maybe I can help you."

She took the handkerchief and blew her nose with it.

"I'm sorry," she said. "I shouldn't be here. I'm so stupid."

"What happened, Mayra?" I tried my kindest tone.

"Don Tomás fired me. And it's all my fault." She started crying all over again.

I dared to place my hand on her back. "Calm down, now. I can't understand you when you cry. Can you tell me why he fired you?"

"Because . . ." She covered her eyes with the handkerchief. "Because I'm expecting a child."

I glanced at her stomach. I'd noticed a small bulge, but I thought it was because often times women of lower strata didn't wear corsets. I recalled the loose dress she'd been wearing the day I met her. Perhaps she'd been trying to cover her growing stomach then. Her tearful visit to the *curandera* made sense now.

"I'm going to burn in hell," she said.

"No, you're not. Women have been having babies out of wedlock since the beginning of time."

"Yes, but not with holy men!"

Holy men? She covered her mouth with her hand.

"Mayra, what are you talking about? Who is the father of your child?"

She dropped the banana peel on the ground as if she'd lost all her strength.

"Look, I just want to help you." Hesitantly, I reached out for her arm. "But you have to tell me the whole truth. Who is the father of your child?"

She mumbled a name, but I couldn't understand her or maybe I couldn't believe what she was saying.

"Who?"

"Father Alberto."

My brother? I glanced at her stomach. She was having my brother's son?

My nephew.

"Does he know?"

I knew the answer before she said it. Of course he knew. That was why he'd looked so disjointed yesterday in Vinces.

"Yes."

"How long has this . . . this relationship been going on?"

She lowered her chin. "You won't tell anyone, will you?"

"Of course not."

"It started when I lived in Vinces, over a year ago, before I went to work for Don Tomás."

I was stunned. My brother, The Priest, had been involved in an illicit affair with the lawyer's maid for so long? I couldn't say I was too surprised, though. I'd always thought it was unnatural to ask young men to be celibate for the rest of their lives, but Alberto had seemed so contented with his vocation, so motivated by intellectual pursuits rather than carnal ones. But apparently, I'd misjudged him. Or had he fallen in love with this girl?

"We knew it was wrong." She squeezed Cristóbal's handkerchief. "We thought that once I moved to Guayaquil, we could end it. We didn't see each other for weeks, but one day Alberto showed up at Don Tomás's house. He said he couldn't help it. He missed me too much. After that, he came to see me once a month."

"What does he say about this . . . situation?" I asked.

"He goes back and forth." She sniffed. "He used to say he loved me, he said he would take me away from here, to another town and start a new life where nobody knew us, but that has changed. When I told him that Don Tomás fired me because he discovered I was with child, Alberto said we should go to the *curandera* to see if she could"—she swallowed—"if she could do something about the child."

"And did she?"

"No. He, *we*, changed our minds. He wouldn't even go inside with me, he said it would be a mortal sin."

This also explained why he was wearing his street clothes yesterday.

She covered her face with her hands. "This is all my fault. If only I hadn't been so sick these last few weeks, Don Tomás wouldn't have figured it out."

"He would have, eventually. A pregnancy is not something you can hide forever."

"But I would've had more time to save money."

I could see why my brother had been so tempted by Mayra. She had a frailty about her that must be irresistible to men. Her wet eyelashes curled up stylishly and her lips were full and moist.

"What does Alberto want you to do now?"

"He asked me to give him some time. He promised he would make it right. He says he'll get some money soon. An inheritance, or something like that, and then we can leave, but mister, I don't know if I believe him anymore." Tears gathered in her eyes again. "He's said this before, but the money never comes and I can't wait forever. I have to find a place to live, money to raise my child. This is why I came here, to see if my cousin would help me get a job here. She's the only family I have around these lands. Otherwise, I wouldn't have come nowhere near Alberto's family."

"Does Julia know this is Alberto's child?"

She pressed the handkerchief against her nose. "She promised she wouldn't tell anyone, but I don't know, she was so cross with me. She said I've ruined everything."

Ruined everything?

"What does that mean?"

Mayra shrugged. "Señor, will you talk to Doña Angélica about me working here? Julia is so angry with me I doubt she'll help me."

This was the second person here who had asked me to do something for her on account of me being a man with money. I was surprised—I was a stranger to them with little influences.

"Of course I'll talk to her."

"But Don Cristóbal, promise me you won't tell her I'm having Father Alberto's child. It would ruin him."

If only his reputation depended on me keeping a secret, but it didn't. Sooner or later, the truth would come out and everyone would know what the town's priest had been doing with his free time.

"I promise you I won't tell her, but I don't think you'll be able to keep this a secret for much longer."

I thought about my father and what I'd discovered last night. He'd had an illegitimate daughter with a maid. Now, his son had done the very same thing. Alberto had more in common with Armand Lafont than either one ever knew.

CHAPTER 26

It was so ironic, and unfair, that someone like Alberto—a priest of all people—and this naïve girl, Mayra, were going to have a baby when they hadn't even been trying. Not only that, but they also wanted to get rid of it. Meanwhile, Cristóbal and I had been desperately trying to conceive a child for years through amorous encounters that had turned into an item on a checklist we must complete during specific times and days of fertility. A partnership to achieve a common goal—that was what my marriage had become in the last few years.

Mayra's news had upset me in ways I couldn't have imagined. It had brought back so many memories: the lists of names that Cristóbal and I had come up with for our unborn children, the tight feel of my swelling stomach, the evenings knitting baby blankets, and inevitably, the blood stains in my drawers.

I would take the nausea and tender breasts if it meant that in the end, I would hold my baby in my arms. I dried my eyes. I hadn't been lying to Soledad when I mentioned my melancholy.

"Good morning," Martin said from behind.

I adjusted my glasses and turned to him. Mayra had left a long time ago, but I hadn't found enough energy to get up from the rock where I sat, numbly staring at the banana peel filling up with ants.

It had been a full day since I'd last seen Martin and my annoyance with him had already dissipated. I should be angry after his offer but there was one thought that had appeased me.

If he truly was a murderer, he could've sent someone else to kill me after I arrived at the hacienda, or do it himself. He'd had plenty of opportunities to do so in the last week.

"What are you doing here?" he asked cheerfully.

Would he smile like that if he knew who I was, or if he knew that I was going to decline his business proposition? He was chewing on a cacao bean again. One could easily break a tooth biting on that. What a pity he'd never tried real chocolate.

"Thinking," I said. "Look, there's something I would like to talk to you about. But not here."

I didn't want either one of my sisters to hear our conversation.

"Sure." He scratched his head, looking around. "I have to take care of some business now, but come to my house for lunch."

I nodded. I was dreading my conversation with him, but I couldn't hide forever. I had to give him an answer and see how he reacted. This way, I'd be able to tell the kind of person he was. You could better understand someone's character in moments of anger or crisis. What were his limits? What would he be willing to do to get what he wanted?

A couple of hours later, I arrived at Martin's house. Somehow, I'd tamed Pacha enough to bring me. A woman in her fifties with flushed cheeks and a nasal voice opened the door.

"About time!" Martin called from the parlor. "You almost made it to dinner! But don't just stand there, *hombre*! Come on in. Have an aperitif."

As I entered the house, I took in the aroma of something being fried in the kitchen. I glanced at the skylight ceiling, unable to resist its mesmerizing effect.

The maid excused herself and hurried back to the kitchen, where just the other day, Martin had cooked the line-caught bass for me.

"I didn't know you had a maid," I said.

"She only comes in the mornings, on weekdays. She has six children in Vinces." He opened a bottle of *aguardiente* and served two shots. "Lunch will be ready in a few minutes. You'll have to excuse Bachita, she's running late."

"I understand. This looks like a big house for just one person to do all the work."

He laughed. "I'm sorry, my friend, but here in Ecuador we're not used to palaces and rows of servants like in your country."

I smiled. "I'm sorry to disappoint you, but not everybody in Spain has rows of servants or palaces. My wife and I lived in an apartment that was half the size of your house."

As soon as I sat down, Martin handed me the drink. One could get used to this pleasurable existence of drinking and eating in excess. How different men were. On my wedding day, I'd been cautious not to eat too much, lest my stomach might swell or I might stain my dress. Mamá always said that men didn't like gluttonous women, though I doubt Cristóbal cared or even paid attention to what I ate. As a woman, there had been so many rules to follow.

"Anyway," I said, holding on to my glass. "This morning I ran into Dr. Aquilino's maid, Mayra. I don't know if you've met her? Well, the poor girl is devastated because she lost her job and is looking for a new one."

"So you thought I ought to hire her."

"Yes." I crossed my leg, mimicking Martin's confident gesture. "You could all benefit: Mayra would have a job and a place to live, Bachita would serve your lunch on time, and you would have a cleaner house."

He studied me for a moment. "Sounds like a grand plan. But tell me, if she's so wonderful why did Aquilino fire her?"

I finished my drink. How much should I tell him? He was bound to find out she was expecting, but he didn't need to know all the details.

"She's expecting a baby."

He unfolded his leg. "Absolutely not."

"Oh, come on. You can't be so prudish. Not after what I've seen you do! These things happen."

"It's not a matter of principle. Pregnant women are complicated. What am I supposed to do with a child running around the house?"

"Nothing. The child will have a mother to look after him."

"I don't know."

"Are you going to let that poor girl wander aimlessly without a home? You know what happens to women when they fall in disgrace."

"But why don't you talk to Angélica? She has a lot more money than I do."

"Because she already has two maids and besides, Mayra is Julia's cousin and Julia is vexed with her."

"All right, all right, this is already too much information."

I bit my lower lip. I'd said too much. Cristóbal didn't care for this much detail pertaining to our staff, either. I recalled all the times I'd talked about La Cordobesa and how the entire town had treated her like a pariah. My husband had the same bored expression Martin now had.

"Was that all you wanted to talk to me about?"

I hesitated. To say or not to say.

"You know, you ought to try chocolate and stop chewing on those beans. If you want, I'll make some for you after lunch."

The kitchen filled with the fine aroma of toasted cacao beans. I couldn't believe I had so much Nacional bean at my disposal. They were considered the finest of the beans and as such, they were expensive. I was used to working with Forastero beans, their African counterpart, which were sometimes easier to find in Sevilla. To think that I practically owned a plantation bursting with this so-called golden seed.

Bachita and Martin stared at me wide-mouthed as I ground the beans I had just roasted and peeled in a mortar, transforming them into a creamy brown paste. I wished they had a mill—it would've made the process much faster.

"Hand me some milk," I told Bachita, "and sugar and cinnamon, please."

At first, Bachita and Martin had both been astonished that I, a man, would get into the kitchen and prepare something so complex, but I informed them that the first chocolate houses in Europe were opened and run by men. Besides, Martin himself had prepared bass for me the other day.

Their curiosity about the process and what would come out of it was enough to distract them from their own cultural norms and preconceived roles.

Or so I hoped.

In an odd way, Bachita reminded me of my assistant at the *chocolatería*. The way she lingered by me, attentive and obedient. It was strange that she would remind me of La Cordobesa because they didn't look anything like each other. La Cordobesa was lean and had an angular face, like a wire hanger, whereas Bachita was hefty and her nose had the texture of a ginger root. Martin stood there, watching with the same bewildered expression of a child discovering that hens laid eggs.

And *I* was the one introducing him to this delicacy. There were only a few things I was confident about in my life and making chocolate was one of them. The process never failed me. Since my grandmother first taught me her recipe, I'd felt the same anticipation. The transformation from bean to paste was something I never grew tired of seeing. It was magical.

"And now, the secret ingredient," I said. "Sea salt."

Both of them looked at me as if I should be sent to the nearest asylum.

"Just trust me," I said.

"You have to add a pinch of salt to the chocolate," my grandmother would say, "to moderate the kick."

I initially didn't believe her. I was, after all, trying to make a dessert. But after hesitantly following her instructions, I realized how salt had the strange ability of enhancing the flavor and made the dark chocolate and cocoa a little less bitter.

"Look at that," Martin said.

I loved the admiration in his voice. Right now, I wasn't the lesser man who didn't know how to ride horses or how to act around women. I was the one person in this entire region who could teach him what he'd been working so hard for every year collecting those cacao beans. I was showing him the real value of his beloved *Pepa de Oro*.

After I attained a rich, creamy texture, I dipped a spoon inside and handed it to Martin.

"*¡Dios mío!*" he said, sitting down. "This is much better than the beans."

I scoffed.

He tasted the mix with his eyes closed. He was falling under the spell of this addicting substance, just like everyone else who ate it did. It was with reason that people called it the Elixir of the Gods.

Licking her fingers, Bachita asked me if she could take some chocolate to her children. I handed her a tin box myself.

"You can use chocolate in many ways," I explained to both. "You can drink it or eat it. You can make cakes, pastries, or truffles with it. The list is endless."

Bachita tried to kiss my hand in gratitude, as if I were a priest, but I removed it.

"There's no need for that," I said.

"Thank you so much, señor," she said. "It's been a real pleasure. I must go home now. I'm anxious to have my family taste some of this."

"You're welcome, Bachita."

We stared after her as she headed out, hugging the tin box of chocolate against her chest.

"I can't believe we've had this here all along and didn't know it," Martin said, smearing a piece of banana in the brown mix. "People must pay a lot of money for chocolate in Europe."

"Where do you think Don Armand's fortune came from?"

"All those conceited friends of Angélica's would spend their lifelong savings on this."

"That was exactly what I was thinking yesterday at the café."

He was quiet for a moment. If his mind was racing anything like mine was, then I'd found the one person in the world who understood me, the one person who was just as possessed by chocolate as I was.

Shamelessly. Unapologetically.

Cristóbal had never been that person. Every time I talked about my plans for the chocolate shop or the most recent recipes I'd come up with, he'd get a glassy look in his eyes, as though he'd rather get shot than endure another second of my conversation.

"Have you given any thought to my proposal?" Martin said.

I was deflated by the question. I wanted to explore the idea of producing chocolate here, not sell my land. We could be pioneers.

"Yes." I sat on a stool across from his. "But I'm afraid you're not going to be happy with my answer."

"You don't want to sell."

I shook my head. "I've been thinking about it and the truth is I like it here. I see some possibilities I hadn't seen before."

"What about your book? You can't run a plantation and write a novel at the same time."

He sat back, folded his arms across his chest, and stared at me without blinking.

"Well . . ." I hesitated. "I suppose the novel can wait."

"You know what I think?" His eyes never left my face. "I don't think you ever intended to sell the property *or* write any novel."

The atmosphere in the room shifted. Gone was the camaraderie, the friendly banter. Martin pushed his plate.

"Why don't you just tell me who you really are and why you're dressed like a man?"

CHAPTER 27

If there were a prize for stupidity, I would've won it. Here I thought I'd been fooling everyone around me, but the only fool was me.

"Should I call you María Purificación or do you go by Puri, like the plantation?" Martin said.

I swallowed.

"Puri."

I removed Cristóbal's spectacles and massaged the bridge of my nose. "Did you know all along?"

"I suspected it from the first day when you climbed on Pacha. Women's hips are noticeable on horseback."

Of course, what a dunce I'd been.

"But I confirmed it last night when I heard you singing and swimming in the creek."

Singing? I covered my mouth. I hadn't realized I was singing.

"Did you . . . *see* me, too?" I said in my normal tone of voice.

"Yes. I saw you." He barely moved a muscle.

I averted my gaze. He'd seen me *naked*, which was even worse than hearing my atrocious singing. My cheeks burned.

"You could've at least spared me the shame of making a fool of myself today," I said.

"I guess I could have said something, but I wasn't sure I'd been fully awake last night. I may have had a little too much *puro*."

All along he'd suspected me. I wondered if others in the family had, too. I wanted to scream.

"So that trip to the bar, the prostitutes? Were you testing me?"

"Not exactly. Like I said, I wasn't sure what to think of you. You were convincing otherwise."

Well, at least that. I would've hated for everyone to be laughing behind my back. In a way, I was relieved Martin had found out. That meant no more trips to bars and brothels and faking that I was a "real man," though I couldn't deny the outings with Martin were more entertaining than I would've expected.

"Did you tell anyone your suspicions?"

"No." He leaned over the kitchen counter, arms folded in front of his chest. "You want to tell me what happened? Why are you pretending to be your husband?"

I wasn't sure I wanted to trust him, but I didn't have a lot of options. He'd already discovered me. The best I could do was tell him the truth in the hopes that he wasn't implicated in Cristóbal's death and that instead, he could shed some light on my family and who might have done this.

I started from the beginning: the day I received the letter from the lawyer, back in Sevilla. I'd had another miscarriage a couple of months prior and was eager to leave all the heartbreak behind. The irony was that I really wasn't as unhappy then as I believed.

True heartbreak still awaited.

Was I making the biggest mistake of my life by confessing to Martin? Perhaps the time had come to confront my sisters and my brother, no saint himself. Was that why he'd been so preoccupied with thoughts about goodness being innate or learned?

Martin nodded, pouring me another shot to loosen my tongue. As I needed all the courage I could, I drank. And talked.

"I know your sisters weren't happy with the will," he said as I neared the end of my story. "But from there to wanting to kill you seems somewhat farfetched."

"Then how do you explain the assassin on the ship?"

"A mistake?"

"What about the check and the note with my name I found among his things?"

"I know Angélica has many defects: she's vain, arrogant, and ambitious, but she's not a murderer. And Catalina, well, she's a saint."

"She's not a saint. She's a human being with flaws like everybody else. But if you think so highly of Angélica then what did you mean when you told the neighbor—Fernando del Río, right?—that he should know better than anyone who Angélica was?"

"That has nothing to do with her moral character. A few years ago, before Angélica married Laurent, Del Río asked for her hand in marriage. Don Armand considered it for a while as a partnership between the two men and joining both haciendas would've meant owning the largest plantation in the region, but Angélica declined. Del Río could never forgive Angélica for rejecting him. After that, the Frenchman came along and she married him instead. Del Río and"—he hesitated—"your father had a strained relationship ever since."

"I heard something about the creek."

"Yes, the damned creek."

"And now Angélica is suing him."

He nodded. Under different circumstances, I would admire my sister's audacity to behave as she wanted in spite of what our father, or anybody else, desired. But not when it could also mean that she would hurt her own sister to get her way.

"If Angélica is as harmless as you say, then how do you explain that I found a snake in my room—the same kind she keeps as a pet?"

Martin's face paled. "It could be a coincidence. There are a lot of snakes in this area."

"I don't believe in coincidences."

Martin paced the kitchen, absorbed in thought, hopefully trying to make connections that would shed some light into my predicament.

"I just can't imagine any of Don Armand's children doing something like that. There has to be another answer."

I stared at my empty glass. "What about my father's *other* daughter?"

"Another daughter?"

"Elisa," I said. "Apparently, she used to live here but Doña Gloria sent her away when she found out she was her husband's child with one of the maids."

"I've never heard of her. Elisa, you say?"

"Yes." This time, I added *aguardiente* to my own glass. "What if she's in town? What if she's the woman Soledad Duarte mentioned?"

"I haven't seen anybody new in town. And I spend a lot of time there."

"Then who is the woman who hired Franco to kill me?"

Martin didn't have an answer.

I was about to mention what I'd discovered about Alberto, too, but didn't. I'd promised Mayra I wouldn't say who the father of her baby was and there was no reason to betray her.

"I'd better go," I said. "Are you going to tell my sisters who I really am?"

"No, but they're bound to find out sooner or later."

"I know that, but I need a little more time. I believe that if I come out as Puri, my life would be in danger. The person who sent Franco aboard the *Andes* may still be here, and perhaps closer than we think."

I didn't know how to read his silence. It lingered on me all the way to my father's house. What was Martin going to do with all the information I'd given him? Moreover, why had he given me that inscrutable look?

CHAPTER 28

Angélica

Vinces, 1913

"I aurent needs one last push," my mother said, mashing green plantains for *tigrillo*. "The way to a man's heart is through his stomach."

Once again, my mother and I were talking about my ongoing problem with Laurent: the fact that he hadn't proposed. I knew it bothered my father, too—he questioned me every time the Frenchman visited.

"You haven't proven to him yet that you would be a good wife," she said.

Her comment irked me, though I didn't know exactly why. Then again, almost everything my mother said had that effect on me. I sighed in resignation.

Grabbing a basket, I set out for the orchard in search of ingredients for *dulce de guayaba*, the only dessert I was good at.

Guayabas were a lot like large lemons, but harder and sweeter. When you split them, the food inside was red and full of seeds. I found a tree bursting with them—I used to come here a lot during my childhood—and filled my basket.

"A miracle, ladies and gentlemen!" a voice startled me. "The elusive lady is outside her palace without her eternal companion."

I turned around to find Juan standing there.

I hated his sarcasm. I turned my back on him and continued

picking guavas. I hadn't seen much of him after the party, though I heard through Catalina that our father had given him a job on the plantation. Papá's reasons for hiring him were a mystery to me. I'd never understood his interest in our poor neighbor.

"What do you want?" I said.

He scoffed.

I turned around, a *guayaba* between my fingers. "What?"

He had a contemptuous smirk on his face. "You've become so vain. I don't know whether to laugh or to cry."

"No, I haven't. I'm the same person."

He shook his head. "You used to be so sweet."

Though I would never admit to it, I knew he was right. I'd become so impatient with my sister that when we practiced our music I yelled at her over the most trivial mistakes. Not to mention my mother—she got on my nerves with her mere presence. At my worst, I excused Papá for cheating on her with that mysterious maid and having a child out of wedlock. But then, almost immediately, I would ask the Lord for forgiveness and say a quick prayer.

"Well, you've changed, too," I said. "You're so mean now. You rarely smile, and I really don't appreciate that sarcastic tone you used with me earlier." Once I started talking, I couldn't stop. "You never wrote me. You never came to visit. You were gone much longer than you ever said you would be. And then, one day, you show up here expecting everything to be the same. You want me to be the same idiot who followed you around everywhere you went."

"I liked that idiot."

He caught me off guard. I fought a smile.

"Well"—my tone softened a bit—"that idiot no longer exists."

He took a step toward me. I tried to take a step back, but there was a tree behind me. *Please, don't touch me.*

He removed a strand from my face and placed it behind my ear. I shivered.

"Are you sure she's not somewhere inside there?" he said.

What was it about Juan that always made my knees weaken? I'd already rationalized this. He had no future—other than living off a salary. He was unsophisticated. Next to Laurent, he looked like a Neanderthal. The idea of Juan at one of Silvia's famous gatherings was unthinkable. I'd die of shame before bringing him over. And to top it all off, his family was nonexistent, the only family member we'd ever known was his father, and he'd been an eccentric at best.

And yet, there was something about Juan that I found irresistible. Particularly when he looked at me with the intensity he did at this moment, as if I were the only person who could hold his interest.

He didn't remove his hand. He continued to caress my hair.

"I've always loved your hair. You're the only blonde I've ever known," he said this last part, almost to himself.

I wondered, the same way I'd done so many times during his years of absence, if he'd met other girls, if he'd loved someone else. The thought of Juan kissing another girl infuriated me.

"So tell me, my dear *Angelique*," he said, mocking my father's accent. "Are you going to marry that French parasite?"

Parasite? The insult took me away, for a few seconds, from the trance his fingers were putting me in as he rubbed the nape of my neck.

"You don't even know him," I said weakly.

"I don't need to. I know the type."

He was standing close to me now, and I could smell him—a mixture of man with the woodsy cologne he used since he turned thirteen. The smell brought back so many memories.

I leaned my back against the tree trunk, grasping the basket handle as if my life depended on it. He must have noticed this because he glanced down for an instant and his lips curved into a tiny smile.

"You haven't answered my question."

My mouth went dry. "I may."

"Well, if you must marry him," he said nonchalantly, "then we must say goodbye forever."

He drew back. I didn't know what came over me, but I grabbed him by the shirt and pulled him toward me.

Smirking, he looked down at me. My chest was heaving though I didn't know why or what had changed, only that I didn't want him to leave. The smile disappeared from his face.

"Give me one last kiss before you belong to someone else," he said staring at my mouth.

It was as if he'd hypnotized me. He must have because I couldn't remember what my grievances with him were anymore, or what I was doing here in the first place.

Juan removed the basket from my hand and he must have dropped it next to us—I couldn't tell. I couldn't stop looking at his eyes as he lowered his face and kissed me.

My God, how could I have forgotten what it felt like to be in Juan's arms? It made me realize that when other boys had kissed me in the past, it had felt as if I'd been kissing my own hand. There hadn't been this tingling all over my body, this heat growing inside my core, this lightheadedness, this desire to be closer to him. I'd thought it was because he'd been the first man to ever kiss me, but now I knew it wasn't that. There was something carnal, almost primitive between us that I would never be able to stop. No matter how much he embarrassed me in front of my friends. No matter how many husbands I might have. I could never stay away from him.

He pulled back abruptly, unexpectedly, and to my chagrin, he took a step back.

There was a triumphant smile on his face.

"See? You haven't forgotten me."

Wait, was this a game to him? If I hadn't wanted to continue kissing him, I would've collected my pride and left, but I was still weakened by the effect his mouth had on mine.

"Wait, Juan, don't leave."

"I don't go by Juan anymore," he said. "There were too many *Juanes* at my school in Colombia. I go by my middle name now, Martin."

CHAPTER 29

Puri

April 1920

When I arrived in my father's house, my sisters were in the sewing room, the door slightly opened.

"You will never guess who I saw at church this morning," Catalina was telling Angélica.

I stood by the window. Angélica wore a navy-blue sequin dress with a gorgeous drape that reached the floor. Catalina crouched beside her, pinning the hemline of her dress. She held a couple more pins between her lips.

"Go higher," Angélica told her.

"I already agreed to the short sleeves, Angélica. Don't push your luck."

"You're not my mother! Besides, you owe me obedience. I'm your older sister."

No, dear Angélica, I am.

"Well, are you going to guess who I saw or not?"

"I don't know. One of Mamá's friends? Let's see, who's still alive?"

"No. None of Mamá's friends," Catalina said. "I saw Silvia."

Angélica's body stiffened, making her look even taller. Her cheeks turned red. But Catalina was oblivious to her sister's reaction as her gaze was fixed on the hem.

"She's a widow now and apparently she just got back," she said.

Angélica didn't answer.

"Like this?" Catalina showed off her work.

Angélica nodded absently.

"I never understood what happened between you two." Catalina stood up straight, resting her hand on her lower back. "You used to be such good friends. And then one day, she stopped coming, she got married and left. Just like that." She snapped her fingers. "Without even saying goodbye."

"Can I take this off now?" Angélica reached for the button at the nape of her neck.

"Wait, wait." Catalina stood behind her and undid the zipper.

Who was this Silvia person? But more importantly, why had Angélica reacted so awkwardly upon hearing that this woman was back in town? Could she be the same elusive woman I was looking for?

Catalina raised her head and spotted me through the window. "Don Cristóbal! I didn't know you were there."

Angélica rushed behind an Art Nouveau folding screen.

"I apologize." I stood by the threshold. "I was just admiring your talent. You have a great eye for design and construction." I couldn't help but think of my mother. She was the one who'd taught me the basics of sewing. She'd also been an excellent knitter.

"Catalina is a superb seamstress," Angélica said behind the screen.

Angélica reappeared in the room, wrapping a black silk robe around her slim frame. "I'm so lucky to have my own seamstress here at home." She smiled at her sister. "Catalina sews all my clothes."

"You're a box of surprises, Doña Catalina," I said.

She smiled at me shyly. There was some yelling coming from the kitchen.

"I need to speak to him!" a woman said.

"I told you he's not here!" Julia said.

I immediately recognized the voice.

"Don Cristóbal, I need to speak to you," Soledad Duarte said as soon as she saw me. Had she figured out my sinister connection to her son?

My sisters turned to me with curiosity.

"I'm desperate!" the *curandera* said. "I don't know what to do."

I held her arm. "Doña Soledad, let's go to the parlor."

"I apologize for this intrusion, Don Cristóbal, I tried to stop her," Julia said.

"It's fine." I was already pulling the woman into the living room.

"Wait!" Angélica said. "What is this all about? You can't barge into our house like this, Soledad. I demand to know what's happening."

"It's my son, Doña Angélica. Franco is still missing and it's been a month already."

I glanced at Catalina, whose cheeks turned slightly pink, but she didn't utter a word.

"Franco? What does he have to do with this gentleman?" Angélica said. She seemed so oblivious to Franco's connection to me that for the first time I questioned if she had anything to do with Cristóbal's murder.

Either that, or she was an excellent actress.

"This gentleman promised to help me find him."

I scratched my forehead. I'd forgotten all about Soledad's request. Not that I was seriously considering contacting the police about a missing man. If anything, I would accuse him of killing my husband.

"I said I would help her, but I'm no detective," I told my sisters. "I offered to talk to the police since Doña Soledad said they won't listen to her."

"I just didn't know who else to turn to"—Soledad looked at Angélica—"since you didn't want to help."

Angélica didn't want to help?

"It's not that I didn't want to help, Soledad, don't be stupid. But I told you, Franco is a grown man. I don't see what is so strange about a man leaving this place to find new opportunities. I'm sure he'll be back."

"He didn't *move away*, Doña Angélica. He left all his things, and besides, he said he would be back right away."

"Soledad, don't be so innocent, men are like that. They don't need a lot of things to start over somewhere else. I'm sure he found something or someone interesting wherever he went that is keeping him away."

I had a strange reaction to Angélica's words. I used to make the same assumptions about men. In a lot of ways, I still did. But the more I impersonated Cristóbal, the more it affected my psyche. I almost took offense at Angélica's comment; the way she trivialized men and bundled them all together as if they were one entity. Living as a man was having strange effects on me. For one, it was forcing me to see them as individuals. Cristóbal and Martin, for example, were different in so many ways I could no longer subscribe to the "all men are the same" mentality.

Catalina removed the measuring tape from her neck, her eyes on the floor, and she turned toward the sewing room. I wanted to follow her in, but what would I say? I spoke before she entered the room.

"You're right, Doña Soledad. I made you a promise that I didn't fulfill. Let's go right now to the police station and report Franco's disappearance."

"You don't have to do such a thing, Don Cristóbal," Angélica said. "I can't believe you've been bothering our guest with your problems, Soledad. I'll take you myself." She turned to the maid. "Julia, have her wait for me in the kitchen while I change." With her hands in her pockets, Angélica headed for the stairs while Julia escorted Soledad to the kitchen.

This was my opportunity to talk to Catalina about Franco. I went into the sewing room.

"Are you all right, Doña Catalina?"

She was now sitting behind her sewing machine.

"You look pale," I said.

"I'm fine." She rested her hands on the fabric she was about to sew. "That just took me by surprise, that's all."

"Why? Did you know Soledad's son?"

She averted her gaze. "Of course, his father worked here for years. They lived by the creek."

"Was he . . ." I dragged a chair in front of her and sat down. "Is he a friend of yours?"

"He used to be."

"And what happened?" I was having palpitations, sweaty hands. Was Catalina the woman Franco had been in love with? The woman who'd asked him that perverse favor?

"I don't want to talk about it."

"I think I know what this is about," I said, taking a gamble.

Her eyes widened.

"He was an admirer of yours, wasn't he? I wouldn't be surprised."

"What do you mean?"

"Well, you are a beautiful woman. I'm sure a lot of men would like to be with you."

"You think"—she blushed again—"you think I'm beautiful?"

"Of course. I can't believe you would even doubt it."

She smiled coyly. "I will admit that Franco and I were close, but that was years ago, that was before, before . . ." She squeezed Angélica's dress.

"The fire?"

"Even before that."

I reached out for her hand. "Sometimes it's better to talk about those things that upset us or give us grief. You may find that it relieves your soul."

The moment her tears started trailing down her face, I knew she was ready to talk.

CHAPTER 30

Catalina

Vinces, 1919

The paper trembled in my hands. Franco's handwriting, still childlike, was unmistakable to me—his *M*s looked more like crashed spider legs than letters—but I'd given up on his penmanship years ago.

"*Meet me at the creek*," the note said, "*I have something for you.*"

Franco had been acting strange lately. For years, I'd cherished his companionship. There were not a lot of people our age in this area and those who lived nearby ignored us. We were the outcasts, the eccentric ones. My sister had already gotten married to Laurent and only talked to me during our rehearsals. Juan, or Martin as he liked to be called now, was always busy with my father, and after the Virgin pilgrimage, I never saw Elisa again.

The only friend I had was Franco. And yet, I couldn't quite pinpoint what had changed in the last few weeks, but he seemed different now. He would constantly fidget with stones or wood sticks and would often start to say something only to stop midsentence.

He now worked collecting cacao pods with his father but—it pained me to admit it—he was lazy and often hid from his father to meet with me. This lack of drive was frustrating because I knew firsthand how bright he was. When I'd taught him numbers as a child, he'd learned all four operations in a matter of days and would often figure out an answer faster than I would.

Why was he wasting his life here? I'd asked him, but he said he had a good reason, though he wouldn't say what.

In all truth, we didn't talk much. Mostly, we went for walks and sometimes I read to him while he fished.

This afternoon, he stood by the creek, throwing stones in the water. In his back pocket, as usual, was a slingshot for catching lizards. Even though we were in our early twenties now, he still carried it around. From the puny boy I'd befriended ten years ago, he'd turned into a stocky man with large, callused hands. But in some ways, Franco never grew up.

I came up behind him and whispered a hello.

When he turned to me, there was a glint in his eye that sometimes made me nervous.

He wasn't attractive, nothing like my brother-in-law Laurent, or even Martin, but he had the most expressive and melancholic eyes I'd ever seen.

"I have a surprise for you," he said.

"A surprise? Why? It's not my birthday."

"I know, but I didn't want to wait any longer." He pointed in the direction of his house with his chin. "Don't worry, my mother went to town for rice and flour."

Years ago, when I'd started schooling him, I'd gone to his house when his parents were away. But as we grew older, it seemed improper. That was why we always met here.

"I left my cigarettes there," he said with a wink.

I'd run out of cigarettes days ago. They were so hard to come by. My vice depended on Franco one hundred percent. Even though my mother had passed away two years ago from diabetes, I still hid my habit from everyone in the family. I couldn't explain why. My father paid me so little attention he would've never noticed if I smoked. But years ago, I'd decided that I would live up to the high standards of my reputation. It wasn't always easy, like today when I nodded and followed him to the house. Such was my urge to smoke.

Franco and I had an implicit rule: we never touched. I suspected it had to do with the fact that he considered me sacred, like the rest of the town. I often wished I'd never come up with that lie—I would probably be married by now if I hadn't. Whatever the reason, there was always a tension between us that I didn't know how to break through.

His house was exactly how I remembered it: the same floral wallpaper, the flight of stairs curling up behind the sofa, even the smell of fresh-baked bread. Besides being the town's *curandera*, Doña Soledad was a baker.

From a wooden box, Franco removed a couple of cigarettes and lit them, hands shaking.

I took in a lungful of smoke.

The sun following a long winter.

We stood close to each other, enjoying our cigarettes, and then he broke the silence with his hoarse voice.

"Come."

He held my hand, surprising me. I followed him up the stairs, as inappropriate as it was, but I was curious about his surprise.

On his bed was a small package wrapped in brown paper and tied with a blue ribbon. He handed it to me.

I undid the bow and ripped the paper to pieces. I'd always been impatient when opening presents, even though it was unladylike and disrespectful to the giver, according to my mother.

I gasped.

In my hand was a miniature violin so carefully carved and varnished that it looked like my own violin had been shrunk so Pulgarcita could play it.

"Franco, this is beautiful! Did you make it?"

He smiled. He so seldom did.

"I've been working on it for weeks."

"But you hate classical music."

"But I love anything you do."

He'd never said the word "love" before. Especially close to the word "you."

"This is the nicest thing someone has ever done for me."

"Well, you're the only person who's ever been nice to me." He cleared his throat. "It's the least I can do. After all you've done for me."

Why did this seem like a goodbye of sorts? Was he leaving?

Franco extended his hand and touched my cheek. I could smell the cacao beans on his skin. That scent which invaded everything.

"So soft," he said. "I'd been wanting to touch you for years."

I flinched. I liked the safety of our platonic relationship, but I sensed our unspoken understanding no longer applied to him. He took a step forward and brought his other hand to my face. He smelled of smoke and sweat. We never stood so close.

Please don't kiss me.

Though I'd been curious for years to know what a kiss of love felt like, I'd never imagined Franco to be the one to deliver it. It felt as wrong as if my brother Alberto were trying to kiss me.

I panicked. I didn't know where to go or what to do. If I pushed him away, I might lose my only friend, and I didn't want that.

His lips were wet and salty, too hard. Our mouths didn't belong together, like a lid trying to cover the wrong jar. His fingers squeezed my cheeks, his growing beard scratched my chin, and I stared horrified how he closed his eyes, immersed in this kiss that only produced in me a desire to run away.

What was wrong with me? I'd been wanting for years to have the affection of a man, but this was a mistake.

I didn't love Franco. I pitied him because he had nothing and knew very little. His parents never paid him any attention. Nobody did. He'd been my project, my lost cause, but I couldn't imagine a life married to him. Having his children. Living under the same roof. Goodness, when was this kiss going to end? I didn't want to be the one to end it, but I didn't want it to continue any longer. This was all I could take.

He was breathing hard now, pushing his body against mine. I had to stop him. Angélica told me years ago the consequences of being intimate with a man. I didn't even want to think about Franco, naked, on top of me.

I didn't know where the miniature violin went, I must have dropped it because my hands were suddenly empty when I pushed them against his hard chest.

"Franco, please."

But he ignored my plea and found my mouth again. "Catalina, *mi Catalina*, I've loved you for so long."

What had I done? I'd given him the wrong idea for years.

This had to be a punishment from the Virgin for all my lies. I was losing my only friend. I could see it happening already because I was not going to let this go on for much longer. My sister Angélica used to say I was a romantic; someone who didn't see reality. I now understood what she meant. How stupid I'd been to think that Franco's feelings for me were just as innocent as mine.

"We should stop," I said weakly.

He seemed to be in some sort of trance. He pushed me toward the bed.

"I love you so much," he was saying against my mouth.

"Franco, listen . . ."

As these rational thoughts muddled in my mind—how wrong this was, how I didn't love Franco as a man, how our friendship would be ruined—something unexpected was happening to me.

My body had turned into a noodle, a slave to someone else's will. Whereas seconds ago, I'd been somewhat repulsed by Franco's intimacy, I now craved his proximity. Oh, God, I was being taken over by carnal desire.

My mother's face came to mind. Frowning.

The Virgin's sculpture in the Saints Room.

And Satan laughing.

I shook my head and pushed Franco.

"What's wrong?" he said, his chest heaving. "I thought you were enjoying this."

I sat up. "I'm sorry, Franco, this is wrong. I should have never let you kiss me."

"But don't you love me?" he said, his eyes looking sadder than ever.

Don't give me that look. Please. For once I let my brain govern my heart.

"I do. But not like you'd like me to," I said as softly as I could. "You're like a brother to me."

He was about to say something but didn't. He sat up, his face stone cold. I reached out for his arm.

"I'm sorry," I said.

He recoiled. "Don't touch me."

Oh, no. It was already happening. I'd lost my friend. He would never forgive me.

"Franco, you deserve someone who loves you the same way you do."

"Stop lying! I know exactly what this is about." He hit the mattress with his fist. "You're ashamed of me because I'm not rich like your father, or elegant like your sister's husband, or one of those fancy Europeans who roam around with their chins up, their fancy clothes and champagne glasses."

My eyes were burning and a smell of smoke was becoming stronger as he spoke.

"I'm nothing but a low-class *montubio*," he said, standing.

"Do you smell that?" I said.

Franco tucked his shirt back inside his trousers with hasty motions.

"Franco, what did you do with your cigarette?" I looked around for mine, but I'd left it downstairs, hadn't I?

He paced the room. "I can't believe I've been so stupid all these years. Dreaming about you. Believing that one day you'd be mine. To think that I would've done *anything* for you! *Soy un imbécil.*"

What had I done with my cigarette? There had been an ashtray downstairs, on top of the end table, but I couldn't remember putting it there. And what about Franco? When we came upstairs, he didn't have his cigarette, either.

I jumped out of bed and opened the bedroom door. Flames and smoke emerged from the first story and fanned up to the ceiling. I screamed.

On impulse, I shut the door. The blue smoke filtered into the room through the gap between the door and the floor. Holy Mother, the entire house was made out of wood!

"The window!" Franco said. "Quick!"

He undid the window latch and attempted to lift it, but it was stuck. Franco banged on the glass, then tried to lift it again until it slowly gave in. The glass trembled on its way up.

We heard coughing nearby. Someone else was in the house!

Franco looked at the door.

"My father!"

He turned back to me. "You're going to have to jump," he told me. "I'll get my father."

I glanced out the window. There was not a tree or anything to hold on to, and it looked so high. I couldn't jump. I would break all my bones.

As he turned, I clenched his hand, digging my fingernails into his skin. "No, don't leave me, please." I was being selfish, but couldn't help it. "I can't jump. It's too high."

"You can do it. It's not as high as you think. I've done it before."

He was lying to give me courage, I could tell.

"I'll help you." His anger had faded in the face of our impending mortality. I, myself, had forgotten all the discomfort I usually felt at his proximity.

"Come on." He extended his hand out to me. The flames were eating up the bedroom door and an unbearable heat filtered into the room.

I climbed on the window frame, clinging to his hand. He was trying to let go, but I wouldn't let him. "Just jump, Catalina," he said. Something had happened to his voice. I sensed impatience, fear. His gaze kept going toward the door. There it was, the coughing. His father.

I let go of his hand and shut my eyes. The next thing I knew, there was excruciating pain throughout my legs. The ground was hard, dry, and tiny rocks dug into my palms and knees. Too weak to get up, I looked up at the window, but Franco was gone. He'd gone back inside to save his father.

CHAPTER 31

Puri

Last night I had a nightmare. Cristóbal was lying at the bottom of the ocean with his eyes wide open and his skin bloated and purple. When his hand reached out to me, I woke up panting and covered in sweat. I'd been trying not to think about him ever since I started spending time with Martin. Such was my guilt. Was Cristóbal denouncing my betrayal? Blaming me for his misfortune?

I had to make it up to him. I had to find his killer.

But things were so muddled. I thought about Catalina. She was tormented by what had happened to Franco. She blamed herself for his burns, for his suffering, for rejecting his love. She said that after the fire, he was never the same, but she didn't want to tell me *how* he'd changed and I couldn't see the connection between the incident on the ship and her. Not after knowing that the relationship between Franco and Catalina had cooled after the fire.

I'd often asked myself what I would do once I found out who had tried to kill me. I didn't think I could retaliate in a similar fashion. I didn't see myself killing either one of my sisters or my brother. It was not in my nature. I would probably just collect all the evidence and take it to the authorities. Let them deal with it. I'd thought about paying the police a visit anyway—not for the purposes Soledad was expecting—but to warn them of what had happened aboard the *Andes*. What stopped me was the possibility that they would take the investigation from my hands and ruin everything I'd been working toward. They would probably try to appease me, like Captain Blake had done, and then tell me the investigation had to be conducted under British jurisdiction. But if I presented proof, or better yet, a confession, things would be different. They couldn't ignore me.

After breakfast, I went to Vinces with Laurent with the excuse that I needed to go to church and confess. I didn't want to confess, certainly not to my brother. What I wanted was to *get* a confession from him.

Alberto smiled at me from across the nave. Gone were the pale face and the confused expression I'd seen the other day.

"What a pleasure to have you here, Don Cristóbal, but you're a little late for mass."

"That's all right. I would like to have a word with you, if you may. It'll only take a couple of minutes."

"A confession?"

"You could say that."

Nodding, he led the way to a sacristy saturated with incense. There was an enormous cross behind a desk, where vessels, candles, and other religious items sat. There was also a bench-like couch with burgundy cushions, where the two of us sat, and an open armoire where I could spot cassocks and white, purple, and green robes.

"How can I help you?" He'd acquired that solemn tone that priests often take during sermons. He hadn't seemed so grave when he sat across the table in the bar last week.

I didn't know how to start.

"Did you always want to be a priest, Alberto?"

He was taken aback, probably by my lack of reverence, but recovered quickly.

"No," he said slowly. "I wanted to be an architect."

I remained quiet, expectant.

"In my youth, I went through a period where I doubted the very existence of our Lord." He set his gaze on his cassock, almost apologetically. "Oddly, my love for architecture is what brought me to Him. You see, my father had a book of European churches. It was a beautiful book, filled with pencil illustrations of Notre Dame, the Cattedrale di Santa Maria del Fiore, St. Peter's Basilica, Santiago de Compostela. This book was forbidden to me since it was one of the few precious things my father had brought from France and he said I would ruin it with my dirty hands. But every time I saw him climb onto his horse, I would sneak into his study and look at the pictures for hours. As I grew older and was able to read the text, I learned that throughout the centuries, theology has always been at the core of the aesthetics and construction of these Christian churches."

He glanced at the cross on the wall with reverence. "When my mother would visit family in Guayaquil and Quito, she took me with her and we inevitably went to those impressive churches. I spent more hours than I can count in mass, but I was silently enraptured by the beauty of those cathedrals. And yet, my mother's excessive religiosity frustrated me just like my father's skepticism filled me with doubt."

His words resonated with me. My mother had also dragged me to church for six o'clock mass every morning—the chocolate store had been a wonderful excuse not to go anymore. It was interesting that the two women in my father's life had shared such devotion.

"So, I set out to disprove the existence of God," he said, and a tight-lipped smile followed. "I went to great lengths to do this. I joined the seminary so I could learn everything I could about philosophy and religion and I could come back home filled with rational arguments to support my stance. Of course, I hid my perverse plan from all those around me, but the more I learned, the more I attempted to illuminate my mother of all my findings. And yet, her faith remained intact." He took a deep breath. "Her death was so shocking and painful to me that one afternoon, filled with rage against this so-called God who had taken the person I loved the most away from me, I turned to the very source of my doubt and struggle for solace."

His voice broke a little. He stared at his hands before speaking again.

"I remember praying the rosary, as I'd seen my mother do so

many times, with the hopes that it would calm me—numb me, if you will—as I'd seen happen to her. I sat in this very same church, in front of the statue of Our Lady, her impassive expression maddening me even more. I wished then with all my heart that God truly existed, as I believed that only He could take this pain away. I lowered my head and closed my eyes, resigned to the thought that this anguish and despair wasn't going anywhere. I can't explain what happened then, not rationally anyway. As I knelt down as a first sign of humility, a sort of serenity descended upon me. My body became light, as if floating, and an enormous peace took over me—not unlike the feeling you get when you leave a cold building and the first rays of sun hit your cheeks. It was at that moment that I realized that everything that had led up to that point in my life was part of the Lord's big plan for me." His fingers rubbed the cotton of his soutane. "I've been chasing that feeling ever since."

He sat in silence for a moment, then turned to me.

"Sorry. I'm known to give long sermons. I'm sure this long outpour wasn't exactly why you came all the way here to see me."

I shook my head, confused. I'd always thought priests had blind faith in everything the Scripture said. I didn't know they had doubts just like the rest of us. Moreover, I couldn't reconcile this touching account with what I believed Alberto had done.

I sat up straight.

"Well"—my voice was hoarse after sitting in silence for so long—"a young girl by the name of Mayra came by the hacienda yesterday."

Whatever color he had left his face. He turned as pale as the two candles flanking the metal cross on the desk.

"She claims that she's expecting a baby. *Your* baby."

He slid all the way to the back of the chair.

"I'm not here to judge you," I said. "I'm . . . human, too, and I understand that the expectations the Roman Catholic Church places on young men are, for the most part, unreasonable." I gripped Cristóbal's pocket watch. "I don't know if you're aware but Mayra lost her job with Aquilino."

He covered his face with both hands.

"She's working for Don Martin now."

He remained still for an eternity.

"So, it is your child?" I finally said.

"What I told you earlier is the truth," he said removing his hands from his face. "I believe this is my calling, but Mayra . . ." He shook his head.

I nodded. I knew all about temptation.

"You don't have to explain yourself to me. I just want to know if you intend to do something about her situation."

He spoke in a low voice. "Why do you care about this?"

"She asked for my help," I said, measuring my next words. "I saw her leaving the *curandera*'s house the other day."

He sprang up, paced the sacristy.

"We didn't really intend to go through with that," he said, his usual composure vanished. "We were just desperate."

"Do you know that the *curandera*'s son has been missing for a few weeks?"

My words took him by surprise, no doubt. He stopped his pacing.

"I had no idea. I just assumed he left town."

I examined his expression in minute detail. I'd wanted to get a candid response from him when I mentioned Franco, but his reaction seemed sincere. Anyone who saw him would believe that this was the first time he'd heard the news that Franco was missing, but as I had just learned, he was also an accomplished liar who'd been living a double life for over a year.

His expression was puzzled.

I honestly didn't know what to believe. When I'd first met Alberto, I'd taken an immediate liking to him. He seemed friendly, frank, and well-read. Plus, his honesty about his struggles with his faith and vocation had touched me. But I was disappointed that he'd left Mayra without any resources and continued with his life as a priest as if nothing had happened. I didn't blame him for failing to keep his vows—it was hard to fight nature—what I resented was how he'd washed his hands of the entire ordeal. Why continue with the farce of the decent priest? Ambition? There was, of course, the power the cassock gave him. Some men loved the adoration, the respect, the demigod status the role of spiritual leader gave them in the community. The shame of giving in to his carnal desires by impregnating a young, ignorant maid might be unbearable for him. He was, after all, the son of a rich landowner, the guardian of his sisters. Would he lose it all if the truth came out? Would he let Mayra and their child be mere casualties in order to save his reputation?

"Why are you bringing up Franco? What does he have to do with us?"

That was exactly what I wanted to know.

"Oh, it just came to mind when I mentioned Soledad. I just think it's very unusual that he left town like that. Soledad told me he said he was just doing a favor for a friend and coming back immediately."

His expression was muted.

"You seem to be very well informed about the comings and goings of everyone in town."

I rested my elbows on my thighs and crossed my fingers as I'd seen Martin do many times.

"I'm a writer. I observe people."

Alberto renewed his nervous pacing.

I leaned back. "Mayra said you offered to take her away with the money from your inheritance."

He stopped in front of the cross to straighten it, but perhaps he was asking for guidance. He faced it for a moment while I studied the back of his head, the tense muscles supporting his neck, the disheveled hair behind his ears.

"You know I don't count on that money anymore."

"Yes. It was very noble of you to renounce your portion."

I couldn't read anything in his expression. He fixed his eyes on mine.

"Can I trust that you will keep silent about . . . about the incident with Mayra?"

An incident. For him, that was all it was, whereas for Mayra it had meant her entire life changed forever.

Instead of answering his question, I wanted to confront him, to corner him into confessing if he'd been the one to hire Franco to kill me. But I didn't know how to do that without making myself vulnerable.

What if the things he told Mayra were true? What if he had a plan to make enough money for the two of them to leave Vinces for good and start over where no one knew them? If he found out about the baby after renouncing his inheritance, he couldn't just take it back without making his sisters suspicious. But if this stranger coming to claim his father's money died and her portion was divided among the three remaining siblings, he could take the money and say it was for a charity or any other noble cause. He could leave then with Mayra, say he was going to another parish. Had he done that? Was he capable of not only breaking his vow of celibacy and lying to the community but also committing the major sin of murdering his older sister?

"I have no interest in exposing you," I said finally. "I just wanted to know if the things Mayra told me were true. What you do about the *incident* with her is entirely up to you and your conscience."

With that, I walked out, more confused than ever.

CHAPTER 32

The next day, I awoke to a medley of angry voices downstairs.

I tightened the corset around my sore breasts and donned my husband's clothes as quickly as possible. Fighting my nerves, I stepped out of the room.

Calm down, Puri.

My encounters with Martin and Alberto had made me vulnerable. I'd cornered Alberto with my knowledge of his secret. Martin had discovered my farce. At any given time, someone might confront me and expose me in front of the entire family. And where would that lead? They might call the police, attack me, and if that happened before I found out the truth, all my efforts would've been in vain. My apprehension might not be rational, but emotions generally weren't.

The yelling grew louder as I descended the staircase. Most of the family was gathered in the parlor, including the neighbor.

Don Fernando del Río was screaming at Angélica. Martin planted himself between my sister and Del Río as if he were Angélica's husband. Incidentally, Laurent was there too, sitting by the harp, witnessing the scene as someone who watches a play by Lope de Vega.

What were they arguing about? I couldn't tell. I assumed it had to do with the lawsuit and the elusive borders that had created so much conflict between the neighboring landowners already.

Between obscenities and insults to the mothers of everyone in the room Don Fernando del Río accused Martin of stealing a new client from him "under Angélica's orders, for sure." Apparently, Del Río had extended an invitation to a German acquaintance of his, a man he called Mr. Meier, to his ranch. The man, who happened to be a cacao buyer, was a potential client for a profitable business. It was practically a done deal until the irrepressible Don Martin met the German at a bar in Vinces and persuaded him, conquered him, bewitched him with the cacao from La Puri by offering him the beans at a ridiculously low price with the sole purpose of "ruining" Del Río.

"You don't care about the money," Fernando said. "All you people want is to destroy me. You and that *vile*, no-good father of yours!" His long finger pointed at Angélica.

On a primitive, guttural level, his insults irritated me. It was true that I hadn't seen my father in decades, but I felt a certain loyalty toward him. Who did this man think he was to come here, to the house of a deceased man who couldn't defend himself, and insult his daughter?

"I didn't try to steal the client from you. He just happened to like our product better," Martin said. "It's not my fault that I'm such a good negotiator and you're not."

Honestly, Martin, do you have to gloat? He could at least try to placate the man to keep the peace.

The neighbor clashed against Martin and tackled him to the floor. Before long, they were rolling on the rug, hitting legs of tables and chairs and making ornaments tumble and fall. Leaning over Martin's chest, a disheveled Fernando started to choke him.

Images of Franco and Cristóbal fighting on the deck came to mind. I couldn't allow another tragedy. If Laurent and Angélica were not going to do anything other than scream, then I would. I jumped on Del Río, wrapping my arm around his neck. He turned to me, looking more confused than angry.

"Who the hell are you?"

He stood up, with me on top of him. He was a giant and I a snail holding on to his shoulders trying not to fall. I was taller than most people here, but Del Río towered over me. He dropped me on the ground and punched my face so hard and fast I couldn't even react.

His fist felt like a brick. Had he broken my jaw?

So now I knew what it felt like to be in a man fight. *I guess I can add this to my list of experiences I never want to repeat.*

Luckily and shockingly, my glasses were still in place, and apparently intact. But Del Río wasn't done. I shut my eyes when I saw his fist coming at me again, but something stopped it. I heard a groan and a thump and when I opened my eyes, Del Río was on the ground and Martin over him.

"Stop it!" Angélica said.

Laurent pinned Martin's arms back so he wouldn't hit Del Río.

"Get out of here!" she told the neighbor. "I don't want you on my property ever again!"

Martin jerked his arm free from Laurent's grip.

Heaving, Del Río stood up straight and assessed every one of us for a moment. "*¡Malnacidos!*" He stormed out and continued swearing under his breath.

Martin came toward me, hands resting on his hips.

"Are you all right?"

I nodded, rubbing the side of my face.

"Come on." He offered me his arm and pulled me up.

Angélica and Laurent gaped at me. I didn't blame them. I didn't know what had come over me, either. Only that the fight on the ship—the fight where Cristóbal had lost his life—propelled me to act like I should've done that fateful night. Why did it bother me so much to see that man choking Martin?

I followed Martin through the patio toward the back of the hacienda. I still couldn't believe that idiot had punched me. Then again, he didn't know I was a woman.

But Martin did.

"Where are we going?" I said.

"To my house. I have dressings and an iodine ointment for your bruise." His voice softened as we drifted away from the hacienda. "You shouldn't have attacked him."

"He was choking you," I said.

"I know how to defend myself."

"Really?" I stopped and gave him my meanest look. That was how he thanked my efforts?

"I'm sorry. I'm just not used to anybody defending me." He attempted a smile. "But thank you."

As we entered Martin's house, Mayra rushed to the entrance to kiss my hand.

"Don Cristóbal! What a pleasure to see you here! Thanks to you my baby will now have a roof over his head."

"No, please. There's no need for this," I said, recovering my hand. "It's Don Martin you have to thank."

Martin inserted both hands inside his pockets.

With brimming eyes, Mayra promised the best *bolón de verde* I would ever taste. I glanced at her stomach. My nephew lived in there.

"It hasn't been all roses in here," Martin said as she rushed back to the kitchen. "Bachita hasn't taken the new arrival so well. She says she can manage all the work herself and complains that Mayra doesn't know how to do the simplest tasks." As he talked, he pointed at the stairs. "Come on."

I froze. Now that Martin knew I was a woman, he must surely understand that it wouldn't be appropriate for me to go to his bedroom. My expression must have given my doubts away because he gave me a slight push on the back.

"Come on, you're not going to act prim and skittish with me now, are you? I keep my bandages and ointments upstairs, that's all."

Hesitantly, I followed. He was right. After all the time we'd spent alone together, I couldn't suddenly be bothered by the rules of decorum. I'd broken them a long time ago.

Peering at every detail of his house—from the ceramic vases to the portraits of severe men and women along the walls—I followed Martin up the stairs. I had an insatiable curiosity about him. I wanted to know how he lived, what he did when he wasn't working, what his parents, his family, had been like.

We entered the first room in the hall.

"Have a seat." He pointed at a den next to a set of windows overlooking the forest.

"What a view," I said, admiring the turquoise sky, the lush

vegetation. And then, a little farther down, a fragment of the river where I'd swum naked. *Madre mía*, he'd probably watched me from here.

"This used to be my parents' room," he said. "My mother always sat by this window, cross-stitching, and usually fell asleep while I played with my marbles by her feet. She had such a lulling presence."

He approached a chest of drawers and removed a leather case. Inside were bandages and a round tin box with ointment.

"How old were you when she passed away?"

"Ten," he said. "I remember she had this tic, this small twitch in her nose, especially when she was nervous, and she always dabbed some kind of rose-infused oil on her neck and wrists. Whenever I smell roses, I think of her."

Poor Martin. At least I'd had my mother until I was a grown woman. I couldn't imagine losing her at such a young age.

He crouched in front of me and without a warning, removed my spectacles.

"Such beautiful eyes you have," he said in a soft voice. I was so surprised by his actions and words that I remained static in my seat without uttering a word.

He pointed at my fake facial hair. "May I?"

I nodded and he gently pulled the beard and mustache off.

"It's a little irritated," he said, staring at my chin. "And your cheek is already swollen. You're going to get a bad bruise from that punch."

The last thing I cared about at the moment was getting a bruise. I was mesmerized by his gentle touch, by having his attention. I'd never imagined him to be so kind. At the same time, I thought about my husband and how disloyal I was being by sharing this intimate moment with another man.

Martin opened the tin, filling the area with a sharp menthol scent, and with the tip of his finger rubbed the waxy texture into my face. I breathed in the peppermint and alcohol from his fingers and flinched.

"Sorry," he said, rubbing softer. "You're going to have to wait for this to dry before you put your beard back on."

This was surreal. To think that Martin, the plantation administrator, who should have more allegiance to the family than to a stranger, like myself, was helping me out. Why was he doing this? I was somewhat dazed by his proximity, by his smell, by his body leaning over me, that I couldn't think straight.

Nervously, I ran my tongue over my dry lips. He stared at my mouth for a few seconds.

"I have to say," he said, holding my gaze, "you are much prettier as a woman than as a man."

I tried to suppress a smile but didn't succeed.

"Why are you helping me?" I asked.

"Because I like you."

He was so nonchalant he made it seem as though there wasn't anything awkward about the way we'd met or gotten to know each other. I tried hard not to think about what he meant by "like."

"But what about my sisters?" I said after a long pause. "You must not care about the family at all." And if so, what did that say about his character? As far as I understood, he'd worked for my father for years. Had he no loyalty? Not that I was complaining about having his help, but it was also worrisome.

He pulled up, gathered his things from the table.

"Not any more than they care about me. Ours is a professional arrangement. I'm a free man and can switch jobs or bosses if I want." He returned the menthol to the drawer. "Land can be sold, acquired, or passed down from one person to another, it doesn't belong to one person or one family until the end of time. We don't live in a monarchy."

So which one was it: Did he really like me or did he want to fall in my good graces so I would sell him my property?

He shut the drawer. "Did you ever wonder how Don Armand acquired such a big cacao plantation?"

His question was not only unexpected but also carried a smack of resentment.

"No," I said. "I was so small when he left Spain that I never questioned how he made his fortune."

He folded his arms across his chest. "Well, you will find the answers inside a locked drawer in his study."

"The drawer?" I recalled. I'd tried to open it. "And where's the key?"

"I wouldn't be surprised if he took it to his grave."

"In that case, why don't you just tell me what's in there?" I didn't feel like looking all over the house for the mysterious key.

"No, I've already said enough. Maybe too much."

There was a knock on the door.

"Don Martin! The *bolones* are ready," Mayra said.

I collected my things. Before I put my disguise on, Martin said, "I hope it's not long before I see you without that beard again."

CHAPTER 33

There was something wrong with me. How could I be attracted to another man so soon after my husband's passing?

It was immoral. It was vile.

But I couldn't help it. Martin appealed to me on an animalistic level. I'd never been as attracted to Cristóbal as I was to Martin—even during the early stages of our courtship. There was no comparison between the bleak intimacy and lackluster companionship of my eight years of marriage and the physical sensations Martin was provoking in me as we sat together at the dining table.

While eating Mayra's *bolones*—exquisite fried balls of plantain filled with cheese—I tried my best to ignore the tingle in my stomach, the way my hands were positioned in relation to Martin's, his solicitous demeanor. When had he cared about whether I needed more salt or if I wanted to try some *ají* sauce? In the past, he'd only cared about filling our glasses with alcohol to the rim. Why couldn't I go back to the ease I'd felt before when I was near him? Why couldn't I concentrate on whatever he was saying?

Because I couldn't go back in time. Martin had seen me *naked*. He knew I was a woman. Now he looked at me differently. His tone had also changed. He knew things about me that nobody else in this country did.

Pay attention. Focus.

He was telling me a story about his high school days. Something about him and his classmates fixing a graduation lunch for their teachers—a group of somber Salesians with hefty appetites—and frying frog legs for them instead of chicken.

I grimaced. "Did you get caught?"

He shook his head. "They were licking their fingers by the end of the meal." He patted his flat belly. "I tried them, too."

"And?"

"Not bad. Similar to rabbit." He grabbed the pitcher of water and served me, as if he hadn't just uttered the most disgusting thing. "What about you? Did you ever play a prank on anybody?"

"Nothing that wicked," I said, taking a sip. "I once put salt inside the sugar bowl for my assistant's tea. But only because she annoyed me."

"How so?"

My ears warmed up. "Uh, nothing important."

"Then, why are you blushing?"

"*¡Por amor de Dios!* Do you have to know everything?"

"Yes." He leaned on the table. "I want to know *everything* about you."

I sat back and glanced at the door leading to the kitchen.

"She criticized my singing."

"Oh, your singing."

"Save it!"

"All right, all right." He covered a chuckle with his hand. As if I couldn't hear him. "So, acting like a man. What are your thoughts? Is it what you imagined?"

"Well, aside from the obvious advantages of having more freedom and wearing more comfortable clothes, it's given me a better understanding of my husband, of how his mind worked."

"In what way?"

"By being forced to act like him, I've had to suppress a side of my personality that had been prevalent all my life."

"Which is?"

"The need to persuade others to do what I want."

"You think this is a feminine trait?"

"Not necessarily. But certainly, Cristóbal wasn't that way. He let others act as they saw fit; he was reserved, discreet, and always in control of his emotions. I, on the other hand, couldn't be quiet for more than a minute and constantly had the need to fix everyone's lives."

"Like Mayra's?"

"Like Mayra's."

"Interesting. Angélica has those same traits."

I was still thinking about Martin's words when I returned to the hacienda.

"Don't take this the wrong way," he'd said right before I left, "but you're a lot more pleasant as a woman. Cristóbal is a little too straitlaced for my taste."

I could see why he thought that. It had been such a relief to have a conversation without having to watch everything I said or did every second.

As soon as I walked into the foyer, Ramona flew toward me and landed on my shoulder. She seemed to have taken a liking to me. Interestingly, she never approached Laurent. She repeated something I couldn't understand, something that sounded like the word "*lobo*." From the parlor, Angélica greeted me and invited me to have a drink with her.

I sat down, clutching a glass of whiskey. What could she want to talk to me about? She'd never showed much interest in me. She had at most offered me food and drink and asked if my accommodations were to my liking. But that was about it. We'd never had a regular conversation, an exchange of ideas.

"Where is Doña Catalina?" I asked by means of breaking our cumbersome silence.

"Sewing. She has to finish our dresses for next week."

"The town's festivities?"

"Yes."

She took a sip of wine.

"Don Cristóbal, I'd like to thank you for your help during that . . . unpleasant episode with Don Fernando today." Somewhat flustered, she explained that he'd been her fiancé for a brief time, but after the breakup, relations with the family had turned sour. She mentioned the fencing issues, the lawsuits, and the problem with the German client.

After her long explanation, she leaned forward. "It was touching to see the way you attempted to defend us, but why did you do it?"

Us? The last person on my mind had been Angélica. I just couldn't stand to see him beating Martin.

"It's what my wife would've wanted," I said. "She had a strong sense of justice."

In a way, I was not lying.

Angélica's face lit up. "Tell me about her, about my sister."

It was so rare to hear her call me "sister." She always referred to me as María Purificación, that very formal name I despised especially when pronounced in that sanctimonious tone. It reminded me of the times my school teachers had scolded me for being bad ("Niña María Purificación, stop distracting your classmates."). But today, Angélica had used her sweetest tone to call me "sister." With that angelic expression on her face, it was hard to believe she would ever plot to hurt anyone, especially her own flesh and blood.

What was happening to me? At times like this, it was hard to sustain my anger. What if none of my siblings had ordered Franco to kill me? What if it had been someone else, someone I didn't even know about? But no, I shouldn't continue with that line of thought. I didn't want to face the possibility of what that meant about me, about my actions.

"What would you like to know?" I tasted the whiskey which, oddly, was growing on me.

"Did she ever talk about us? Was she happy to come?" Her eyelashes were thick, her eyes of an unusual transparency.

"She didn't know about you," I said honestly. "Your father never told her he had a new family."

She smoothed the creases on her peach charmeuse skirt. "I thought she knew. My father never hid her from us." She kept her gaze on her lap. "Perhaps because she was his only legitimate daughter." Her last words were spoken in a whisper.

Was that jealousy I was perceiving or just sorrow? In spite of her legitimacy or lack thereof, I'd been the one who grew up without him.

"Puri was excited to come," I said. "She'd dreamt about visiting this land all her life."

Angélica set her glass on the coffee table. "How sad that she died so young. I'd like to have met her very much."

There it was again—the stab of guilt. In an odd way, I wanted her to be the culprit; it would ease the remorse of my imposture. But I had no way of knowing if she was being truthful or not. All I knew was that at that moment, I had a strong desire to tell her the truth—she was bound to find out anyway. Martin could tell her who I was at any given moment.

"There's something I must tell you," I said.

"What?"

There was something about her reaction: the slight crease between her brows, the sharpness of her tone, the sudden shift of her knees away from me—something that made me reconsider what I was about to say. If I told her the truth, then what? I recalled the feel of Franco's rope against my throat, the knife threatening Cristóbal, the snake in my bed. No, I couldn't confess while I was living under this roof. Not when things were so unclear to me.

"Yesterday, I received word from Panamanian authorities that there have been some complications with Puri's death certificate and it will take a little bit longer for the documents to arrive."

She didn't move a muscle.

"I wouldn't want to impose or take advantage of your kindness any further so if it's more convenient, I can find accommodations in Vinces."

"Of course not," she said. "You're no bother, Don Cristóbal. Why, we barely see you around here."

I thanked her and added, as a truce, "I would like to reciprocate your kindness with a small token of my appreciation, something that I'm certain my Puri would've liked very much."

I spent the rest of the afternoon preparing chocolate drinks and truffles for Laurent and my sisters. Just like Martin and Bachita, my sisters were in awe as the beans transformed in the mill. Laurent, not so much. He said he'd tasted better in his native country ("It must be the ingredients. They are purer in France."). But my sisters didn't care about those details and they didn't even bother waiting for the truffles to cool down completely. They were captivated and ate chocolate until their stomachs ached. I forgot I was supposed to be on guard around them and laughed as they licked their fingers—all etiquette gone—and their mouths were filled with chocolate. If only my father would've brought me here when I was younger, I would've grown up with these women. How lonely I'd been in my mother's quiet apartment, always surrounded by adults.

When my sisters were done indulging, they went to bed, satisfied, and Laurent went to town to play Corazones, his "favorite card game and far superior to Cuarenta," with his friends.

With all the eating and drinking, I was certain I wouldn't see my sisters until the morning. It was my one chance to see what was inside that infamous drawer in my father's study.

When the house was quiet, I descended the staircase, candle in hand, and snuck inside the room. I checked the drawer, but it was still locked. I felt under the desk, checked floorboards and bookshelves, but there was no sign of the key.

I sat in my father's leather chair, deflated. The only thing left to do was convince Martin to leave the mystery aside and tell me what was inside the drawer. I crossed my hands behind my head and stretched my back. I was so tired of wearing this damned corset around my breasts.

In front of me was an oil painting of three windmills sitting on top of a hill. In the foreground was a field of wheat and behind it, rows of olive trees. It was La Mancha—the land of Don Quijote—a region I'd passed by on my way to Toledo many times. Funny, my mother had a similar painting. It looked like it had been painted by the same artist. My father must have brought it from Spain.

And then, I remembered.

I sprang from my chair.

My mother used to hide the key to her trunk behind the frame of that very same painting. She would hang it on the hook that held the picture up.

I lifted the painting from the hook.

And there it was.

An inexplicable lump came to my throat. My parents had more in common than I'd thought. How often had they thought of each other, I wondered, how much had they missed each other's company, and how many habits and idiosyncrasies had they shared? I grabbed the key and tried it in the drawer's lock. It worked! But nothing would've prepared me for what I found there.

A chess set?

I removed the wooden box to check underneath. There was nothing. But this couldn't be it.

Why on earth would anyone hide a game? And what did this chess set have to do with my father's plantation?

I set the board on the table to examine it. There was nothing extraordinary about it. On either side were drawers to hold the pieces. I shuffled through them and found another key.

This one was tiny and had a weird shape to it. It looked like the key to a safe. I groaned. Couldn't my father be a little more straightforward? Now I had to look for a safe? Then I remembered that most safes usually had combinations, not keys. Maybe this was a key for those safety boxes kept at banks?

Yes, that had to be it.

In the morning, I would go to the bank and see if there was a match.

As I tiptoed across the patio, a quick movement to my side caught my attention. I turned toward the back door that Martin and I had used earlier today to leave the hacienda, and made out the shape of a woman in a cloak.

I spotted a flash of blond hair flying about. It could only be Angélica's.

She didn't see me as she opened the door and left the house, mingling with the shadows of the night.

CHAPTER 34

The bank manager was hesitant to let me open my father's safe deposit box, but after I told him that Don Armand Lafont himself had left the key for my wife—the majority holder of all his properties—and that I would be willing to pay him a small fee for his help, he acquiesced. He added, as a means to justify his actions not only to me but also to himself, that he already knew that my father had made María Purificación the primary beneficiary of his will.

After showing me to my father's safety box, he left me alone in the vault, a room with walls made of iron—a claustrophobic's nightmare. My mother would've hated it. She couldn't stand closed spaces and always left the windows open in our apartment, even when it was cold outside.

I unlocked the safe and remove a rectangular metal box. I tried to guess its contents. Money? Jewelry? A gun? But I was wrong. The only thing inside the box was a package of letters tied with a string.

I sat on a nearby bench and looked through the envelopes. There were about a dozen letters for my father from his daughter Elisa and, according to the stamps and addresses, they'd been sent from different locations in the country: Guayaquil, Manta, Machala. A couple were sent from Quito, the capital. They were piled up in order of dates: from the oldest to the most recent. Her handwriting had changed with time. On early envelopes, her letters were large and ended in curly tails, but in later ones her strokes were fast and reflected the evolution of a girl into a woman. If I had to guess, I would say she was an artist, though I didn't know much about calligraphy readings. I checked the date on her last letter: it had been sent three years ago from Quito. Why had she stopped writing him?

I turned to the first envelope, dated 1909, and removed the letter.

> *Dear Papá,*
>
> *It's been two years since the last time I saw you. Did you see me on the hill when your daughter said she saw the Virgin? I gave her my doll so you would know that I came to visit. Do you remember me? I'm 12 years old now, but people say I look young for my age. I have been studying hard to be able to write to you. My teacher says I have good penmanship and "dedication." I like school but sometimes I just feel like lying around, belly up, thinking.*
>
> *Since we left Vinces, we've lived in many places. My mother is now with a puppeteer named Benjamin. She says they're married, but I don't remember any ceremonies. I just remember her coming to me one day and introducing him as my new father. She said to call him Papá, but I told her I already have a French father and his name is Armand Lafont. Did I do right, Papá?*
>
> *I'm now learning to handle the puppets because Benjamin needs help with the show, but I'm a little tired of always performing the same story:* La Caperucita Roja. *I told him people already know it by heart and are getting tired of seeing the wolf eat the little girl and the grandma. The worst part is some silly tune I have to sing whenever Caperucita is wandering about the forest. I can't get it out of my mind all day!*

I told Benjamin people want love stories, but he says puppets are for the little ones. I sometimes pretend the puppets are all a big family living in La Puri.

Right now, we're in Machala. We usually stay in the Costa because Benjamin says the Sierra is too cold and here we can sleep outdoors. Sometimes Benjamin takes other jobs, like fishing or collecting cacao pods, because he says we can't only live from "art." My mother goes from house to house offering to wash people's clothes and when she gets a job, she takes me with her to do the washing. I hate it. I keep asking her if we can go back to Vinces and live with you in that big house like we did when I was small, but she says we can't. She says your wife doesn't want us there.

When am I going to see you again? As soon as we have a permanent address, I'll send it to you so you can come visit.

I miss you,
Elisa.

I opened the next envelope.

April 30, 1910

Dear Papá,
We're up north now, in Manta. My stepdad is working as a fisherman. I've seen the ocean and I'm not afraid of it. My face is so tan now I don't think you'll recognize me. Also, my hair has gotten really curly!

I've made some friends here. Mostly young fishermen and cocada vendors (have you ever tried them?). The bad thing about all this traveling is that I can't go to school. I'm not complaining too much because I know a lot of kids would love my life, but I want to learn all I can so one day I can go back to Vinces and help you with La Puri. Mamá says you write a lot when you work, so I have to learn how to spell and do sums and subtractions, too.

Back in Guayaquil, I used to sneak into a school.
The arithmetic class was so big that the teacher never
noticed me. He didn't even know his own students'
names! My classmates didn't seem to care or notice
me, either, though once in a while, someone was mean
to me.
    That's all for now.
    Your daughter who misses you,
    Elisa.

I checked the dates and skipped a few letters until I reached a
letter from 1914.

    Papá,
    Mamá says you're never going to write back even
though I've had this same address for a year. I tell her
you probably didn't receive my other letters so you
don't know where to send yours. We all know that the
post office in this country is lousy! And besides you're
a busy man and according to my calendar, the harvest
must be at its bloom.
    My life has somewhat settled now that I have a
steady job here in Quito. After an unpleasant incident
in Guayaquil, which I'd rather not talk about, my
mother and I decided to move to the Sierra. Benjamin
is no longer with my mom, but I think she would take
him back in an instant if he ever finds us.
    I now work at the telegraph office. The days are
long and tiring, but I like it, and at least I don't have
to travel anymore. Mamá and I rent a room at a
boarding house in the center of the city. The house
where we live is surrounded by churches. I've never
seen so many in one single place! They're so big, too!
Sometimes on weekends, I like to visit them. I don't
pray, like my mother, who takes a list of favors she
wants from God. But I find the silence and the smell
of all those candles soothing. Mostly, I like to look at
the artwork inside and the stunning domes and ceil-

*ings. Can you believe human beings can create such
beauty?*

*If you're ever in town, come see me. (Address
attached.)*

Elisa.

I skipped to the last letter; such was my impatience.

Papá,

*Mamá died last week. The doctor said she had a
bad case of pneumonia. I'm not sure how I'm going to
go on with life after this. I haven't been feeling too well
myself. I've been locked in my room for the last couple
of days with a fever and didn't go to work, even
though my boss had warned me that if I skipped one
more day, he would fire me. But what was I supposed
to do? Someone had to look after my mother. I
couldn't think about work when she was dying.*

*I don't care about anything anymore. I wish I
could've seen you one last time, but apparently, it was
not meant to be.*

Elisa.

Wait. Was this a goodbye? I reread the letter. That was all. I
checked the return address. Elisa had been in Quito when she
sent this last letter, but what could've happened to her? It had
been sent almost four years ago. Had she died?

I skimmed through the letters I'd skipped but they sounded a
lot like the earlier ones, where she told my dad about her day to
day, the people in her life, etc. Nothing else about the "unpleasant incident" in Guayaquil or what had prompted the breakup
between Benjamin and her mother. If I hadn't been so immersed
in resolving things here, I might have been tempted to go to
Quito to find Elisa.

I returned the letters back to my father's safety box and left
the bank, submerged in thought. Why hadn't my father ever
written Elisa back? He always wrote to me. Was it an issue of fluency in Spanish? As far as I could recall, he always wrote to me in

French. But no, he could've asked someone else to translate if he truly wanted to communicate with her. It seemed like he'd abandoned this daughter—even worse than when he'd abandoned me. Why her and not me? Was it an issue of class? After all, she was the daughter of the maid—someone who Elisa describes as having little education and who washed other people's clothes for a living, a woman who traveled the country like a nomad with a man who wasn't her husband. It was apparent that my father had been ashamed of this daughter, or else he wouldn't have hidden her letters here. However, he *had* saved them, which meant he had some sort of emotional attachment with Elisa.

"Don Cristóbal!"

Someone touched my shoulder. It was Soledad Duarte, the *curandera*.

"I've been calling you for a whole block!" she said, her chest heaving, her cheeks as red as a bullfighter's cape.

"I'm sorry. I'm hard of hearing," I said as a sole explanation.

"Did you find out anything about my Franco?" she asked.

I hesitated. I hated to give her hope when I knew the truth about her son, but at the same time, I needed her help. Maybe I could strike a balance between giving her some information without disclosing my connection to Franco.

"Yes," I said. "Apparently he went to the Caribbean."

"What? Where is that?"

"Someone saw him aboard a ship on the island of Cuba."

"What would he be doing there?"

"Well, didn't you mention a favor for someone? Maybe it had to do with that."

Soledad rested her hand on her forehead. "Cuba? I have to talk to the police."

"Wait. The police didn't tell me this. It was someone else, someone who wishes to remain anonymous."

She studied me for a moment.

"Well, at least he's still alive," she finally said.

Why did the sight of this woman, this suffering mother, produce so much guilt in me? She was the mother of my husband's killer, for God's sake! I shouldn't feel anything other than contempt for her after she'd raised a criminal.

She gripped my arm.

"I found something," she said, "but I don't know if it has anything to do with his disappearance."

"What?"

She looked down the block before speaking. "Come."

We walked a couple of blocks to her place, which had acquired a particular stench reminiscent of mud and moist grass. There seemed to be even more clutter than before, if such a thing were possible.

Soledad zigzagged toward a walnut chest of drawers. From the bottom one, she removed something—a black velvet pouch—and handed it to me. Inside a gold case was a pocket watch. The case, engraved with vines and flowers, was somewhat tarnished. I wound the watch and the hands started to move around a series of Roman numerals.

"Where did you find this?" I asked.

"Hidden under Franco's mattress."

"This looks expensive," I said. "Like real gold."

She nodded.

I turned it over. The brand was engraved on the back: *Bolivar e Hijos, Guayaquil. 1911.*

"How do you think your son got this?"

"I don't know. I'd never seen it before yesterday."

Could this have anything to do with that woman he was so in love with? Was this part of the payment for his services? Only a few people in this town had the kind of money to afford this watch.

"Doña Soledad, was your son close to Catalina Lafont?"

"La Santa and my son? Oh, no, perhaps as children, but not lately. Since the accident, Catalina hadn't come to see him once. The only times I see her in Vinces is for mass on Sundays and during the festivities. Why do you ask?"

"Did anybody else come to see him after the accident?"

"Just the workers from the plantation. Franco didn't have many friends."

"Any women ever come by?"

"Not that I saw."

"Would you let me borrow this?" I asked. "I think I have an idea."

She hesitated. Of course, she would doubt me, I was a stranger to her. I removed Cristóbal's pocket watch, which was also valuable and newer, and handed it to her.

"I'll leave you this in exchange. Please don't think I'm trying to shortchange you. I believe this watch may help us figure out what happened to Franco."

Soledad, whose hair had grown grayer and whose skin seemed more ashen in a matter of days, sat down.

"Take it," she said. "You're the only person in this rotten town who's shown any interest in helping me anyway. If I weren't so poor and weak, I would track my son down myself."

 CHAPTER 35

With the Fiestas de Vinces coming up, tracking the history of Franco's watch wasn't as easy as I'd originally thought it would be. I'd planned to go to Guayaquil with the excuse of visiting Aquilino. In reality, I would pay a visit to the watchmakers, Bolivar and Sons, but I had no luck finding transportation at this busy time of the year.

My sisters, who were warmer to me since I prepared them chocolate and fought the neighbor "to defend Angélica's honor," invited me to partake in the festivities. That evening, the two of them were to perform in a theater with other musicians and poets. Directly after, they were invited to an exclusive party for the landowners of the region, Los Gran Cacao, as Martin had called them. Angélica was mortified at the thought that Don Fernando del Río might attend. "If he has decency left, he won't show his face in public. Not after the scandal he caused here."

My sisters looked radiant tonight, particularly Angélica. She wore a navy tunic with a turquoise sash draped around her waistline, the garment Catalina had sewn for her. A blue velvet turban hugged Angélica's skull. She was so fashionable!

Catalina, on the other hand, wore one of her customary black dresses, but this one was made out of the finest silk. Hard as she tried, she couldn't hide her generous behind, which I later noticed became the focal point of many male glances across town.

Her hair was pinned up and held together with a satin wrap fixed in a bow. She was a natural beauty and didn't need all the enhancements that Angélica used. Some might even consider Catalina lovelier than her sister.

Laurent joined us after much grooming. He was impeccable, as usual, in a white suit and brand-new leather slippers which, he bragged, had been brought from the Real Paris especially for him. As he spoke, he smoothed the nearly imperceptible wrinkles in his pants.

I wore one of Cristóbal's nicest outfits: a three-piece gray suit that would certainly stand out among the light linen suits men wore in the region. Angélica commented that I ought to visit the tailor so he could make me a new wardrobe that would be more weather-appropriate. I nodded agreeably, but no human power would send me to the tailor. I knew all about the heat—the summers in Sevilla could be dreadful, too. In fact, there were lighter fabrics in Cristóbal's trunk, but how would I explain to Angélica that I required several layers of clothing to conceal my breasts?

As Laurent drove us into town, Angélica explained that early in the morning, Martin had taken their instruments to the theater. ("God bless him!" was Catalina's excited contribution.) Ignoring her sister's outburst, Angélica said there would be a variety of events during the week: parades, folkloric dances, art shows, and even tango dancing on the last day. One of the highlights of the festivities, Catalina pitched in, was the election of the Queen of Vinces, which Angélica had won some years ago. I already knew this. Julia had mentioned it during breakfast. In the last couple of days, the maid had also opened up to me. I wondered if she was mimicking her mistresses' recent kindness—being that she seemed to look up to her so much—or if she was grateful that I'd found a new job for her cousin Mayra at Martin's house.

"It's so bright tonight," I said. Vinces seemed more alive than any other night, as if the city itself also wore its best garments for the festivities.

"President Baquerizo Moreno has a special fondness for us because of all the cacao we've produced," Angélica said. "We were one of the first towns in the region to have electricity."

"After producing eighty thousand tons of cacao a year, he ought to be grateful," Laurent said, surprising me with his insight. It was the first time he'd said anything remotely interesting.

I stared at him as he absently rubbed Angélica's hand. Maybe his frivolous image was just a façade.

Teatro Olmedo was small but impressive. The auditorium was crammed with red-cushioned seats placed in a semicircle and raised boxes on either side. Cream-colored columns flanked the stage and a pair of carmine velvet curtains descended from an elliptical arch.

The place slowly filled up. I recognized a few faces from Bingo Night. Some greeted me with a nod, but others blatantly ignored me. The chatter around me was mostly in French rather than in Spanish. Apparently, this was the place where the Parisian community gathered.

Minutes before my sisters performed, I found myself in a strange state of nervousness—glancing behind me every so often, drying my hands on my pants. Meanwhile, Laurent was more interested in the people behind us than his wife onstage. As soon as the curtains opened, the room became silent. A sense of pride took over me. Sitting with their instruments under the warm lights, my sisters formed a breathtaking view. Their backs were perfectly straight, their necks elongated and graceful, their heads slightly tilted. They sat with such elegance and poise it was impossible to look elsewhere.

On cue, the two of them started playing. Their strings vibrated in flawless harmony to the sounds of Strauss, Chopin, and Debussy. Halfway through the recital, Catalina stood, holding her violin and performing with such concentration she seemed to have forgotten that half of the town was watching her. I'd never seen her more focused and unrestrained than tonight.

The master of ceremonies, a slender man with an overgrown

white mustache that perfectly matched his bow tie and vest, announced that there would be a poetry reading in honor of President Alfredo Baquerizo Moreno, a poet himself. People applauded and cheered the absent president, whom Laurent seemed to have a lot of respect for and branded as a "liberal."

When the poetry readings began, several audience members started to yawn. I, myself, had a hard time keeping my eyes open, but I was certain that my Cristóbal would've enjoyed this evening of arts and culture. My eyes watered. I longed to see him again.

After the recital ended, I met Catalina and Angélica backstage. I congratulated both and candidly hugged them for the first time.

When we arrived at the party, the parlor was already full. Busy waiters in black tuxedos carried trays of appetizers and French wine. Cradling a glass of champagne, I observed the people around me. Flushed and invigorated from the performance, Catalina attempted to talk to a cluster of women who had greeted her with side kisses and forced smiles.

Much like on Bingo Night, Angélica was more comfortable than ever. She thrived among this type of crowd: the elegant, the tall, the beautiful. She always had the right compliment and the perfect anecdote. People swarmed around her, especially men, and Laurent didn't seem to mind. In fact, he gravitated toward a young man I'd seen that evening at the hacienda and he engaged in a conversation that seemed to be continued from another encounter. I recalled the silence in his bedroom while I hid under the bed and the close distance between the two pairs of shoes. I involuntarily glanced at Laurent's new slippers.

When I looked up, I met a face I was not expecting to see tonight: Martin's.

He raised his glass to me and I followed suit. The room turned warmer. He was one of those men who grew more attractive the longer you knew him. To me, he seemed the most striking in the group—not because of his looks, but by the way he carried himself. He moved across the room with a self-assurance that demanded attention. I took a long sip of champagne as he approached me.

But before he could reach me, I sensed a change in the atmosphere. The room became quieter, all laughter ceased. There was a tension I couldn't quite pinpoint. My first thought was that Don Fernando del Río had arrived, but I didn't see him anywhere.

At the center of all the glances were Angélica, who'd turned quiet and pale, and another woman, whom I'd never seen before. The first thing I noticed about the other woman was her eyes, the color of honey. She was just as fashionable as my sister in a silver silk frock embroidered with beads and rhinestone and a hat adorned with two feathers. But there were dark circles under her eyes, as if she hadn't had a good night's sleep in weeks.

With a serious demeanor, she walked toward Angélica and extended her hand toward my sister. Without removing her eyes from the strange woman, Angélica accepted the handshake, though it looked like their hands barely touched. Instead of a shake, it was more like a polite squeeze done through their gloves. How different were the handshakes I'd received from men in my Cristóbal persona. They had been firmer and had transmitted a genuine openness that I'd never perceived in women, even in my closest relationships. But first, there had been challenge in the men's gazes, an assessment of sorts that seemed to end with the truce of the handshake.

After the forced handshake between Angélica and the newcomer, the conversations slowly renewed. Catalina's comment in the sewing room came to mind. She'd mentioned something about a woman coming back to town. And Angélica hadn't looked pleased. What was the woman's name? This was probably her.

Martin greeted me with a low "hello." His attitude had definitely changed since he'd found out I was a woman. He was no longer relaxed and uninhibited around me. Now he seemed to plan every gesture and every word before opening his mouth. I missed our old camaraderie.

"Who was that woman?" I asked him, ignoring my racing pulse as his sleeve brushed against mine.

He avoided my eyes, looking around the parlor without saying a word.

"Martin?"

"I heard you."

"Well, who is she?"

"A friend of Angélica's, I think," he added, as an afterthought.

"They didn't seem too friendly."

He didn't comment.

"What's her name?"

"Silvia."

Yes, that was the name.

"So, what's wrong with them? Why was everybody staring when they greeted each other?"

"You should ask Angélica."

He didn't say he didn't know. In fact, he gave me a feeling of knowing more than he let on. Since he'd reached me, he hadn't looked at my face once and he seemed as uncomfortable as a freemason in ballet class.

"So, what are you doing here anyway?" I said. "I thought you didn't like social engagements."

He loosened his tie a notch. "I don't, but this is a good business opportunity that only comes once a year. During the festivities, new buyers come. It's the perfect time to make new connections."

How odd that being business partners of sorts, Angélica and Martin never seemed to spend time together or work as a team (except when they fought with Don Fernando). It was the opposite—they appeared to repel each other, to make separate decisions. Another thing that was strange was that Laurent had no involvement whatsoever in any of the business decisions.

"Are things different now that my father is gone?" I asked Martin in a low voice.

"Like night and day."

"You don't see eye to eye with Angélica."

"It's that obvious?"

Martin was tense and distracted with the people parading behind me.

"Do you want to go?" he said, out of the blue.

"But what about your potential customers?"

"We have a whole week ahead of us. There will be other opportunities. I don't like the atmosphere here today."

I glanced at my sisters, each one immersed in separate conversations with their friends and acquaintances—although Catalina kept looking at me with eyes that screamed of boredom and discomfort. Angélica, on the other hand, seemed to have forgotten the uneasy encounter with her former friend and had returned to her charming self. But I didn't believe those forced smiles and her phony laughter. It was a good thing that Fernando del Río had not shown up, or he would've shattered Angélica's calm façade.

"Yes, let's go," I said now that Catalina had peeled her eyes off of me to greet an old woman who spoke to her with the same respect and adoration people reserve for priests and nuns.

La Santa.

I could see now, firsthand, how the town viewed her, how her loyal followers surrounded her.

Martin set his glass on a nearby table and, without another word, led the way toward the entrance, squeezing between arrogant guests and hectic waiters.

Though it was a warm night, it was a relief to be outside, away from the scrutiny of folks whose biggest preoccupation was their image and how they compared with others. I was both fascinated and repelled by this micro-society, this Paris in the tropics. I'd observed similar glances in my chocolate shop sometimes, but I never got involved. As the hostess, I had bigger concerns than what so-and-so was wearing or who was sitting with whom.

Martin said he needed a drink so the two of us walked to the *cantina*. Oddly enough, I'd grown more comfortable in this cheap bar filled with cheerful men and salacious women than surrounded by the wealthy.

"I didn't realize there was so much money in this region," I said, sitting in my usual spot and ordering my customary *puro*.

"Oh, yes," Martin said, as if I'd opened up the most fascinating subject in the world. "Cacao completely changed the economy and politics of this country. It used to be that all the money and power was in Quito—with the traditional elite and the Church—but after the cacao boom a new oligarchy was born in Guayaquil and we finally have a say in national politics. The last few presidents have been liberal and have pushed for modernization and the separation of Church and State. Am I boring you?"

Martin leaned over the table, resting his arms on the flat surface while he watched me.

"Not at all," I said.

He continued telling me about local politics and regionalism. He smiled often, but it was a guarded smile, one might even call it rehearsed. His voice was not as loud as it used to be nor was his laughter as boisterous. He was also careful with his language. Not a single curse word was voiced in my presence anymore.

It was driving me crazy.

I missed the old, unrestrained Martin, and I told him so. He sat back with an amused smile.

"All right, I'll throw an *hijo de puta* here and there if it pleases you."

I laughed.

"I was getting exhausted with having to watch everything I say or do anyway," he said, and ordered two more *puros*.

When the prostitutes came, Martin told them we didn't need their services tonight. I was grateful for being spared the sight of that woman sitting on Martin's lap and kissing him. The two of them gave us a baffled look and hesitantly left. As they walked away, Carmela whispered something into her friend's ear.

Martin and I talked for a long time. He wanted to know everything about my childhood in Spain, about the scarce memories of my father, about how my mother and I had survived all those years without a husband and a father. I told him my father used to send us money, plus my mother had a small inheritance from my grandfather, who'd been a merchant of fabrics. I also told

Martin about my grandmother, María Purificación García, and how she'd invented a cacao roasting machine in 1847, which could also be used for coffee beans. He was extremely interested in this invention. He borrowed a fountain pen and ink from the barman and asked me to draw the contraption on a napkin.

"Where is it?" he said after I was done drawing and explaining how the roaster worked.

"I left it with my former assistant, La Cordobesa. It's the only thing I have left in Spain."

He said I should send for it "once this was all over." That was the only time he mentioned my precarious situation.

After we'd finished an entire bottle of *aguardiente*, Martin wanted to know about my husband. I loosened my tie.

"My mother and Cristóbal's mother were childhood friends. Ours was an arranged marriage."

"Did you love him?"

"Of course I did, though I don't think I was ever *in love* with him." I nestled my drink, remembering. "I'd seen Cristóbal throughout the years, but was only properly introduced to him during a tea at his mother's house after he had just graduated from the Universidad de Sevilla. I was only nineteen years old and he was the only person I'd ever known with a university title. I was impressed by his scholarly achievements, by his good looks, but I really didn't have time to get to know him. From our sporadic encounters, I could tell he was a quiet and gentle man, and I liked that. I needed a stabilizing presence in those years when I was cross all the time and only wanted to find the next ship that would take me to see my father. But my mother would scream that I would only leave *over her dead body*, which is ironic because that's exactly what happened," I said, finishing my drink. "I've always thought that the reason she pushed my relationship with Cristóbal was to keep me in Spain."

"Did you ever regret marrying him?"

"Not really. We had a good life together. At the beginning of our marriage, he worked as a schoolteacher and at his father's bookstore on weekends, but that had all changed when his father died and I convinced him to turn the bookstore into a chocolate shop."

"So, it was your idea."

I nodded. "He would do anything to please me. How could I ever regret being with someone like that?"

To my chagrin, my eyes filled with tears. I never cried in public. Worse, I was crying in front of Martin, of all people. I wiped my tears with a napkin, looking around to make sure nobody was watching.

"If I hadn't convinced him to come here," I said, "he would still be alive."

"You don't know that. So many things could've gone wrong if you'd stayed in Spain. He could've slipped in the tub and injured his head or rolled down some stairs, or he could've caught the consumption. You never know what's going to happen. That doesn't mean you shouldn't follow your dreams for fear that something bad might happen. You did what was right. You followed your heart, and he could've always said no."

I could tell he wanted to hold my hand, to offer some comfort, but he didn't make a move. He just stared at me for a long time, and his eyes, expressive and warm, told me he couldn't have had anything to do with the plot to kill me.

I pressed the palm of my hand against my warm cheek.

"Tell me about your chocolate shop," he said.

I told him how my grandmother had taught me the chocolate-making process with patience and determination; how I'd improved some of her recipes and made them my own; how I'd decorated the shop and even got a latrine in the back for our customers. From time to time, our hands accidentally touched. I recoiled as if his fingers were flames. As much as I liked his proximity, I had an image, a reputation to maintain. And so did he.

"So what did you do for fun?" he said.

"For fun? What do you mean?"

"What else did you do besides work?"

I was quiet for a moment.

"Well, my work was fun. I did what I loved."

"Yes, but there's more to life than work, even if it's fun, right?"

I folded the napkin with my drawing into a tiny square. "What do *you* do for fun?"

"Well, you've seen my life. I come here, I fish, occasionally I go on long walks, I read."

I lifted an eyebrow.

"I do." He flashed a smile—it was disarming.

"And you go out with numerous women."

He turned serious. "Not really, Puri. I may have exaggerated my amorous conquests some, just to test you, back when I didn't know if you were—"

"Including those women?" I pointed my chin toward the door, where the prostitutes had just walked through.

"Including those women."

"What about your family?"

Martin sat back. "We should go. They're about to close."

I was starting to think it was no coincidence that Martin always avoided going into details about his past.

Martin offered to drop me at the hacienda, but I thought it would be strange for two men to ride a horse together.

"Nobody's watching," he said.

It was dark outside and the weather had finally cooled down. I hadn't realized until I stepped out of the bar how dizzy I was. People often said it was the cold air that got you drunk, not the alcohol. I never believed it—until now.

"No, I'll go back with my sisters." My speech was slurred.

"They probably left already. It's one in the morning."

I noticed then that the crowd had already dispersed. How unkind of me not to tell my sisters I was leaving the party with Martin.

I hesitated, but climbed on the back of his horse, Melchor, nonetheless. I did my best not to touch Martin, and instead, rested my hands on the horse's rear, attempting to hold my balance as the animal started to move.

My arms and legs were so stiff they started to get sore. Worse yet, the ride was making me dizzier—I couldn't go on. Martin said I could stay at his house; he had a spare bedroom I could use. I agreed, mostly because I feared that if I continued on that horse, I would end up retching every piece of food I'd consumed in the last two days. When I climbed off of Melchor, the world spun all around me. Martin helped me into the house, which was quiet and dark.

I nearly tripped on one of the steps and yelped.

"Shhh, Mayra is already asleep," Martin said.

With Martin's arm around my waist and my arm over his shoulders, we walked up the stairs. He led me to a room at the end of the hall, where I noticed a portrait of a man that looked like an older version of Martin. I pointed at it.

"That was my father," he said.

There were still things I wanted to ask about his parents, but I couldn't produce any words. He set me on the bed and helped me remove my jacket and my boots. Then, he stood up.

"Well, have a good night," he said.

"Wait," I said with a hiccup. "Would you help me remove this?" I pointed at my corset. "I can hardly breathe with it."

Suffocated by the dense air around me, I unbuttoned Cristóbal's shirt. I might have choked if I didn't remove the pressure from my breasts right away. Gently, Martin assisted me in unwrapping the fabric around my chest until I was left in Cristóbal's undergarments. After I removed my facial hair, something came over me, something I couldn't explain. It could've been his scent— a blend of sweat and alcohol masked under his citric cologne; or maybe the fact that I'd been alone for too long and I yearned to be embraced, or the way Martin had watched me all evening— and was watching me now that I no longer looked like a man. Whatever it might have been, I didn't care. I clasped my fingers around his neck and brought his face down toward mine. Off came my glasses, the buttons of my undergarment, his shirt. We kissed with the urgency of two people who'd been thirsty for too long and had finally stumbled upon a glass of water. Martin's kisses had an unexpected tenderness to them. He was gentle, yet vehement. His hand traveled softly over my breasts, his lips on my neck.

"Puri," he said. "*Mi Puri.*"

I'd never experienced a more intense and sublime moment. It was almost as if my entire life had been leading up to this moment of complete communion. Martin seemed to have known my body all along—in ways that Cristóbal never did. He knew exactly where to touch, where to kiss, how to make me feel alive. Above all, I was touched by his kindness—I'd never imagined him to be so giving.

After it was all over, he lay next to me, staring at the ceiling. I kissed the line between his eyebrows. He smiled and asked me if I was all right. I said yes, I said I'd never been better. Our fingers interlaced. I expected him to say something along those lines, one of those trite words lovers say when they're feeling satisfied. But he only kept that faint smile on his face, a smile that—in ways I couldn't understand—made me shiver.

HAPTER 36

I woke up like one of those heroines in a fairy tale: the sun filtering in through the translucent curtains, the sounds of the birds in the forest vivid and sharp, a soft sheet covering my nakedness.

Martin was nowhere in sight. I refrained from calling out his name. Maybe Bachita had already arrived and Mayra might be tidying up the house. The door to my room was shut. I wasn't sure if Martin had slept here with me, or if he'd gone off to his own chamber.

There was a dent in the mattress beside me, but his clothes were gone. Mine had been collected and piled on a chair by the armoire.

The door opened. I covered my breasts with the sheet.

Martin snuck inside the room with a small tray in his hands, shutting the door behind him with his foot. He signaled with his free hand that I should be quiet. The tray had a cup of tea and bread and something that looked like caramel. I was delighted. In my twenty-eight years of life, nobody had ever brought breakfast to my room.

"Mayra is already up," he said, "so we have to be very quiet. I told her you had spent the night here for you were too sick to get home."

I smeared the caramel-like texture onto the bread.

"This is delicious," I said. "What is it?"

"*Dulce de leche*. Some people call it *manjar*. It's made out of milk and brown sugar loaf. Bachita makes it once a week."

"I love it," I said, taking another bite of my bread.

"You're so beautiful," he said unexpectedly. "I always knew there was something different about you. A man could never have such fine features."

"Do you think other people might have noticed, too?"

"Nobody has said anything to me."

Smiling, I took a sip of tea while he opened the curtains. He stood by the window for a moment, looking outside, and his smile vanished. He tensed up and shifted forward, fixing his gaze on something I couldn't see. Forcefully, he shut the curtains and rushed to the door.

"Stay here. And don't open the door for anybody until I get back."

Before I could say a word, he darted out of the room, shutting the door behind him.

I set the tray on the night table and dashed to the window to see what the source of his distress was.

Angélica.

She climbed off Pacha with a mastery I didn't think I would ever achieve with this horse or any other. Lifting her skirt as to not dirty the hemline, she started toward the front of the house with a determined gait. What had happened?

Before I'd finished putting on my trousers, I heard her screechy voice, more upset and unhinged than I'd ever heard her. She was already inside.

"Where is she?" Angélica said.

She?

Oh, no, she'd figured out who I was. But how? Nobody but Martin knew and he'd been with me the entire evening. At least I thought so.

I tried to lock the bedroom door but the knob seemed to be broken.

She was climbing the stairs now, her feet stomping against the wood, her voice getting closer. Martin was telling her to calm down, to come downstairs, calling her by her first name instead of señora. This familiarity of theirs, Angélica's demands, her ringing voice. It almost sounded like she was jealous. They *both* sounded more like lovers than work associates.

"I know Silvia is here! I know! She left the party right after you did! Oh, I know her so well. She couldn't wait until her husband cooled down in his grave before coming to see you! Silvia, *Silvia!*"

She was in the hall now. I was halfway through putting on my corset.

"Silvia is not here," Martin said. "Stop with this nonsense."

"You're such a liar!" Her voice was filled with contempt, but also pain. She was vexed, yes, undoubtedly, but at times it sounded like she might break down and cry.

I was tucking my shirt inside my pants when I heard the door opening in the adjacent room.

"Stop hiding, Silvia! I know you're in here!"

¡Virgen de la Macarena! I'd never moved faster. I didn't even have a mirror to glue my beard and mustache. Should I try to hide somewhere? The first place she would look would be under the bed.

When the door flew open, I'd just managed to attach the beard to my chin, but I had to hold on to it with my hand so it wouldn't fall off. I was sitting in the chair where my clothes had been with my legs crossed, my spectacles crooked, and my hand on my chin.

"Don Cristóbal! What are you doing here?"

She stopped sharply by the door. Her eyes taking in the scene in front of her. The bed was still unmade, the breakfast unfinished on the night table, her sister's husband holding on to his chin as though it might fall.

"Good morning," I mumbled. "Don Martin was kind enough to let me spend the night here. I'm in horrible pain, you see, I think it's my molar."

I only wished she wouldn't ask to see it.

"Yes," Martin said promptly. I wouldn't look him in the eye. "We left the party because Don Cristóbal could barely handle the pain in his mouth, but he didn't want to ruin your evening, Doña Angélica. Hard as we tried, we couldn't find a single doctor to help him, so we just came here so he could rest."

I couldn't bear the sight of him. He was so good at lying. It had come so easy to follow my lead.

"I'm so sorry to hear that, Don Cristóbal." Her breathing had slowed down, but her cheeks were still red. "I can arrange for Laurent to take you to the doctor today. I'll have him come over immediately to pick you up." Then, adjusting the sleeves of her sheer overblouse, she turned to Martin. "I wish you would've told me right away that Don Cristóbal was here."

"I *tried*," he said between clenched teeth.

"There's no need for anybody to bother taking me. I can walk to town," I said. "If you'll excuse me for a moment while I finish getting ready, I'll be on my way."

"Of course." Angélica walked out of the room. Martin raised his finger, as though asking me to stay, but I avoided his face and put on my jacket.

I somehow managed to attach the facial hair and swiftly left the room. Angélica was already climbing on her horse. Martin was telling her something, and she was nodding. I circled the house so neither one of them would see me leave, and I then I hastened down the road in the direction of Vinces.

There was an unbearable pressure in my chest that my hand couldn't soothe.

I didn't want to talk to Martin, and I certainly didn't want to go back to the hacienda. I just wanted to be alone and think about what I'd just learned.

Martin and Angélica were lovers. It had been obvious.

Everything made sense now: why Angélica had left the house that night while her husband was away playing cards and she thought everyone was sleeping; why at times Martin seemed so irritated by Laurent's presence or his nearness toward Angélica. My suspicions about Laurent liking men, and why there seemed to be a mere companionship, not affection and certainly no sexual tension, between Angélica and her husband. It also explained why Martin was a still a bachelor. A man his age would've found a woman to settle with by now instead of fulfilling his urges with prostitutes until Angélica could come to him during Corazones night.

For how long had this been going on? And what did Silvia have to do with them? Had Martin cheated on Angélica with this woman? Catalina had mentioned a rupture between the two friends. And then, last night at the party, Martin had wanted to leave as soon as that woman had arrived and had avoided talking to either one of them.

I'd been such a fool. I'd fallen directly into Martin's trap. He'd been on Angélica's side from the very beginning. He'd wanted my father's land all along. The worse part was that *I'd known this*. He'd even *made an offer* to buy my share of the estate. He'd been trying to get his hands on the plantation in every possible way he could: if not through Angélica, then by purchasing my part, and since neither one worked, he was going to get it through *me*.

What better way to get full control of the plantation than by having the majority holder fall in love with him? That was why he hadn't told Angélica about me. Because I was certain now that she didn't know. I could see it in her humiliation a moment ago. If Angélica had thought for a second that I was a woman, her jealousy would've multiplied. Instead, her anger had dissipated when she realized that I wasn't a threat, that I didn't want her man.

How could I have been so stupid?

I walked for a long time and, without realizing it, I reached the first houses in Vinces. I slowed my pace, more out of surprise than tiredness, and continued toward the plaza. I reached the park next to the miniature Eiffel Tower and sat on a bench. Undoubtedly, Martin would tell Angélica about me now. There was no reason to keep covering up for me.

I sat there for a few minutes, leaning forward with my hands pressed against my eyes until I heard a familiar voice.

"Don Cristóbal?"

I raised my head and recognized Aquilino, who waved at me and crossed the street in my direction.

"Don Tomás, what are you doing here?"

"Oh, just taking care of some business for one of my clients, but I'm heading back to Guayaquil now."

I hoped this business had nothing to do with the bank manager telling Aquilino about me and my inquiries.

"How are things going with you?" he asked.

An idea came to mind. I felt the pocket watch in my trousers. "You said you're going to Guayaquil now, right?"

"Yes, Paco is waiting for me at the docks."

"Would you mind if I came with you? There's someone I need to see in Guayaquil."

He adjusted his hat. "Sure."

As we headed toward the docks, Aquilino mentioned that he hadn't heard anything from the Panamanian government concerning Puri's death certificate.

"Have they contacted you?" he asked.

I considered telling him the truth, but I would have to think about it some more. Once the truth was out, there was no turning back, and I had to learn everything I could before I became exposed to all.

"No," I said, and renewed my walk. "I met your former employee, Mayra."

He removed a handkerchief from his back pocket and dried the sweat from his neck. "You did, did you?"

"Yes, she's now working at Don Martin's house."

"She is?"

"Well, the poor woman was desperate. It's not easy being an unwed mother and not having a job."

Aquilino stopped. "An unwed mother? What are you saying?"

"You didn't know? Mayra is expecting."

"I had no idea."

He seemed honestly surprised, or maybe he was a good liar.

I lowered my voice. "She said that was why you fired her."

"She did? But that's a lie! What kind of man would do that? Who do you think I am?"

"I apologize, Don Tomás, I'm just telling you what she said."

"Well, that's a rotten lie meant to cover up her own dishonesty. Do you know why I really fired her?" He didn't wait for an answer. "I found her snooping through my things, and it was not the first time. I'd caught her going through my papers once before and I warned her that if she ever did that again, I would fire her."

Snooping through papers? What interest would she have in his affairs?

"That's strange," I said.

"Indeed." He pressed the handkerchief against his forehead. "The first time was over a month ago. I thought it was peculiar because I'd always thought she was illiterate." He faced the front. "You know what's even stranger?"

"What?"

"She was reading the telegraph you had sent me from Málaga with your itinerary."

CHAPTER 37

The rest of my trip to Guayaquil happened in a daze. It was a good thing that both Paco and Aquilino were quiet men because I could do a lot of thinking while we traveled from one river to the next until we reached the Guayas.

So Mayra had been interested in knowing when Cristóbal and I were arriving in Guayaquil. As I recalled, Cristóbal gave Aquilino all the details of our trip: the dates, the names of our ships, the ports.

Could she be the mysterious woman who'd hired Franco? My first thought was that Mayra might be Elisa, but she'd claimed to have a relationship with Alberto, to be carrying his child, and my brother didn't deny it. Elisa knew Alberto was her brother. I found it hard to believe she would've been intimate with him. It made more sense to think that she'd been gathering information for Alberto, who may have found out about Mayra's pregnancy after he'd renounced his share. Perhaps when my father first died, my brother hadn't foreseen he would be needing any money, but this baby changed everything. Now he had to hide what he'd done or maybe start a new life with Mayra.

Either way, he needed capital.

As soon as we arrived in Guayaquil, I thanked Aquilino for his help and got lost among the dozens of pedestrians heading toward downtown without giving him a chance to make further plans with me, or to find out anything about my mysterious visit to Guayaquil.

I removed the pocket watch and turned the case over. Engraved on the back was the watchmakers' name, *Bolivar e Hijos*.

I asked at least ten people if they knew where the jewelry store was. After much confusion, I finally found a man who, without hesitation, pointed in the right direction.

A sign in cursive letters told me this was the right place.

As I pulled the door open, three austere men turned toward me. Bolivar and sons? They were standing behind a massive counter, working on some pieces. The older one, closer to the door, sported a curly mustache over his upper lip and a blue smock. The other two men looked like the younger and older version of the same person: the same angular nose, the large forehead, but one had a fuller face and a thicker frame.

"Can I help you?" the old man said.

"Yes," I said, "I have gotten a hold of a pocket watch manufactured here nine years ago. I need to know if you have any record of whom you sold this watch to. I need to track down its rightful owner."

He stared at me over his spectacles.

"It's an issue of life and death," I added, in an attempt to move him. At moments like this, I wished I could be myself. A woman could always use her charms to recruit the help of a man for any endeavor.

"Let me see," he said.

I placed the pocket watch on the counter. He picked it up and examined it. "Lizardo, come."

The one with thinning hair and fuller face approached us. Up close I could discern faint lines in the corner of his eyes.

"Do you remember this?" the father asked.

Lizardo took the watch. "God, yes. I can't believe it."

"What?" I said.

"This watch," Lizardo said. "Where did you find it?"

"A woman in Vinces had it but she didn't know how her son had gotten a hold of it."

"I thought we'd never see it again," the father said.

"It was one of the first watches I ever completed on my own," Lizardo said. "I was so proud of it."

"That damned woman," the old man—Bolivar?—said.

The younger son stared at each one of us, expectant, his fingers leaving traces of moisture on the glass counter.

Bolivar turned to me. "I believe it was in 1914 or 1915. This girl, what was her name?"

Lizardo shrugged.

"Well, let's call her María," the father said. "She did our cleaning for us for a couple of months." He turned to the younger one. "Do you remember her, Carlos?"

Carlos nodded. "She had a beautiful voice."

"Oh, yes," the old man said. "She was always singing while she swept and mopped. This one"—he pointed at Carlos—"this one was enchanted by her voice. He thought there was no one more charming in Guayaquil."

"Papá . . ."

"But I do agree that there was something special about her. Even though she was poor, she was very neat. Her clothes were always clean, her skirts always starched. She had what they call class, and she was smart. I don't know how, but she knew how to read and write, and she started helping this simpleton with his additions and subtractions." He pointed at his youngest son with his chin. "You should have never trusted her."

"We all did, Padre," Lizardo said in his brother's defense.

Bolivar shook his head. "One day, she didn't come to work. We thought she was sick and didn't make much of it, although she was always efficient and timely. But then, that evening we noticed that there were some watches missing. This was one of them."

Lizardo rubbed the case slowly.

"We called the police, of course. Well, I did. This one was in shock and swore on his mother's grave that the girl would never rob us." He stared at Carlos, sighing. "Men in love are idiots, you know?"

I pretended not to notice that the younger son was blushing.

"But she did," the old man said. "A couple of days later, the police found her. She was part of a ring of thieves who sold stolen things. It turns out she worked for her stepfather."

Her stepfather? My pulse raced. "What happened to her?"

"She went to jail for some time. Then, we lost track of her."

"We recovered all the merchandise but this watch," said Lizardo.

"It goes to show you," the father said, shaking his head. "You can never fully trust people. You think you know someone, but then, as soon as you turn your back on them, they'll stab you." He pointed his finger at his elder son, as though teaching him a lesson that had escaped his younger one. "The only God out there is money. It's the one everyone follows."

"Papá . . ." Lizardo said.

"Anyway." He looked at me. "That's the story."

"I would like to pay for this watch and keep it," I said, "if you don't mind."

"That's generous of you," the older brother said.

"Well, it's the fair thing to do. You deserve payment for your work, even if it's nine years late."

The father banged the counter. "I got it!"

The three of us turned to him.

"Her name." He smiled as if he'd uncovered one of the biggest mysteries in the world and spoke in an ominous voice the words that only confirmed my suspicions. "Her name was Elisa."

CHAPTER 38

I spent the night at Aquilino's house. The lawyer was discreet enough not to ask me where I'd been and I didn't offer any explanations, either. I returned to the hacienda the next day. When I arrived, it was already nighttime and the house was silent and dark. I hadn't eaten all day so I headed directly to the kitchen. The sobs inside the room stopped me. I could tell it was a woman but didn't know whether it was Catalina or Angélica.

I really needed to eat something if I didn't want to pass out, but I didn't want to intrude in this private moment.

Before I made up my mind, Angélica opened the door, handkerchief in hand. Had Martin told her who I was? I held my breath.

"Don Cristóbal! I'm sorry. I didn't know you were coming back tonight. Someone in town said they saw you leaving with Tomás Aquilino yesterday."

"Yes. He offered to take me to a dentist in Guayaquil."

"Oh, good." She pointed at a silver teapot on the counter. "I just prepared some Hierba Luisa tea. Would you like some?"

Her eyes were swollen. I'd never seen her hair this untidy. Even in the mornings, she was well-groomed.

"No, thank you. Is something the matter?" I said.

"No. Yes." She blew her nose, sitting on a stool.

"Do you want to talk?" I said.

She nodded.

I sat beside her.

"I must explain what you saw yesterday," Angélica said. "My . . . familiarity with Don Martin."

Yes, please explain!

"I've loved Martin since I was a little girl," she said. "Growing up, he was the center of my world, but it all changed after he left for school. Our relationship cooled down considerably and I was . . . what shall I call it? Enchanted with Laurent when I first met him and frankly disillusioned with Martin's rash manners and lack of sophistication. It was my mistake, I admit it. It was a time of confusion for me. I thought I loved Laurent, but I didn't really know what he was like." She covered her mouth with her hand.

We sat in silence at her revelation, but I needed to know more. I squeezed her hand.

"I think I understand what you mean."

"You do?"

I nodded. "It's not that uncommon. I've met men like him before."

She breathed out, seemingly relieved.

"I don't know what it is about you, Don Cristóbal," she said, "but sometimes I feel I can talk to you about things I've never told any other man."

It was a compliment, but instead of being pleased, I experienced tremendous remorse in the face of my lies.

She lowered her voice. "Laurent tried to"—she sniffed—"change at the beginning of our marriage to no avail. In the end, we reached an agreement. We both had things we wanted, things we needed. He wanted a wife, he wanted to be part of an important family. I wanted a French husband to please my father. Of course, I would've never considered marrying Laurent if Martin hadn't betrayed me."

She wiped her tears with her handkerchief.

"I know Martin is a womanizer but I can't deny that I'm partly at fault for what happened between us."

"What happened?"

She looked at me for a moment, as if debating whether she should speak more. "I hope that what I'm about to share stays between us." Her finger traced the glossy tile on the countertop.

"Of course."

She took a deep breath. "When Martin came back from school, I was horrible to him. First, I ignored him. I wouldn't even speak to him. But I'd just met Laurent and was enthralled by him. You can understand that, right? Look at Laurent, there are not many men as handsome as he is."

I shifted uncomfortably on the hard seat.

"Martin felt rejected by me," Angélica said, "even though there was so much chemistry between us that, at times, I couldn't deny him anything. He has that kind of power over women."

Didn't I know that.

"As a worldly man, you must understand how important the first time is for a woman? Well, I was no exception. After my first time with Martin, I didn't want anything to do with Laurent, but my engagement was too far along and I couldn't simply break things off with my fiancé out of nowhere, especially when my father was so happy with the relationship. I asked Martin to give me time to end my engagement and he did—initially—but as more misunderstandings and humiliations took place, he took the ultimate revenge." Her voice turned into a whisper. "He was intimate with my best friend."

Silvia, just like I'd imagined.

"That was the last straw. I married Laurent one month later."

"And now?"

"And now, Laurent and I have an understanding. He has his friends, and I have Martin. It's a comfortable arrangement and I thought I was fine with it until Silvia came back." She squeezed the handkerchief. "I can't stand the sight of them together! After seeing them at the party, I haven't been able to think of anything else but the two of them in bed, laughing at me."

"Did he . . ." I couldn't even word my question properly. "Did he express an interest in her again?"

"No, but I know him. He can't resist any woman." She tightened the belt of her burnt-orange silk robe. "That's why I refuse to have kids; why you saw me at Soledad's house the other day. She gives me some herbs to prevent pregnancy."

My thoughts were still on her earlier comment.

"But if he's not a faithful man," I said, "then why are you still with him? Why do you continue to suffer when you made your choice a long time ago?"

"Because Martin is mine. I will never give him up."

CHAPTER 39

I'd barely been able to sleep after my conversation with Angélica. My head had been spinning all night with thoughts of Martin. He was not only my sister's lover; he was apparently the lover of every pair of legs in town. My initial reaction had been to believe her, to think the worst of him. But now, I wasn't so sure that everything she said was true—not after what Martin and I had shared. Was I being obtuse to think that what happened between us had been special? Had he been using me all along?

Enough!

I couldn't let my feelings for him distract me any longer. I had to *focus*. I needed to end this farce once and for all. And in order to do that, I *must* figure out who was behind Cristóbal's murder.

I was almost certain that Elisa had paid Franco with the pocket watch to kill me. She must be in town—or had been recently. Now the only question was whether or not Mayra had something to do with her. She was the only one who'd had access to my traveling plans. Could it be possible that Mayra was, in fact, Elisa?

Maybe she didn't care that Alberto was her brother, maybe she just wanted to take revenge on the family by ruining them.

My head would explode at any moment now. There was too much information to sift through. I couldn't make sense of anything anymore.

I just wanted to flee this place and never come back.

Either that or confess who I was and wait until Elisa or whoever was behind Cristóbal's murder would come forward.

"More coffee?" Julia asked, holding a metal pot with warm milk in one hand and a small glass container of coffee essence in the other. I was alone in the dining room attempting to have breakfast, but I hadn't touched my fruit salad yet.

"Yes, please," I said.

Julia poured milk and coffee into my cup.

"How is your cousin doing, Julia?" I asked.

"Mayra?" She shook her head. "That girl is incorrigible, but I think she's fine with Don Martin."

The sole mention of his name hurt.

"I never got a chance to thank you for what you did for her," Julia said, setting the plates on the table for the rest of the family.

"Don't thank me," I said. "Thank Martin." I grabbed a croissant from a wicker basket. "So how are you and Mayra related?"

"Our mothers were sisters," she said. "I'm the one who got her the job at Mr. Aquilino's after her mother passed away and she needed a place to live. If I'd known the kind of person she really was, I would've never recommended her."

"Don't be so hard on her," I said. "She just fell in love."

"I suppose. That's what she says, anyway."

I took a bite of bread, but nearly choked when I saw Martin entering the room.

"*Buenos días*," he said.

"Don Martin, you're here early," Julia said. "Would you like some breakfast?"

He wouldn't take his eyes off me. "Sure."

Julia dashed into the kitchen while Martin took a seat in front of me.

"You deserve an explanation," he said, his body leaning forward, his voice urgent.

"There's nothing to explain. Angélica already told me you've been lovers since you were youngsters."

He rested his palms on the table. "I know it looks bad, but I had nothing to do with what happened to you on that ship. I swear."

"What about her?"

He glanced over his shoulder, lowering his voice. "I don't know, but I don't think so. I admit that she wasn't pleased when she learned her father had left you the control of the estate. And neither was I, for that matter, but I doubt Angélica would hurt someone for money." He attempted to hold my hand but I moved it away. "Look, my relationship with Angélica is complicated. It's something that has tormented me for years. I'm sorry I didn't tell you, but even I can't explain it."

"Explain what?"

"The effect she has on me."

I stood up. I didn't want to hear another word. I didn't want to hear how much he loved and desired her and how he'd been playing with me, using me, or worse yet, helping her, even if he denied it now.

I darted out of the room without looking back. I needed air. He was following me, trying his best not to run.

I crossed the patio and headed for the stables. My throat was tight, my eyes stinging. I wouldn't let him see me cry. What was wrong with me? I'd never been so weak to cry for the love of a man.

A young boy, whom I'd seen before tending to the horses, was brushing Pacha just a few meters away. I told him to put her saddle on.

"English or Western?" he asked.

"Whatever!"

"Cristóbal!" Martin said, behind me. "Wait!"

The boy grabbed a brown leather saddle and I helped him strap it around the horse. He was still adjusting the mount when I climbed on top. Now, Pacha and I weren't the best of friends, but we'd grown to respect each other—at least I thought so. However, Pacha didn't seem to appreciate my urgency or my abruptness and being that she was not particularly fond of me, she reared, just like she'd done when we first met. Again, I slid to the ground, but this time I hit my head so hard that everything circled around me before turning pitch black. The boy's voice became so distant and faint that after a moment, all I could hear was the ringing in my own ears.

* * *

When I woke up, I was lying on a bed in a dim room with the curtains drawn. It was a tiny room—I'd never been here before. Martin was sitting on a chair next to the bed. Behind him was a shelf filled with ornaments of all kinds: vases, glass containers, dolls. He spoke as soon as I opened my eyes.

"You're in Julia's room," he said. "Julia is here, too."

I took this as a warning not to say anything about us in front of her. I looked around some more. Indeed, Julia was standing by my side with a moist cloth in her hand. Oddly, Ramona was there, too.

"Don Cristóbal, you scared us! We thought we'd lost you. You have to be careful with that mare," she said. "Not even Don Armand liked to ride her, and he was an experienced rider."

And yet Martin had made me ride her the first day. I fixed my eyes on him, then sat up.

"What are you doing?" she asked.

"Getting up."

"Oh, no, Don Cristóbal. You have to rest here for a while and wait until the doctor arrives."

A *doctor?* So he could see what my body—my female body—looked like?

"That won't be necessary," I said, trying to stand, but the entire room started spinning around me.

"Benito already went to town to get one," she said.

"Who?"

"The boy that takes care of the horses." She approached the bed.

I lay down again, my breathing agitated.

"Look at you with that suit. You must be suffocating. Let me help you with that." Julia proceeded to undo my tie. "I told Don Martin that we needed to remove these clothes, but he wouldn't let me." She turned to Martin. "You see? The poor man is sweating. He's going to catch a cold now."

"Just leave him be, Julia. You shouldn't be moving his head. I'll help him out of his clothes later when he's feeling better. Now go back to the kitchen. I'm sure your mistresses are up already."

Grumbling, Julia walked out. What a relief.

I closed my eyes.

"Puri," he said. "I'm sorry I didn't tell you about Angélica, but I don't want you to think that I've been using you or anything like that. The truth is . . ." He stopped.

I opened my eyes and looked at him.

"The truth is I like you. Very much."

"Is that why you wanted me to ride the most finicky mare here?"

"Well, in the beginning, I was angry, too, but it was only meant as a joke. I didn't want you to get hurt." He held my hand. "For whatever it's worth, I'm sorry."

I removed my hand, avoiding his face. I looked around Julia's room—it was so neat and organized, just like she was, but she owned a lot of things. I would've never imagined she collected so many things. There was a porcelain tea set, ceramic birds, dolls and marionettes of different sizes, jars, candles.

"I don't know if this makes any difference to you," he said, "but I haven't been intimate with Angélica in a few weeks."

Was that why she'd been crying that night in her room?

"It doesn't," I said. Knowing that Martin had loved my sister was devastating and I didn't think anything would make it better. "But if you truly like me, then answer this. What was all that nonsense about looking through my father's drawer? You know what's in there?"

"A chess board."

"Yes. What's so important about a chess game?"

He covered his face with his hand. "My father lost this entire plantation over a chess game."

"What?" I didn't think I'd heard him right.

"My father became consumed with chess. It was all he thought about night and day. At first, it was just a hobby. He just wanted to learn the game, but then he started buying books, learning all the tricks, all the possible combinations. He had manuals sent from Spain and some from the United States that he translated into Spanish vehemently. He studied them thoroughly. He would pose problems that he tried to solve all day long. He stopped working. All he wanted was to master the game. Your father took advantage of that. Don Armand was an innate chess player, and my father couldn't stand it. One day, they made a bet. My father was out of his mind by then. One day, he just came and told me and my mother that he'd lost the hacienda. Just like that."

So the hacienda belonged to Martin?

"It ended up killing my mother. Her heart couldn't take the shame of having to move to the guest house and everybody in town knowing it. She tried for a while, but it eventually killed her."

"You can't be serious," I said. His father couldn't have lost his fortune to a game of chess, could he?

"That chess set you saw belonged to my father. It's the board they used for the bet. Armand kept it as a trophy."

I felt sorry for him, for the loss of his mother, of his father's legacy, but at the same time, I was outraged.

"Is that why you're still here?" I said. "Why you want the hacienda so badly?"

He didn't answer.

"You thought that by marrying Angélica, you would get the hacienda, the entire plantation back?" I shook my head in disbelief. "But Laurent wasn't in your plans, was he? And now, you thought you could get it through me?"

"No. I told you, I'm fond of you, I've developed feelings for you. I know it looks bad, but I've never felt such a strong connection to any other woman. That's why I was never faithful to Angélica. I now see that Angélica was an obsession, a habit, and not much else."

"But it's also convenient that I'm Armand's oldest daughter."

"I guess for a moment I considered that," he admitted. "But I can't deny that there is chemistry between us, an affinity. You must feel it, too."

"There was chemistry before I knew who you really were," I said.

"But you lied to me, too, and I overlooked that."

"Because it was convenient for you."

He sighed, rubbing his eyes. "No, it's not convenient to be involved with two sisters, or to have all these feelings and not knowing what to do with them."

Catalina came into the room.

"Don Cristóbal." She was still in her robe. "Are you all right? Julia just told me what happened to you."

"I'm fine," I said.

"You shouldn't be here, in this cramped room." She turned to Martin. "Don Martin, let's take him to his bedroom."

"I said I'm fine. I don't need anything." I set my feet on the floor. "And I don't need a doctor, either."

With that, I let myself out of the room while everything I thought I knew about my father, about my future on this plantation, about my feelings for Martin collapsed.

CHAPTER 40

I slept all morning and woke up at two o'clock in the afternoon. After the blow to my head, I needed the rest. I looked around the room, disoriented. Still in my clothes. I recalled hearing Julia's voice, a couple of hours ago, knocking on the door incessantly, saying something about the doctor. But I didn't open. I didn't want to see any doctors. All I wanted was to sleep—I hadn't slept this much in weeks. There was something else bothering me, though, something in the back of my mind. A concern. Something I had to remember. What was it? Had I dreamt it?

My head throbbed. There was a bump on the crown of my head.

Slowly, I got out of bed. I was hungry. Thirsty. Maybe if I ate something, I would feel better, maybe even remember this detail, this idea that tormented me. I checked my beard to make sure it was still in place and donned my spectacles from the night table.

The house was quiet.

Holding on to the banister, I descended the staircase and headed toward the kitchen. There were subdued voices in the parlor.

"I think he's up," someone said. A man. Was that Laurent? Martin? No, it sounded more like Alberto. What was he doing here?

Angélica, with that charming smile of hers, came out of the room and met me in the hallway. It was hard to reconcile this image of pleasantry and confidence with the devastated woman I'd encountered in the kitchen the previous night.

"Don Cristóbal, how are you feeling?"

"Much better, thank you." I hesitated to take another step.

"Would you come in for a minute? We've been waiting for you."

We? Exactly who was waiting for me? I didn't feel like seeing Martin right now.

I followed Angélica into the parlor. Laurent, Catalina, Alberto, and Tomás Aquilino stared at me from their seats around the coffee table. Where was Martin? Had he told them the truth? No, he'd covered up for me in front of Julia. But what was going on here? I'd just seen Aquilino the previous day.

I shook hands with the lawyer. His handshake was weak and he avoided my eyes the entire time. Come to think of it, everybody seemed to be avoiding my eyes.

"Shall we wait for Martin?" Alberto said.

"No," Angélica said. "He's not part of this family."

So she was still irritated with him. But little did I care about the complexities of their relationship at the moment. I dug my hands in my pockets to hide their tremor.

Aquilino turned to me. "Señor . . ." He cleared his throat. "Padre Alberto was kind enough to bring me over to discuss with the family some disconcerting news I received this morning."

Disconcerting?

"I received a letter from a British captain—I think his last name is Blake—from a ship called the *Andes*. He's trying to locate Doña María Purificación de Lafont y Toledo to notify her that her husband's remains have been found. Apparently, the only address he has in connection to Mrs. Lafont is mine since her husband had sent me a telegram from Cuba."

Cristóbal was found?

I leaned on the arm of the couch, light-headed. My face was on fire, my chest thumping. How had they found him? I wanted to see him! But then, as soon as I realized the extent of the news, I looked around the room at all the puzzled faces staring back at me. They didn't understand a thing—obviously. How was it possible that *my* remains had been found when I was alive and well, standing right in front of them?

Here it was, the moment I'd been dreading. I looked around the room. Catalina, Angélica, and Laurent were staring at me. Alberto was simply nodding as if nothing could shock a man in his line of work.

"But if Don Cristóbal passed away weeks ago," Aquilino said slowly, "then who are you?"

"An impostor!" Laurent said. "I knew it!"

"I don't understand. Didn't our sister die on the ship?" Angélica said. "Where is she now?"

Catalina had turned pale. She merely looked from one face to another trying to make sense of things.

"It was to be expected," Laurent said. "A fortune like this one attracts all kinds of scoundrels."

A scoundrel? He was the only scoundrel here! I was about to respond, to defend myself, but Angélica spoke first.

"Well? Aren't you going to tell us who you are?"

"Yes," Laurent said, pointing his finger at me, "and how did you find out about my father-in-law's fortune?"

At that moment, Julia entered the room with a tray filled with espresso cups. I thought of the word "scoundrel" and suddenly I remembered what it was that I needed to recall, what my unconscious mind had been trying to tell me since I woke up.

As my siblings and my father's lawyer stared at me, I removed my spectacles and set them on the coffee table, then I pulled off my beard and mustache, relieved that this would be the last time I would ever have to wear that dreadful thing.

Their faces transformed from confusion to shock.

As I removed my jacket, so relieved as if I'd been unlocking a pair of handcuffs from my wrists, I spoke with my regular voice. "I'm María Purificación."

I raised my chin. I was not ashamed of what I'd done, especially now that I'd figured everything out.

Catalina covered her mouth.

"What? Purificación?" Angélica looked at me as if a sculpture had come to life. "Why would you do this? Why would you deceive us?"

"Because I needed to know which one of you had sent Franco to the ship to kill me; because I feared for my life and didn't trust any of you after Franco murdered my husband."

All of them spoke at once. In their faces, I read incredulity, confusion, and in Catalina's case, an intense pain.

Finally, Angélica's voice rose above the rest. "You're mistaken. Nobody here would do such a thing!"

I glanced at each one of them until my eyes landed on the guilty one.

"Yes, one of you did." I lifted my chin. "Since we're all here confessing, why don't you tell them the truth, Elisa?"

Still holding the tray, Julia looked directly at me, her eyes filled with tears of what I could only read as rage.

My sisters turned to the maid, incredulous.

"Elisa?" Catalina said.

Julia, or Elisa, set the tray on the sideboard. For a moment, I thought she was going to flee, but she simply stood there, staring at her hands, which were shaking even more than mine.

"I don't know what this . . . this person is talking about."

"Don't deny it," I said. "I saw the puppets in your room. Your stepfather was a puppeteer. I read about it in one of the letters you sent to Armand."

That morning, when I'd been talking to Martin, taking inventory of the things in Julia's room, I'd seen the puppets of Red Riding Hood and the Wolf sitting on one of the shelves, buried between other dolls and ornaments, but I hadn't thought anything of it. Not at the time, anyway.

"And Ramona," I said. "She's always repeating something about the wolf, *cuidado con el lobo*. I heard you sing that tune this morning. Ramona must have learned it from you."

"What on earth is she talking about?" Angélica asked Elisa.

Elisa frowned. For the first time, I noticed how much her gestures resembled Catalina's, and yet they were so different.

Everything made sense now. Elisa had put Mayra in Aquilino's house to get information about me and my father's will. She'd forged my father's check. Of course, she had access to his checkbook, to his signature, and she'd paid Franco with the pocket watch and promises of a fortune she would share with him. I glanced at Catalina. *She* was the woman he'd loved and he'd done this to be worthy of her.

"*Caperucita*," Elisa said, void of emotion. "It was a show we put up for the kids."

"Why didn't you tell us you were Elisa?" Angélica said. "You've been living here for three and a half years!"

"I was going to do it," Elisa said, unable to look Angélica in the eye. "I came here with every intention to tell the truth. After our mothers died, there was no reason to hide anymore, but Don Armand, with that problem in his brain, couldn't remember me. At first, I told him who I was, and he hugged me." Her voice broke. "But then, the next day, he'd forgotten all about me. He asked who I was again and again. In his mind, the only daughter he remembered and who really mattered was María Purificación, his firstborn, his legitimate, *European* daughter." Her voice turned bitter. "I was an embarrassment to him because I was the daughter of a *mestiza*," she scoffed, "the *maid*." She dried her tears and straightened her back. "And his wife didn't want us here."

Catalina sat down, pressing her hand against her forehead.

"I know that!" Angélica sounded annoyed. "My parents argued about you all the time."

"You knew?" Catalina asked.

"But there's something I don't understand, Ju . . . Elisa," Alberto said, his voice rusty. "Why did you think that if Puri died, you would get her part of the inheritance?"

Elisa crossed her arms.

"I knew Angélica would do right by me. I heard her speak to our father a few days before he passed and she told him that they needed to find me, that it would be fair that I received part of the inheritance. She remembered me as a little girl, and how her mother had kicked me and my mother out of the hacienda. She knew it was unfair and I deserved a part of the money, too. Our father agreed, but he died before he could speak to Mr. Aquilino about it." She turned to me, her eyes brimming. "But you would've never understood anything. You would come here and collect all the money and all the land you didn't deserve. You were never here for our father, you didn't tend to him when he was dying like we did. You didn't clean his vomit, or his dirty sheets, or give the injections he needed. And yet, he loved you so, he never stopped talking about you."

"I don't understand why you didn't tell me who you were," Angélica said.

"Because you were so upset about Purificación that I thought you might send me away, too. I wanted to fix things for you, for all of us." She appealed to her other siblings. "Don't you think it's unfair that our father would leave almost everything to this woman, to this . . . this person that we hadn't even met before?"

Neither Alberto nor Catalina would look her in the eye.

"The irony of it all was that my grandfather was also a Spaniard," Elisa said, facing me again. "He'd been my grandmother's *patrón* at another *finca*. So I guess history repeated itself. My father loved you the most because of your European blood, but I had it, too."

Everyone stood in tense silence. Aquilino broke it.

"What you did was very serious," he told Elisa in that somber voice of his. "A crime."

Elisa reached out to Angélica. "*Hermana?*"

"I'm afraid I will have to contact the authorities, señorita," Aquilino said.

Angélica removed her arm from Elisa's grasp.

Elisa fixed her eyes on me with a hatred that made me shiver. "Why did you have to come? Nobody wanted you here. *Nobody.*"

I looked at the faces around me. Nobody said anything.

"This is all your fault!" Elisa came at me with a strength that I never imagined she could possess. I fell hard on the floor. Elisa raised her hand, but before she could hit me, Alberto restrained her arms.

"Calm down!" he told her.

I came to my feet, dusting my trousers with my hands, and gave one last glance to my father's portrait before walking out of the room.

CHAPTER 41

I didn't bother going back to my bedroom. I needed to get out of the hacienda *immediately*.

But there weren't a lot of places to go. I didn't want to go to Martin's house or to Vinces, either; it was too long of a walk. There was one more option, though not ideal.

I headed toward the creek. I needed to think about what had just happened. I needed to understand what I was feeling, to put my thoughts in order. A tingling sensation ran through my body, energizing me. I had an urge to break something.

Things had not gone as I expected them to *at all*.

But *what* had I been expecting? Welcome hugs? Tears?

Not after my deception.

"Nobody wanted you here. Nobody."

Elisa's words kept ringing in my mind.

None of them had denied what she'd said. They weren't even mildly relieved that I was still alive. Though I understood their surprise and shock, their coldness hurt. It reminded me that I didn't mean anything to them, that they didn't know me. They only knew the façade of Cristóbal.

And that was my own fault.

Not even Catalina seemed pleased. And I thought she genuinely liked me.

I didn't stop until I reached the neighbor's house.

Don Fernando stopped cold when he saw me sitting in his parlor in men's clothing but without looking particularly masculine with no facial hair or spectacles.

"Señor . . . ?"

"Señora," I said. "I'm María Purificación de Lafont y Toledo, Don Armand's oldest daughter."

Such was his shock that instead of shaking my hand, he sat on the couch, gaping.

"But I thought Doña Purificación passed away. At least that was the rumor around town."

I shook my head.

"Wait, weren't you supposed to be her husband?"

I explained to him, as succinctly as I could, the entire situation. By the end, he had an amused expression on his face that I didn't particularly care for. Still, I proposed a deal to him. If he let me stay in his house while the inheritance was being processed and distributed, I would renegotiate with him, in more favorable terms, the border issue that had caused such a headache for him and my father. My siblings might not be happy with the agreement, but it was about time that I started making decisions regarding the plantation—it was what my father had wanted. And maybe he had a good reason for it.

Don Fernando looked at me with apprehension, but after a moment, he smiled.

"All right, you have a deal, Doña Puri."

"One more thing," I said, before shaking hands with him. "I'll need you to send one of your employees to collect all my things from my father's hacienda. I don't want to set foot there until this is all over."

Things were far from over, though. The next few days proved challenging. I remained locked in my neighbor's house, the odd guest wearing his employee's dresses and occasionally my husband's trousers. Don Fernando was not as annoying as I'd originally thought. He'd traveled widely and offered interesting conversations about the places he'd visited in Latin America and Europe. He was fond of bullfighting, one of the most popular activities in my hometown, and enjoyed a good meal and drinks after dinner. The more enthusiastic the story, the more he snorted.

In the beginning, he couldn't make sense of me and whether he should treat me as a man or a woman. It was apparent that neither one of us could forget that he'd punched me once, though we never mentioned it. Yet, the memory was always there, in the middle of our conversations and our silences, though it seemed like it had happened in another lifetime.

Thanks to Don Fernando's assistance, I paid a visit to Aquilino in Guayaquil and brought all the paperwork to prove my true identity. He promised he would start moving things along, but he was sorry to say that an unexpected event had taken place: my three siblings had united in contesting the will, claiming that my father had not been in his right mind when he wrote the inheritance.

The news felt like a bucket of iced water thrown in my face.

Aquilino added that the day I'd left the hacienda, the authorities had taken Elisa to Guayaquil. She was now in custody until a trial date was set.

I was conflicted by the news. On one hand, I was glad that justice for my husband would finally be served, but I couldn't help but think of the little girl who wrote those letters to my father—how much she'd wanted to be loved by him, how much she'd wanted to better herself by attending school and learning. A spirit like that didn't deserve to be imprisoned by the past. It was ironic that, like me, she'd tried to connect with my father through incessant letters.

By now, Soledad must have learned the truth about her son, too. I felt sorry for her, but Franco had made his own decisions and unfortunately she would have to live with the consequences.

I'd thought that knowing the truth—finding Cristóbal's killer—would give me peace of mind, but I was more heartbroken than ever.

As I held the ticket for the ship that would take me to Panama to give my husband a proper burial, I thought of Cristóbal and how naïvely he'd followed me across the ocean, unaware that this trip would signify the end of his life and his dreams. Yes, he deserved justice. He deserved all the things I'd taken away from him. For the first time, I admitted that it had been a mistake to come here. I'd ruined the lives of all of those around me—not just Cristóbal's. As I lifted my skirt to board the ship, I couldn't help but think of Martin.

Aside from Cristóbal, Martin was the only other man I'd ever been intimate with. I couldn't dismiss what we'd done—what I felt for him—as if it was a casual act like drinking a glass of water. Perhaps he could do that, but I couldn't. Not only had I disgraced my husband's name by being intimate with another man out of wedlock and so soon after his passing, but on top of it all, Martin had been my sister's lover. I was so humiliated, so vexed. And yet, I couldn't stop thinking about him. I hadn't seen him or heard from him in days. I was certain that by now, everybody in town knew that I'd been staying at Del Río's hacienda.

But Martin never came to see me.

I must forget him. I would have plenty of opportunities to do so since I doubted that he would continue to work at La Puri—not when his dreams of owning the plantation that had once belonged to his family had come tumbling down with my very existence.

CHAPTER 42

May 1920

The sight of my husband's casket unleashed a turmoil of emotions. It was like opening a faucet; out poured all the pain and tears I'd been suppressing for weeks. Not only for my husband's sake, but also for everything that had happened since my arrival in Ecuador.

For Martin. For my father. For my siblings.

I'd been doing everything wrong.

I hugged the casket, asking for forgiveness, and was unable to maintain my composure as the Panamanian authorities explained that Cristóbal's body had washed ashore and a Jamaican fisherman had found him. The man had contacted the local authorities, who'd been aware that a couple of men aboard the *Andes* had been missing.

"But we suspect he died on impact," said the somber officer, squeezing my shoulder.

Upon my return to Guayaquil, I learned that a judge had dismissed my siblings' contention of the will since my father's doctor, the bank manager, and Aquilino had all testified that my father was in his right mind when he wrote his last wishes. When hearing the news, Angélica, Laurent, and Catalina had left the plantation and were staying with friends in Vinces.

"But I never wanted them to leave," I mumbled, fixing my gaze on the intricate carvings on Aquilino's bureau. I'd been thinking, innocently perhaps, that they would come to resign themselves to my father's desires and we would all live in harmony at the hacienda, like sisters.

I squeezed the handkerchief in my hand—I hadn't been able to stop crying since the funeral.

"Aren't you satisfied with the news?" Aquilino said. "As the majority holder, you're free to take possession of La Puri now if you wish to."

I nodded, but I never thought that good news could taste so bitter.

I dabbed the corners of my eyes with the handkerchief. "Why have you been helping me?" I asked. "You've known my siblings for much longer than me."

"Because it's the right thing to do. I worked for your father for many years and he always confided in me the remorse he felt about leaving you and your mother behind. He said his fortune was built thanks to your grandmother, who introduced him to chocolate. Without her influence, he would've never left Europe. So, he thought it was only fair that you should benefit from your family's legacy. He felt he owed it to your grandmother and he made me promise that I would make sure you got your part—I think he suspected that his decisions might cause problems between his children."

"What about Elisa? Did he ever talk to you about her?"

"He mentioned her a few times, but he always had doubts that she was truly his. Elisa's mother didn't have a good reputation around town. She was known to have had many"—he cleared his throat—"friends, so he was never sure that Elisa carried his blood. This is why he never truly accepted her, why he didn't leave her anything." Aquilino stood up. "Now if you'll excuse me, I have another appointment." He removed a key from the pocket of his vest. "Here's the key to the hacienda. La Puri is yours."

When I entered the house, my hacienda, I felt a chill. My heels echoed across the foyer. I met my father's gaze from his portrait, sitting proud, oblivious to all the havoc he would cause after his passing. In the parlor, everything was in order: the elegant furniture intact, the grand chandelier dangling above my head, not a single ornament seemed to be missing. I ran my finger by the sideboard, where the porcelain figurines of three ballerinas were covered with a thin layer of dust.

There was an empty space in the corner of the room; it was the spot where Angélica's harp had always sat—apparently, it was the only thing she'd taken. It almost seemed as if my sisters had left in haste and would be back any second.

But that wouldn't happen.

Somehow, the sight of these elegant furnishings was more painful than if I'd encountered a demolished house with tables split in half, lamps turned upside down, sliced curtains, and shattered glass all over the floor.

The excitement I'd first experienced when I boarded the *Valbanera* to come to Vinces was no longer there. I couldn't even identify with the woman I'd once been, the one who'd innocently believed a grand cacao plantation would give her everything her life lacked.

The truth was that this perfection, these beautiful objects surrounding me, held no meaning for me.

CHAPTER 43

Martin looked like he hadn't slept in a couple of days—large circles darkened his eyes—his hair was longer and disheveled, and his beard, unshaven. Had the realization that he would never own the plantation affected him this much? Or was it Angélica's departure? He'd said their relationship was complicated.

I was annoyed at my own quickening pulse as he walked into the hacienda.

"I heard you were back," he said, studying me as if seeing an apparition.

I realized why. This was the first time he'd seen me in women's clothes. I wore a black dress with silk chiffon sleeves and a leaf-like design embroidered on the collar, which I'd purchased in Panama, among other gowns. I was finally paying Cristóbal the proper respect by donning mourning clothes.

I grasped the doorknob; mostly because I didn't want Martin to see the involuntary tremor in my hands and how his presence affected me.

"Please come in," I said, leading the way across the foyer.

He followed me in silence.

"I went looking for you at the warehouse this morning," I said, sitting down. "But nobody was there." I studied his muted expression. "Look, I understand if you don't want to work here anymore. I can find someone else, but I was hoping we can put our differences behind us. I need people who know and understand the business. I'm not a fool to believe that I can run this plantation on my own."

When I was done speaking, he approached the sideboard.

"May I?" he asked, opening the cabinet and grabbing a bottle of *aguardiente*.

I nodded.

He took out two glasses and filled them. Then, he handed me one. He sat in front of me and gulped his drink at once. I took a cautious sip of mine before speaking.

"I understand you might be . . . frustrated with what's happened," I started. "With your father, with the inheritance, well, with everything, but the truth is I need you here, and I want to make you a business proposition."

"No."

"I'll raise your salary."

He shook his head.

"I had no idea you disliked me this much."

"It's not you," he said, staring at his glass.

Angélica, then. He was this distraught because she'd left.

"Well, I'm sorry if my arrival here has posed an inconvenience for your *complicated* relationship with Angélica." I wasn't proud of the bitterness in my tone.

"It's over."

"It can't be over if you're this troubled about it."

"I don't mean my relationship with her. *This* is over."

Did he mean *us*?

I fingered my string of black pearls, my sole ornament. "I know that."

He banged the armrest and stood up, dragging the chair's legs back, making an unbearable screeching sound.

"I mean this plantation! It's over!"

"I'm sorry you feel that way."

"It's not about you, woman! The plantation is dead. Yesterday, we got confirmation from a technician from Guayaquil that there are traces of witches'-broom and frosty pod rot in most of the plants!"

"What are you talking about?"

"I'm talking about diseases that are killing this entire planta-tion. In fact, all the region is infected!"

"What?" I sprang up. "How come you're here getting drunk instead of doing something about it?"

"What am I supposed to do? There is no cure for either dis-ease. Everybody knows that once the *escoba de bruja* and the *monilla* appear, a plantation is doomed. It's a good thing your fa-ther didn't live to see this."

I shook my head, my mouth dry as a bone. "Surely, there's something we can do about it. Bring another technician. Get help. I'll go back to Spain, to France, and find someone."

I was frantic, pacing the room back and forth. Martin blocked my way and squeezed my shoulders with his hands.

"Stop. There is nothing you or anybody else can do. These diseases are well known to wipe out entire regions. Don't you think that if there was a cure, I would've done something about it? I would've traveled to every corner of the world to find a solu-tion, but there's nothing. Every landowner knows this and lives in terror of these diseases. I'm telling you. This is the end of the cacao bonanza for this entire country."

I slapped his chest with my hands, tears trickling. "You brought this on! Out of jealousy! Because you wanted the planta-tion for yourself! This is all your fault."

He let me hit him, and then, when I was exhausted, when the tears were so abundant that I could no longer see the sadness in his eyes, I took a step back.

"I need to get out of here," I said, turning around.

He called my name, but I left the house before he could say anything else. I left knowing that he was right, that I'd lost everything before I ever had it.

CHAPTER 44

I didn't want to believe Martin. I walked around the plantation for hours. I talked to every worker I could find and demanded that he show me the disease up close. My former informant, Don Pepe, pulled out a cacao pod and showed me the white, moldy spots spreading all over the fruit. I looked around me: leaves were withering, pods were filling with fungus, the entire region was rotting, like my family.

No, I couldn't accept this. My father didn't abandon us, he didn't work for twenty-five years, so fungi would wipe it all away. On my way to my neighbor's house, I encountered dozens of workers walking toward Vinces along the dirt road, their heads lowered, their feet dragging. They carried with them all of their belongings.

Don Fernando del Río confirmed that everything Martin had said was true. He also seemed anxious, but in a different way than Martin. Instead of drinking, he was pacing his living room like a madman. He was still wearing his night robe and he would twitch and talk to himself. Any minute now, he would lose his mind and would have to be admitted to an asylum. I tried to calm him, asked him to sit down, to have a *valeriana* tea for his nerves, but he barely listened, he kept repeating something about the witches'-broom, and calling it a curse, he went as far as blaming Soledad, the town's *curandera*, who at Angélica's request must have done something to the plants.

Yes, that was his explanation for things. Those women were witches and they'd cursed the entire region. When there was nothing else I could do or say to calm him, I left his house and went home.

The hacienda felt lonelier than ever. Prior to leaving the house, my sisters had apparently fired Rosita, the cook. But little did I care now about food or housekeeping. I collapsed on the sofa, watching the bottle of *aguardiente* on the coffee table and Martin's empty glass. I hugged my knees and gently rocked back and forth until the night closed in.

CHAPTER 45

This was, perhaps, the hardest visit of my life. I stood in front of the sky-blue door for a few minutes. It was impossible not to compare the grandeur of the hacienda with the humble house that now stood in front of me; a house where, according to the rumors in town, my sisters were now living.

I rang the doorbell. A part of me understood that they might not open the door. After all, the last time they'd seen me—that horrible day at the hacienda where I'd disposed of my disguise—I'd left on less than amicable terms, one might even call them downright hostile.

The movement of the door startled me. So did the face in front of me.

I'd expected to see Catalina, even Angélica, but in front of me stood Alberto. It took me a moment to recognize him. He had shed off his cassock and was wearing gray trousers, a buttoned-up shirt, and suspenders. He looked so young.

I didn't know what to expect from him. An insult? A sarcastic remark about the doomed plantation we'd fought over?

Instead, he nodded.

"Hello, Puri."

He opened the door wider for me to come in. I hesitated before entering, but at least my long black gown was good for hiding the tremor in my legs.

The living room was a cozy combination of Angélica's impeccable taste and Catalina's discreet simplicity. There was a long, maroon sofa in front of three windows framed in oak wood. They were furnished with soft beige drapery, and there were plants scattered throughout the room. I noticed, without intending to, that there were no portraits of my father in sight.

Catalina stood upon seeing me and set her embroidery by her side.

There was something different about her, too. She no longer wore black. Instead, she'd picked a pink gingham dress with a belt that crossed over and buttoned in the front.

I greeted her first. She offered a coy smile. The silence between us prolonged for a few, unbearable seconds.

"Would you like something to drink?" Alberto said. "A fruit tea?"

"Yes, please." I wasn't thirsty, but I needed something to do with my hands, something to distract us from the tense silence.

And Angélica and Laurent weren't even here yet.

"Any preference?" he asked.

"Whatever you have will be fine."

"I'll go get Rosita," he said.

So they'd taken the cook with them. Well, I couldn't say that I was surprised.

"Have a seat," Catalina said.

I sat on the edge of a rocking chair that looked familiar—it might have been in Catalina's room before. The old me would have known exactly what to say, how to engage Catalina in conversation and defuse our mutual discomfort. But after living like Cristóbal for a couple of weeks, I'd learned to appreciate silence. In some ways, I'd become more contemplative and introspective.

"You look so nice," Catalina said. "So different."

"And you look beautiful in pink," I said.

"Thank you."

I sat with my ankles crossed and my hands clasped in my lap. Someone was at the door. Catalina stood, nervously.

"I'm home!" Angélica said from the foyer.

Catalina stared at me, uncertain. I remained in my seat, though I could feel my pulse speeding up.

"I found the loveliest fabric at Le Parisien," she said, entering the room, wearing a lovely mint frock. She nearly dropped the parcel in her hands when she saw me.

"*Buenas tardes, Angélica,*" I said.

She stood up straight and raised her chin.

"What are you doing here?"

My mind went blank. I had a speech planned. I knew exactly what and how I was going to say it, but the whole, rehearsed speech died on my lips.

"Visiting." Alberto reentered the room, followed by Rosita carrying a metal tray with a teapot and three porcelain cups. The color drained from her face when she saw Angélica and me in the same room. Alberto spoke louder, with an almost annoyed tone, "What else would she be doing?"

"I don't know," Angélica said. "Maybe *she* wants more money?"

"Oh, stop it, Angélica. Haven't you caused enough damage already?" He turned toward Rosita. "Just set that tray on the table and leave, please."

Alberto sounded more assertive than ever. Gone was the youthful friendliness I'd seen at the bar when I'd just met him.

"*I* have caused damage?" Angélica said.

"What do you call that lawsuit you made us sign?" he said.

"Nobody forced you."

"You took advantage of our vulnerable state. We were confused, angry, hurt."

I stood up. "Please. I didn't come here to fight. I don't want to cause more conflict between you. Between us."

"Then what do you want?" Angélica said, the veins in her forehead visible.

"I want . . . I came to make a truce."

The three of them stood silent.

"It was wrong of me to deceive you. I should have been less of a coward and confronted you with the truth of what happened on the ship, but I was so angry, so filled with hatred, with fear." I squeezed my hands together. "But then, I got to know all of you, to like you. I didn't realize until much later that none of you were at fault over what happened to my husband. None of you ever had any intention to cause me harm. I now see that a big injustice had been committed against you, against all of us. Our father should have left us an equal share of the money and properties. It wasn't your fault that he abandoned me. I now understand your frustration."

"Nice thing to say now that you've lost everything," Angélica said.

"I didn't lose everything. All of us did. But you know, the loss of the plantation, of that dream I'd had for so long, was nothing compared to"—my voice broke—"losing my family."

Angélica lowered her gaze, squeezing the package in her hands.

"I understand if you never want to see me again." I searched through my purse, avoiding their gazes. "I caused you a lot of harm, even if I didn't intend to." I removed a key from my purse's inner pocket and set in on the coffee table. "Here's the key to the hacienda. You may do with it whatever you choose. I know it's not worth much anymore, but maybe one day, the plantation will rise again." I dried the tears from my cheeks. "At any rate, it's not fair that you should live in this tiny house any longer."

None of them said a word as I snapped my purse shut and walked out of their house with the fear that this might be the last time I would ever see my siblings.

PILOGUE

Vinces, 1922

The cacao beans were almost ready. The roaster my grand-mother had invented was truly wonderful. I'd refused to use it back in Spain because I kept it as an heirloom—a souvenir from my grandmother to be revered and admired as an art piece. But ever since La Cordobesa had sent it to me across the ocean and the contraption had gone through perilous waters and an uncertain destiny aboard two transcontinental ships, I was so grateful to see it again that I'd installed it in my new *chocolatería* and had been using it faithfully.

I'd gotten back into the habit of singing *zarzuelas* aloud, and my new assistant, Mayra, had also acquired La Cordobesa's old (bad) habit of sticking cotton balls in her ears. I didn't care because at least Alberto's two-year-old son, Armandito, seemed to enjoy my singing and often followed me around the kitchen, learning the lyrics of my songs, or asking me over and over again all the ingredients in my truffles, which he loved more than life itself.

"Chocolate, butter, *leche*," he recited in baby-talk.

How I loved those round, rosy cheeks of his—I could watch him all day long. Although Mayra had initially been guarded with me because her cousin Elisa had ended up in prison, she eventually understood that it had been Elisa's own doing, not anything I'd done.

It also helped that I encouraged Alberto, slightly, to marry her. I must admit it wasn't easy. It took a while for him to make the decision to marry Mayra—after all, he'd been preparing to be a priest for years—but he finally came to terms with his feelings for Mayra and decided to give Armandito a family.

After the cacao industry collapsed in the region, most of the French landowners returned to Europe, including Laurent and Angélica. The four of us sold our land and hacienda to Don Fernando del Río, who decided to start a new cultivation from scratch. He tore down the old, infested trees, and replanted new ones. It was a project that might take years to succeed, but that was no longer our concern.

With the money from the sale, Angélica bought tickets to Europe and planned to spend the next few months traveling all over the Old Continent. She seemed more than a little excited to embark on this new adventure and even smiled at me the last time I'd seen her.

Begrudgingly, the two of us had realized we had more in common than we ever thought: our sense of adventure, our impatience for the town's tattletales, even a dislike for beets. It was bittersweet that once I started to know her and make amends, she had to leave.

I ended up buying the coffee shop I had once visited with Martin. It took a small investment, but with my experience and the excitement of being the first chocolatier in the region, the business was paying off. In the few months since I'd opened the shop, I'd acquired a small, but regular clientele. People came all the way from Guayaquil to try my chocolate. As it turned out, I had access to very exclusive and fine cacao beans, which arrived from a new and promising plantation in Colombia, owned by none other than Martin Sabater.

After the turmoil of the plague, Martin stayed for a while, offering to help me in any way he could. But when there was nothing left to do, he collected his life's savings and bought a property of his own in the south of Colombia, in a region called Valle del

Cauca. In honor of our friendship, he offered me cacao beans at discounted prices and extended an invitation for me to visit his land one day, which he grew more and more excited over with each letter.

When he parted, leaving me a goodbye letter where he apologized for the pain he'd caused me, I considered returning to Spain. There was nothing left for me here. But a fortuitous encounter with Catalina at the Vinces marketplace made me change my mind. She told me, over a cup of coffee and *pristiños*, that she'd never been close to Angélica and that she'd always longed to meet me and have a relationship with me. She told me about her lonely childhood locked in the hacienda—her golden cage—and then she squeezed my hand and asked me to stay, at least for a while longer. Her request made me postpone my trip time and time again until one day, after leaving her house, I saw a FOR SALE sign outside the coffee shop where I'd eaten with Martin. I knew then that I had to stay.

I never regretted my decision. I was happy to introduce the people of this country to the wonders of chocolate. I worked hard, but not as intensely as I had in Sevilla. I now took the time to enjoy a *tinto de verano*, a good conversation, or a sunset.

Since Catalina moved to town, she progressively shed her saintly image among the eligible bachelors in the region. I must admit I'd been pushing her a little bit. Since I often met people at my chocolate shop, I'd been systematically introducing men to Catalina. But she was hard to please. Still, I held hope that one day I would find her perfect match.

After Laurent and Angélica left the country, I agreed to move in with Catalina. So far, it was working out. I loved those late-evening talks with her or watching her sew for the women in town.

The peal of the doorbell woke me from my ponderings. I asked Mayra to keep an eye on my cacao beans and went to open the back door.

The postman stood before me with a parcel.

"It's from Guayaquil," he said, handing it to me.

There was no sender's address, so I impatiently tore the packaging paper to shreds and removed a small cardboard box. Inside was a doll with a pillow for a dress. It looked old, her face dirty, and her blond hair, matted. Underneath the doll, there was a paper folded in half.

I recognized the handwriting immediately.

> *Purificación,*
> *I gave this doll to Catalina years ago. I recently found it inside a box in the storage room of the hacienda and took it with me. This is the only memory I have of our father, the only gift he ever gave me when I was a little girl.*
> *It is, also, the only thing I can give you as a peace offering and an apology for all the suffering I caused you with my petty, rash actions. Perhaps one day you will find it in your heart to forgive this girl who only wanted to be close to her father, but didn't know how to do it right.*
> *With much regret,*
> *Elisa.*

I refolded the letter and carefully stored the doll behind the shop's glass counter, right next to my husband's typewriter. Then, I headed to the room in the back of the shop, where my twenty-month-old son, Cristóbal, napped in his crib. I picked up his chubby hand and gave it a soft kiss. He was more perfect than I'd ever envisioned my child would be—with long curly eyelashes and bright eyes, just like his father's.

I'd discovered I was expecting shortly after Martin left. I'd been afraid to lose this baby, too, but somehow my pregnancy came to fruition and my baby was born healthy and strong. I often wondered why I could carry Martin's child and not Cristóbal's. Had it been the conditions of this land, my more leisurely life, maybe even fate? I would never have an answer. To everyone's eyes, though, this child was the son of Cristóbal de Balboa, a man of simple ambitions who knew that true happiness lay in the things we couldn't own.

Author's Note

In an obscure corner of the internet, I once found a list of women inventors that included a Spanish woman who allegedly developed the cacao bean roaster in 1847. Her name was María Purificación García. My imagination wandered after learning this piece of information—whether it was true or not. What would have prompted a woman in the nineteenth century to come up with such an invention? Despite my many attempts to confirm the data, I never unearthed more details about who she was, but I found her name in a historical archive in Spain, which proved that she had, in fact, patented the idea.

While studying women inventors, I learned that in the past, many of them had to have their patents registered under their husbands' names, which led to another interesting discovery. Since women were not allowed to develop in several fields, such as warfare or medicine, they cross-dressed.

I had to do something with all this information.

I could've written a story about María Purificación García, but I was also fascinated by a historical event that took place in my native country: the arrival of a group of French landowners to the coast of Ecuador where they grew cacao for export, and as a byproduct, replicated their own Little Paris in the town of Vinces. During the early twentieth century, Ecuador became one of the top cacao-exporting countries in the world, but the cacao bonanza ended in 1920 with two devastating plagues that wiped out the entire region.

That's how my protagonist, Puri, was born—the granddaughter of this wonderful lady inventor, the daughter of a French land-owner, and a chocolatier herself who introduced an exporting country to the irresistible allure of chocolate.

Acknowledgments

My infinite gratitude to the following people:

My wonderful agent, Rachel Brooks, for her perseverance and drive—not even a pandemic could stop her from finding a home for this novel.

To Norma Pérez-Hernández, an editor whose vision and enthusiasm for my work made not only this book possible, but also a sequel to explore Puri's further adventures.

To Susie Salom for her astute eye which helped me pinpoint what wasn't working with the book—I believe your guidance and energy were pivotal to this story.

To María Elena Venant for always rushing to clarify my many historical and fashion doubts, and for lending an ear when I need one.

To Marriah Nissen for her ruthless line editing and historical accuracy.

To Shea Berkley, a kindred spirit who's always there to bounce ideas off and do anything artsy I propose.

To my early readers: the talented Robyn Arrington and the amazing Jill Orr, your excitement and encouragement pushed me to continue to pursue this project.

To the equally talented Brenda Drake for helping me polish that very important first chapter.

To Father Emmanuel Delfin for his trust in me and for sharing his wonderful story of heartbreak and transformation.

To Jackie Padilla for her assistance in chocolate-making, her recipes, and for giving me Puri's secret ingredient.

To all the readers who reached out to me and kept asking when the next novel was coming out, especially Ana Gracia and Beatriz. Well, here it is and I hope you enjoy it!

To my mom for continuing to feed my imagination with her memories, and my dad for teaching me about hereditary law.

To my family in Ecuador and in the US for their unconditional support, especially to Mónica and Alfredo, who are nothing like Puri's siblings.

And last, but definitely not least, my gratitude and love for Danny, Andy, and Natalie, who have the perpetual task of correcting my ESL and hearing all about my imaginary worlds.

THE SPANISH DAUGHTER

Lorena Hughes

ABOUT THIS GUIDE

The suggested questions are included to enhance your group's reading of Lorena Hughes's *The Spanish Daughter*.

DISCUSSION QUESTIONS

1. It's not until after the death of her father that Puri learns he had three children in Ecuador—her half-brother and sisters. Are there any uncovered secrets in your family history? If so, did that discovery change your relationships or your feelings toward certain family members?

2. Do you think Puri was justified in deceiving her family? Why or why not?

3. Have you ever heard of real-life women cross-dressing in order to protect themselves or to perform activities that used to be only reserved for men? Could you cite some examples?

4. Just like cacao beans transform into chocolate, Puri goes through a transformation herself after her experience of posing as a man. What are some things she learns about herself and the opposite sex? How do her preconceptions regarding men and women change by the end of the novel?

5. What were your first impressions of Puri's half-sisters, Angélica and Catalina de Lafont? How did your opinions about them change over the course of reading the novel?

6. The story repeatedly mentions how each sister's physical appearance greatly impacts how they are perceived (and received) within society. How do you think the dynamics within the story would change if each sister looked differently from how they were portrayed?

7. As a dynamic adventurer and business owner, the character of Puri can be seen as a feminist of her time. But dressed as a man in Ecuador, she is able to closely examine, as an outsider, the strong social hierarchy among women. How might a contemporary woman have reacted

in her situation? Conversely, how would a woman of her times view these relationships?

8. How did you feel about the relationship between Catalina and Franco? Do you think Catalina was ever truly in love with Franco?

9. Martin tells Puri that his relationship with Angélica is complicated. Do you think they loved each other or were they just accustomed to one another? Do you think Puri is better suited for Martin? Why or why not? Do you see a future for them together?

10. Despite his transgression, do you think Alberto had a true religious calling? What are your thoughts regarding the Catholic Church's expectations for young men who enter priesthood?

11. Don Armand's cacao farm in Ecuador is referred to as a "plantation," an accurate word to describe an estate where cash crops are grown at a large scale, but one that comes with a complicated history and negative connotations for some American readers. What do you think about the ongoing cultural debate over the use of words in historical fiction that may bring about negative associations for contemporary readers?

12. Did you know anything about Ecuador before reading this novel? How has your perception of this country changed since you read Puri's story? What were some of the cultural and historical details that surprised or interested you?

13. When Puri arrives at the cacao plantation and sees the sign at its front gate, she learns her father had named his hacienda after her, "La Puri." Why do you think Don Armand made that decision? Do you think it was fair to Puri—or her siblings?

14. Family and jealousy are important themes in the novel. Puri always longed for an intimate relationship with her fa-

ther, and when she learns about her half-siblings, she envies the closeness they had with him. Similarly, her sisters experienced a desire to meet her, but were also jealous of her. What do you think was the root source of their jealousies? Were you satisfied with the way their stories ended, or would you prefer a different outcome for them?

Connect with U(s)

Visit us online at
KensingtonBooks.com
to read more from your favorite authors, see books
by series, view reading group guides, and more.

Join us on social media

for sneak peeks, chances to win books and prize packs,
and to share your thoughts with other readers.

facebook.com/kensingtonpublishing
twitter.com/kensingtonbooks

Tell us what you think!

To share your thoughts, submit a review,
or sign up for our eNewsletters, please visit:
KensingtonBooks.com/TellUs.